B.L. OVERMAN

FLESH FOREST

Other Books by B.L. Overman

THE PRIMEVAL ONES UNIVERSE
(The Publication Order is The Reading Order)

The Amazonian Uteroboscis (Book 1 | Lena's Story)
The Yoni Flower (Book 2 | Allie's Story)
Lizzy's Flower Glizzy (Book 3 | Lizzy's Story)
The Amazonian Uteroboscis: Outbreak (Book 4 | Lena's Sequel)
Flesh Forest (Book 5)
Blight of The Yoni Flower (Book 6 | The Crossover)
The Horned One (Book 7 | The Next Crossover)

THE DEVIANT ONES UNIVERSE

Tijuana Burger Girl
Sentenced to Glory
Blackmailed Into Servitude
The MasqueRave

B.L. OVERMAN

FLESH FOREST

SCIROTIC
BOOKS
Scirotic.com

**SCIROTIC
BOOKS**
An Imprint of Masterless Press

Scirotic.com

Flesh Forest

Cover design by Thea Magerand

First Scirotic Books print edition: February 2026

Printed in the United States of America

ISBN: 978-1-7350801-3-0 (print)
ISBN: 978-1-7350801-4-7 (ebook)

<u>FOREWORD</u> & *<u>CONTENT WARNING</u>*

Welcome back to the **Primeval Ones Universe**! And thanks for buying *Flesh Forest* (*Primeval Ones series* Book 5).

CONTENT WARNING: <u>This book is a straight-up body-horror/sci-fi novel with splatterpunk themes</u> that deals with certain Lovecraftian-like organisms from earlier works. If you want an idea of the vibe of this book, think one of those movies where a bunch of best bros journey to a party, but then imagine that it rapidly spirals into nightmarish, surreal horror. Expect gruesome descriptions, plenty of "guy talk," and strong language. If you're squeamish or have any triggers related to the kinds of things typically found in splatterpunk-style fiction, you might wanna skip this one.

CHRONOLOGY: This story begins 3 days after *The Amazonian Uteroboscis: Outbreak*'s final chapter, which itself takes place 1 day after the end of Lizzy's storyline. It follows a new cast of characters—Danny Holland and his friends—as they stumble across the nightmare that Allie Hannigan and Lizzy Rutherford inadvertently unleashed in the woods of Yelm, WA. So, for the best experience, the series is best read in publication order. As for the free prequel ebook, **Flesh Forest: Origins**, it may be read either before or after this book, depending on whether you prefer to enter the story fully informed or if you'd rather discover its mysteries alongside the characters! If you haven't downloaded the companion ebook, please visit the freebies section on the publisher's site (<u>www.scirotic.com/scirotic-freebies</u>) or check the back matter to find out how to get it!

<u>**FOR THOSE WHO JUST STUMBLED ACROSS THIS SERIES**</u>**: If you're just looking to read a messed-up body horror story without having to catch up on the other books,** *Flesh Forest* was written to serve as an entry point for new readers. While it lightly touches on the lore and science surrounding the Uteroboscis parasites [which have become a household name by this point in the chronology], it presents the mystery and horror of the other organisms from books 2 and 3 [but with new twists] through the perspective of characters encountering them for the first time. So, if you're new and want maximum shock factor, and if you don't mind having some major events from earlier books spoiled, jump in here 'blind' then go back to the previous installments afterward to learn more about the other characters/the science behind the organisms.

<u>**No AI was used to write this story or to make this cover!**</u>

Alright, that's all!

Now, go get your read on! I hope you enjoy it!

PROLOGUE:

NICK CRAWFORD
Wednesday?

Woozy… Delirious… Sedated…

Drugged.

My eyelids slowly open, revealing a darkness rivaling the one I've just awakened from.

Never in all my twenty-seven years of life have I felt this awful. This altered…

This dreamy, tranquilized haze reminds me of how that anesthesia left me feeling after my hernia surgery, mixed with the crippling malaise of the brutal flu I had freshman year of college. But what I see around me this time isn't a hospital room. Not that my blurry eyes can see much right now.

Even if I were in a dark hospital room, no nurse or doctor would let me lie contorted like this. My chest, abdomen, and the right side of my face are flat against this bizarre, cushioned surface, while my arms are stretched out in front of me like I passed out mid push-up. However, my lower half is twisted so that I'm lying on my right hip, my left leg awkwardly curled on top of the right, both knees pointing in the direction I'm facing.

I'm normally a side sleeper who doesn't roll around much, so waking up contorted like this is unusual. My current position reminds me of how I've found drunk friends on the couch the morning after a crazy party. It's the kind of position you'd expect to find a corpse in after someone collapsed mid-run.

I try sitting up, but no part of me budges. I can't even lift my head.

Am I… paralyzed?

On my second attempt to move, I feel the muscles in my arms and legs flex, and my painfully swollen erection throbs. Everything feels so numb that it's barely noticeable.

No… not paralyzed. Just too weak to move, I think, sighing quietly in both relief and frustration. *I'm numb in the same way I am in dreams.*

Am I dreaming?

While I wait to muster more strength, I lie still, slowly blinking to clear the blur from my vision. Blinking in what feels like slow motion isn't a choice. It's just, when I try to move my eyelids faster, they feel too heavy to cooperate.

What's wrong with me?

Eventually, my vision clears enough for me to make out the silhouettes of bushes and towering trees a few yards away—moonlit outlines of a woodland landscape encircling this small clearing like a curved wall. The grassless, lumpy ground between me and the woods ahead is coated in a glistening sheen that stretches as far as I can see, making it look like I'm lying on an ocean of wavy mud frozen in time. Rising from that glistening surface are the shadows of tall, skinny plants—long stalks topped with egg-shaped bulbs—standing between me and the tree line. Some of the farther stalks are perfectly erect. A few of the closer ones bend in my direction, as if reaching out to touch me.

Plants usually grow towards the sun, not towards the ground…

My eyes drift upward, and I stare sidelong at the crescent moon and the starlit sky through a lopsided opening in the tree canopy.

At that exact moment, I become aware of the chirping crickets and the rustling of small critters moving through distant shrubs.

Mustiness mixed with something extremely sweet and floral suddenly fills my nostrils.

Then I notice the cool night air sweeping gently across my back, arms, and legs.

I passed out in the middle of the woods, is what crosses my mind as I fight against the sedation that makes my limbs feel both nonexistent and too heavy to move. *I passed out in the woods? Naked?* As I focus harder, it dawns on me that my butt and upper thighs are the only parts of me shielded from the breeze, and that my painful erection is straining against something held taut against it. *Boxers…* My toes slowly curl against fabric. *I'm wearing boxers and socks.*

Another intense wave of drowsiness washes over me, as though someone just injected me with anesthesia. It takes all my willpower to keep my eyelids from shutting.

Get up…

"Grrugh," I groan softly while shifting and digging my fingers into the ground.

What I feel beneath my palms and digits isn't mud or dry soil. This surface I'm pushing against feels… *spongy* yet firm in the most bizarre, unsettling way—like soft clay covered in skin. No… it's more like pressing against a thick slab of raw beef or pork. And as I claw and writhe against it, a horridly wet, sticky sound comes from beneath me, immediately making me picture myself squirming atop a bed of mac and cheese.

It isn't until my fingers begin to slide against the meatiness beneath me that I realize they're coated in something slick.

That's when I realize how warm this squishy ground is—far warmer than the earth should be at this time of night.

What the hell am I lying on? It's wet…

No, not wet… Slimy. Feels like I'm on a giant bed of slightly warm steaks, glazed in something slippery and sticky, like syrup…

I shake my head. *Don't worry about why the ground feels weird as fuck. Just get up!*

My limbs flex and tremble harder than before, and though I don't feel as weak as I did when I first regained consciousness, I still can't push myself up. Which is concerning, considering I've been doing a hundred pushups every other day for nearly a decade.

C'mon, Nick… Get up!

I picture Heather and remember the last thing we said to each other at the airport last night. *"See you in a week! Love you!"*

I think about the sonogram of our daughter from Monday's second trimester appointment, and I will myself to find the strength to get home to my wife and our child. *You can't die out here. You've gotta be there for the birth of your first child, so get the hell up!*

The harder I try, the more violently my limbs shake.

And when I finally start to push off this strange surface, I feel resistance, like something is pulling me back down. Something tugs at the flesh on my cheek, chest, left arm, and thighs all at once. The first thing that comes to mind is that I must've fallen face-first onto a glue trap big enough for a human. Eventually, it starts hurting so much that my eyelids reflexively squeeze shut.

"GRAAH!" I roar, thrashing harder while pushing against the muscular ground with more force.

Whatever is adhered to my skin stretches between me and the surface, like gum stuck to a shoe. But it doesn't tear apart the way gum should. This… *rubbery* material tethering me to the ground just keeps stretching, getting more taut and pulling harder at my skin until—

Something completely stops me from pulling away any further.

Something coiled tightly around my right wrist and both legs.

Whatever it is feels too thick and too *fleshy* to be rope or chains. And whatever's constricting my limbs, it's… pulsating? Not noticeably. Subtly. Each *throb* is spaced about 5 seconds apart.

Snakes… Boa constrictors, I think, going limp again now that I've exhausted what little strength I had. *Feels like snakes are coiled around my limbs.*

Now that I'm focusing harder, I notice the same gentle pulsing beneath my abdomen, coming from some lumpy thing I hadn't realized was there this entire time.

I'm also lying on a snake… A smaller one… And it's got a big head… A head girthier than its body.

As I lie here trying to make sense of this nightmare that I've found myself in, I realize that my line of sight has changed. I'm now staring at the silhouette of my left arm instead of the shadowy woods that my head was awkwardly angled toward before. It dawns on me that now that I've stretched out whatever has me adhered to the ground, I might be able to lift my head and look over at my right arm to see what's coiled around it.

Groaning, I do just that. And sure enough, whatever's tethering my face to the ground stretches with me, slowly but surely.

Wait, I think, looking back at the glistening patch on my left arm that just caught my eye. *I should figure out what's got me stuck to the ground first.*

With the side of my face resting back against this meaty surface, I lift my left arm and watch in horror as a thin, continuous, glistening membrane that spans from my palm to my bicep stretches between my limb and the spongy surface like a sheet. No, like a batwing that's grown between me and the ground instead of between my arm and my body. Whatever it is, it's tan and lumpy, and it's wrapped around my muscle like a gooey bandage.

"Whuh-thuh-fuhhk," the expletive comes out as a slurred mumble. As panic sets in and my breathing turns ragged, I lift my head and fight through the pain of the membrane pulling at my cheek as I turn to the right. "GRUHH!" I groan, wincing.

Right as the pain gets bad enough for me to want to turn back around, I catch a glimpse of the tubular thing wrapped around my right arm like a snake—a spiked silhouette emerging from the same glistening, spongy surface I'm stuck to.

A beat after my body goes limp with panic, hazy memories begin flickering through my mind.

I went for my usual hike from our house to Fiander Lake in the middle of the afternoon.

Alone.

And I didn't tell Heather—or anyone else—where I was going today… But my car is still in the garage, so she'll know where to look for me when she comes back. Right? She knows where I usually hike.

There's no official trail, but the 3.25-mile trek through the dense woods behind my neighborhood is traveled often enough by local nature lovers that there's a beaten path leading to the point where you need to start heading straight east. From there, a compass is all one would need to navigate to the lake. Either that, or hikers can follow the carvings in the trees made by students from the high school where I teach—arrows pointing toward the best path to the unofficially named Yelm Lake.

Maybe a mile or mile and a half into the hike, I remember noticing a horribly musty smell in the air, a stench that grew stronger the closer I got to this spot. I expected to find a dead skunk. Instead, I saw something so horrific and incomprehensible it couldn't be real.

Through a gap in the trees ahead was a clearing about half the size of a basketball court, its ground covered in some kind of horrific biomass. The fungus—or whatever it was—was shiny, lumpy, this tan color tinged with a bit of yellow. It reminded me of the SCOBY used in kombucha production, but it was also webbed with fleshy cords that looked like veins, with black roots strewn across the top of it.

It wasn't until I got closer that I realized it wasn't just the ground within the clearing that was covered. The organism spread across maybe a quarter acre of the surrounding area, and the fleshy mass was growing up all the tree trunks in its path. Not a single blade of grass rose from the affected region. And the bushes and trees growing within it—and along its perimeter—were either leafless or in the process of losing their leaves.

My initial thought was that I stumbled across a film set for some movie or show set on an alien world. Because in all six years of university, I'd never learned about anything like *that*. As a high school science teacher with a master's in biology, I concluded it had to be some kind of fungus. Or perhaps a slime mold. A thick one. One that was thin as deli ham at the edges and thick as a ribeye toward the center.

My instincts screamed at me to get the fuck out of there. But the curious scientist in me urged me to investigate what could very well be a new discovery.

Just as I was about to listen to my gut, I saw something in the distance. Beyond the freaky stalks rising out of the biomass, I spotted a wavy-haired brunette girl with what looked like some kind of skin condition, sitting slumped over at the organism's center.

"Hello!" I shouted, hitting record on my phone as I crept toward her.

When she didn't respond after the fifth time I called out, I stepped onto the edge of the biomass. I remember shuddering at the squish it made beneath my boot and instantly thinking that it was like stepping on someone's abdomen.

A beat later, I heard something that compelled me to keep going.

The surface was incredibly slippery, forcing me to shuffle forward the way I used to cross black ice during winters back at UPenn. What I discovered next horrified me enough to turn around. But then I saw and heard something that made me believe continuing was the right thing to do.

It didn't take long for me to realize why I should avoid letting the stalks' black spikes touch my clothes or my flesh. By that point, though, I was too committed to turn back.

It wasn't until I was a few feet away from the girl that I realized what was wrong with her skin. It wasn't until I stopped focusing on dodging the quilled stalks that I finally looked up and understood why she wasn't responding.

That's when I panicked and slipped during my retreat.

That's when everything went sideways.

As I recount the traumatic, painful, nightmarish moments that led to me lying here mostly naked, I feel a tickling sensation across my arms, legs, and chest as another wave of intense drowsiness washes over me. The tickling instantly reminds me of what I saw beneath my flesh when I woke up from a deep, sedated slumber sometime earlier—sometime in the late afternoon or early evening. It's too dark to see it now, but I can feel them. The crawling beneath my skin is several inches farther along than where I last saw *them*.

The realization of what's happening to me sends me into a fit of groaning and thrashing as tears start rolling down my face.

Heather… Heather will find me before it's too late.

With each passing second, my attempts to break free of this nightmarish organism grow more and more pathetic.

As my body begins giving up on me, I suddenly remember why my wife won't get to me in time, and I go completely still.

Her new job has her training at the main site for a full week…

And since the school year doesn't begin for another two weeks, my coworkers won't think to request a wellness check anytime soon…

That means if Heather doesn't take my lack of texts and failure to call her back as a sign that something's wrong, it'll be at least a week before anyone knows I'm missing.

Not good, considering that I've got maybe two days left before I die of dehydration.

The panic that hits me in that moment gives me just enough strength to resume thrashing.

"Hel-luhhh!" That's how the word hello comes out. "Suhmwuhh hell-puhh mehh!" My facial muscles feel weak. My tongue is too heavy to move.

With each passing second, my body grows weaker and more tranquilized.

Dreaming…

I've gotta be dreaming… Because there's no way any of this is real…

My heavy eyelids flutter as I begin losing the fight to stay awake.

Consciousness slips away.

"HALLLPUHH!" I cry out like a zombie trying to speak for the first time after reanimating from the dead.

A moment later, my eyes shut. And no matter how hard I try, I can't reopen them.

Dreaming… I've gotta be dreaming… That's why I feel so numb all over. This is all just one fucked-up nightmare. That's all…

The instant that thought finishes crossing my mind, the chirping crickets go silent, the sound dropping away as my consciousness plunges into a thoughtless black void.

CHAPTER 1:
END-OF-SUMMER PARTY AT YELM LAKE

DANNY HOLLAND
Friday Afternoon, August 26th

Through the showerhead's high-pressure hiss and the rap song blasting from the Bluetooth speaker by the sink, I can just barely hear the intermittent buzzing of my iPhone against the countertop. Like most teens, I only ever get phone calls when I'm late getting home, or when my parents or friends are trying to figure out where I am after we've gotten split up. Given that Mom and Dad are right downstairs—and considering my sisters never call me—a phone call this early in the afternoon probably means Tucker's here. It means he texted me a while ago saying he's parked outside, and now he's calling to tell me to hurry my ass up.

I don't have to check my phone to confirm that, but I pull the shower curtain back anyway to see if I need to rush.

Crap, it is him, I think, yanking the curtain closed.

Like I'm late for school or some shit, I drape my washcloth over the shower caddy hook, step back under the spray, and start feverishly rubbing the soap off my body. It doesn't hit me until a few seconds later that I never washed below the thighs.

Ah well, I think, watching the suds from my torso run down my pale, hairy legs. *The parts that matter are clean…*

Plus I showered last night…

Besides, you're just gonna get sweaty on the hike to the lake anyway.

'Pshhh. *Guy logic*'—that's what my mom or sisters would say if they ever heard my reasoning for skipping the leg scrub.

Sure, I could take a few seconds to soap them up, but every second wasted is another second my overly caring mother might invite Tucker inside. If that happens, she'll ask what we're doing today. And if he slips up and says anything even slightly different than what I told her this morning, there's no way she'll let me go to the end-of-summer party at Yelm Lake. Hell, she'll probably call his mom too, which would likely end with Mrs. Williams forbidding him from going as well.

Because why wouldn't she after what's been all over the local news these last few months?

I towel off so fast that I damn near give myself friction burn. Then I scramble out of the tub the way I would if I just spotted a spider crawling toward me. After texting Tucker that I'll be down in 5, I resume drying off, staring at myself in the mirror as I do.

Today's the day, Danny, I think, locking eyes with my reflection like I'm trying to intimidate myself. *Today has to be the day.*

My hazel eyes flick up to my shaggy mess of brown hair, and then I focus in on the wet locks plastered to my forehead. Those few strands and the edges brushing the back of my neck are the only parts that are wet. Because I didn't bother washing my hair either. Didn't need to since I already did that last night.

Should I have gotten a haircut?

Nah. It's the same length as when she said she liked it like this, is what I think as I look down at my torso and arms.

My body type is what people would call an athletic build, which feels inaccurate considering I don't play any sports. Whatever muscle and definition I have comes from working out alone in my room—push-ups, calf raises, curling 20-pound dumbbells. Most days, I'm proud of being toned with flat abs instead of all hefty and potbellied like Gavin. But now that I'm about to head to the lake, where a bunch of girls from school are going to see me shirtless, I feel weirdly self-conscious.

I wish I looked more like Kyle, though, I think, picturing his noticeably bigger muscles forged by years of playing lacrosse.

The tan cargo shorts and green T-shirt that I laid out before hopping in the shower are what I race to put on. Even though my backpack's already packed, I rummage through it anyway, just to make sure I have everything.

Towel… Check.

Change of clothes… Check.

Deodorant… Check.

Toothbrush and toothpaste… Check.

Water bottle… Check.

Backup condoms… Check.

Flashlight… Check.

After zipping the bag shut, I pat down my cargo shorts. *Phone, wallet, keys…* I nod when I feel each one. Then I dip a hand into the bottom-right pocket. *Condom… Check.*

What are the odds you even get a chance to finally use one of these?

I think about how flirty Morgan Gallagher's been in her texts lately, and how she's been nonstop DM-ing me memes.

Hopefully my odds are good, I think, slinging my backpack over my shoulder and heading for the door. *Hopefully tonight's the night. At the very least, I need to kiss her. I refuse to start senior year without at least having my first kiss.*

"Would you like to come in and wait for Danny?" Mom says from the foyer as I'm starting down the stairs.

The second step groans beneath my foot.

"Oh, never mind," she continues, "he's coming down now!"

"About time!" Tucker shouts, just loud enough for me to hear him from the driveway.

When I'm halfway down, I see Mom leaning against the open door, arms crossed, hazel eyes already locked on me. Past her, the left half of Tucker's blue Honda Civic is visible, the mid-afternoon sun glinting off the windshield. The passenger window's down, and my dark-haired, pasty-skinned bro is leaning over the center console, grinning and bobbing his head to the music.

"See ya tomorrow, Ma," I say with a smile while powerwalking past her.

"You *sure?*" Mom says with a smirk, patting my overstuffed backpack. "Looks like you're packed for a few nights, *Daniel.*"

I spin around to face her but keep walking backwards. "That's because there's a towel and a hoodie taking up all the space."

"Whose house did you say you were staying at again?" she asks, eyeing me suspiciously.

"Kyle's," Tucker and I answer in unison.

She squints. "Kyle's the one who lives in Fox Hill, right?"

"Yup," I say, my heart racing as I pull open the passenger door.

"And isn't Fox Hill the community right by those woods where they said all those disappearances happened?"

I turn back to her while slipping off my backpack, doing my best to keep a straight face. "Mom, we're just gonna be chillin' in the house—playing games, watching movies, and stuff."

She squints harder. "So, you're *not* planning on going to that lake you boys went to earlier this summer, *right?*"

"Nope," I groan, climbing in and pulling the door shut, still maintaining eye contact through the open window.

"No, ma'am," Tucker adds.

"Alrighty then…" Mom says, sounding slightly skeptical. During the brief silence that follows, her hazel eyes study my face. "Text me when you get there! And if you go anywhere *other* than Kyle's house, *please just text me,* okay?"

"Alright, alright," I say, annoyed. "Bye, Ma."

"Bye, Danny! See ya, Tucker! Tell your mom hi for me!"

Tucker shifts into reverse. "Later, Mrs. Holland! Will do!"

"And tell Mrs. Turner hello for me, sweetie!" she adds.

Can't do that, since they won't be home until Sunday evening…

"Okay!" I say, forcing a smile to sell the lie.

The second Tucker starts backing out of the driveway, I roll up my window. And once it's up, I turn to him and let out an exasperated huff. "For a second there, I thought she knew about the Yelm Lake party."

Tucker snickers. "Dude, me too. You think one of your sisters said somethin'?"

"Doubt it. Chloe was never in the loop about parties during her high school days, so I doubt she'd even know about anything happening now." Because she was introverted as hell until she started college.

"Valid point."

"And Jess mentioned she might show up later with her friends, so I doubt she'd snitch. Especially with how bad my mom's been freaking out over the disappearances."

"True, true. Oh! Speaking of disappearances, you know Mr. Crawford?"

"Uhh… the bio teacher?" I say, picturing the bearded guy with slightly long hair who always seemed way too fit and cool to be a science nerd like me.

"Yeah."

"I didn't have him, but I know of him."

"Ah, okay. Well, he lives in Fox Hill. Like, six houses down from Kyle or some shit. And before you hopped on Xbox last night, Kyle told me some woman rang his doorbell late last night and asked his parents if they'd seen Mr. Crawford around the neighborhood lately."

My eyes widen. "No shit?"

Tucker turns to me, nodding. "Apparently, his wife left on a trip Tuesday night, and she hasn't heard from him since they texted the next morning. She called him nonstop from Wednesday afternoon until midnight. But he never answered. And when she tried calling again yesterday morning, it just kept going straight to voicemail. So, Mrs. Crawford called up this neighbor lady—the one who rang Kyle's bell—and asked her to check on him. And she also asked her to see if the Amazon packages that got delivered Wednesday were still on the porch. Because she figured if they were gone, it meant he brought them in. Not only did he not answer the door, but the packages were all still there."

"Well, shit, dude…" I mutter as the thought of this hike suddenly fills me with a sickening dread.

If Mr. Crawford really is missing, that makes six people who've vanished under mysterious circumstances in Thurston County these past few months, I think as I begin zoning out.

Back during the second week of July, this twenty-something-year-old guy visiting our area from New York went missing.

A little over 4 weeks ago, Jake Landau—a kid who just graduated from our school—randomly walked out of his house in the middle of the night without his phone and was never seen or heard from again. I didn't know Jake, but I knew *of* him. Because he was popular and played varsity lacrosse with our bro Kyle.

Exactly two weeks later—sometime after midnight on August 10th—the same thing happened to a guy named Eli Rutherford. The creepy part? Eli and Jake were neighbors. And Jake was best friends with Eli's younger sister, Lizzy—a girl who had also just graduated.

Then, in the middle of last week, the local news put out a missing person's alert for Savanna Lockhart—another one of Lizzy Rutherford's best friends.

And *then*, 3 or 4 days ago, a bunch of people started posting on social media asking if anyone had seen Luke McCarthy—*another* recent Yelm High grad who'd been dating this hot girl named Whitney Emmerson. Apparently, Luke was driving home after only a few days of being at the University of Washington and disappeared after pulling over on the side of the road somewhere during the trip. Something like that. Hearing about it shook me even more, because Whitney was *also* best friends with Lizzy… which made her friends with Jake too…

Since 5 out of the 6 disappearances involved kids from our school who were all connected, a bunch of Yelm High kids and I started obsessively Googling every article about local disappearances, trying to piece together the mystery. Current students and alumni took to TikTok, which is why the story blew up. It went so viral that hardly anyone was posting about the Amazonian Uteroboscis outbreak that'd been dominating the news since late July. And once the vanishing-teenagers story took off, internet "detectives" with zero connection to Yelm High started digging too. That's when they found two similar disappearance cases elsewhere in Washington that happened within the last three months.

The first semi-related case involved a 22-year-old girl from Seattle named Julie Bloom, who vanished while hiking off-trail in Olympic National Forest around June 4th or 5th. Coincidentally, she'd been hiking that weekend with a girl named Allison Hannigan—someone who *also* graduated from our school, like, 4 years ago. And where things get really weird is that Allison and

Julie also just so happened to be friends with the guy from New York who disappeared in late July…

The other semi-related case happened during the second week of July. A dude named Matthew Barlow from Seattle left his phone in his apartment and vanished the same way Jake and Eli did. The only connection social-media sleuths could find was that he lived close to that Julie girl. That, and some people claimed they'd seen them at the same bar *at the same time* a few nights before they both disappeared.

The disturbing part is that the cops don't think the missing people were kidnapped or murdered by a serial killer. Well, at least not in Jake Landau and Eli Rutherford's cases. Because their parents were home when those boys left, and there were no signs of forced entry. Which means something weirder is going on. Something like a cult. A bunch of TikTokers think it's aliens. And with all the soft disclosure lately from the government and military about UFOs, UAPs, and aliens in the mainstream news, I don't totally rule it out. Honestly, I'll be surprised if it's *not* aliens.

"Maybe we shouldn't hike to the lake anymore," I finally say after zoning out for half a song.

"Don't be a pussy, Danny! We're goin' to that damn party!"

"No, I'm not sayin' we *shouldn't* go!" I say quickly. "I'm just sayin' maybe we should drive to Tailgater's Lot instead of hiking."

"Yeah, *no*. Not on a big party night where every teen in town'll be there. In case you forgot, the reason we gotta hike there is because on the rare occasions when cops show up to bust the party—like they did at the end-of-school-year party two years ago—they block the one and only dirt road to the lake. Which forces everyone to run into the woods to avoid getting arrested and slapped with underage drinking citations. And do you know what happens to whoever leaves their car behind?" He turns to me.

I bobble my head. "They trace the car to the owner's house."

"Exactly. And if me or Kyle get a visit from the cops, our parents tell your parents—and then everyone's parents. Now, I don't know about you, Danny Boy, but the last thing I want is to start senior year being grounded. And unlike you, I don't just risk not being able to hang out. I also risk getting my car taken away. And I really don't fuckin' want that."

I nod slowly. "Shit… yeah… I wouldn't even get grounded. My mom would straight-up kill me for drinking and lying about being out in those woods."

"Exactly. Your mom would disappear you, and then everyone would just think you're out there somewhere with Jake Landau." He barks out a laugh.

I snicker while shaking my head. "You dick! Too soon, bro… Too soon."

Tucker lets out a more sinister laugh. "Yeah, you right…" he says, looking up at the ceiling. "My bad, Landau. R.I.P., homie."

The car swerves.

"Eyes on the road, fucker!"

"Relax, *relax…* Anyways… Uhh… What the fuck took you so long to come outside? Our food's been ready for pickup for, like, ten minutes!"

"I—"

"Wait," he interrupts. "Lemme guess… Jess took forever in the bathroom again?"

"That, and—"

"And you spent too much time jacking it to pictures of Uteroboscises?" He smirks and waggles his eyebrows.

Uteroboscises, A.K.A. womb-worms, are these newly-discovered parasites that live in and feed on the uterus of mammals—mainly humans. What's even wilder than where they live is that those pink, unsegmented worms are basically the exact size and shape of a well-endowed, circumcised dick.

So basically, Tucker's making a gay joke…

While I obviously don't like dick or things shaped like them, what those worms do to get into a chick's uterus *is* something I've definitely fantasized about during tug sessions. The way Uteroboscises migrate into a host is by slithering into the birth canal, inducing cervical dilation with their proboscises, and then wiggling their way into their *preferred habitat.* If that's not insane enough, they also root into the organ with microscopic threads that sprout from their red tail-tentacle things and start sucking blood using their branched proboscises. And once they're rooted, they can't be removed without dire consequences. Oh, and while those slithering dongs are going all vampire-mode on their hosts' blood supply, they basically turn their host into sex-zombies so that the chicks can spread their worms' eggs in the wildest way possible…

"No, weirdo!" I shout. "I got up hella late. And since Jess took forever in the bathroom, I didn't even get to shower and all that until, like, ten minutes before you called."

"Damn. How late did you sleep in?"

"Got up 'round eleven? Ate breakfast, went back to sleep an hour later, then woke up again at two-ish."

"And here I was, about to blame your sweet, pretty little sister for our food being cold."

I shake my head. "First of all, stop calling my fifteen-year-old sister pretty. It's creepy… Second, *you're* to blame. Because you had us all up till four a.m. playing Warzone, *Mr. One-More-Game!*"

"Bro, we were doin' too good to stop! Besides, you're a teenager—not some old-ass thirty-year-old who's gotta wake up early for work five days a week. So you got no business cryin' about late-night gaming," he says, turning into the restaurant's parking lot.

"That'd be true if it wasn't three nights in a row of late-night gaming."

"Yeah, yeah, yeah," he groans, pulling into a spot right out front of the restaurant. "Now quit your bitchin' and go get the food, would ya?"

Scowling at him, I reach for the door handle. "You're not comin' in?"

"Nah."

"But… I'm gonna need help carrying out the food."

"You had me waitin', so this is your penalty. Besides, I've got bitches to text before we hit the road again. You know, to set *thangs* up for us. Now chop, chop, broski!"

I huff as I open the car door. "Fine. Whatever."

Farrelli's without a doubt has the best pizza in town. And since it's literally an 8-minute walk from school, it's the go-to spot for our crew and pretty much everyone at Yelm High. From my house—16146 Prairie Creek Loop SE in the Prairie Creek subdivision—it's just under a mile and a half away. About the same distance from Tucker's place in Nisqually Meadows at 10437 Brighton Street SE, which is roughly two miles southwest of mine.

That's great for us. But the problem is that we usually hang out at Kyle Turner's house, which is thirteen miles west—on the complete opposite side of the forest where people may or may not have been disappearing. So even when I don't keep Tucker waiting, the food still usually needs reheating by the time we get there.

Sure, it sucks not being able to enjoy fresh-out-of-the-oven pizza and having to drive twenty minutes every time we want to kick it with the boys at Casa de Turner's, but it's worth it. Because Kyle's parents are never home, and he's got a sick-ass gaming setup in his basement with a bunch of old consoles and an always-stocked beer fridge his parents don't mind us raiding. On top of all that, there's a combo ping-pong and pool table.

"Pickup or—" the large, hairy guy behind the counter asks when I'm a few feet away.

"Pickup," I cut in. "For Danny—I mean, for Kyle Turner."

He turns to the rack and eyes the two pizza boxes with a big plastic bag of Styrofoam containers balanced on top. "Large meat lovers, large pep, five dozen wings, and fries?"

"Yup."

Since Kyle already paid online, the guy just hands it all to me. "Here ya go! Enjoy."

"Thanks!"

Leaving Farrelli's while two-handing the boxes isn't an issue since the exit opens with a push. Getting back into the car, though, won't be as simple without some help. And when Tucker glances up from his phone as I'm passing the front bumper, only to look right back down at it, I know I'm not getting any help unless I ask.

"Yo!" I shout. "Can you get the door?"

He smirks. Then he scowls. "Dude, if I can open a car door while holding that same amount of shit by myself, *you can too*."

"Bro, I don't have a good grip. Just open the fuckin' door so I don't drop all our food!"

Tucker sets his phone in the cupholder with an annoyed huff. "Fine." He leans over the center console and cracks the door just enough for me to wedge my knee in. "Happy?"

"Was that so hard?" I ask, prying the door open with my leg.

"Yes," he says flatly, taking the boxes. "Yes it was."

Shaking my head, I sigh and climb in. The second I shut the door, he drops the warm boxes onto my lap.

"Alright," Tucker says, shifting into reverse, "let's see if I can make up for all the time you set us back." He guns it out of the spot.

"If you get us pulled over, we won't make it there at all."

He smirks at me as the car accelerates. "When have I ever gotten pulled over for speeding?"

"Never."

"Exactly. Because I know all the spots where cops hide. Now shut the fuck up and watch a precision driver do what he does best!"

His tires screech as he drifts out of the parking lot, hanging a right onto the main road.

CHAPTER 2:
PREGAME

DANNY HOLLAND
Friday, August 26th

Yelm Highway is one of those annoying two-lane roads with a single lane going in each direction, so there's no safe or legal way to pass slow drivers. But that doesn't stop Tucker from doing it anyway. Whenever there's a long stretch of tree-lined road with nowhere for cops to hide, he guns it around anyone not doing at least 65 in a 50-mph zone, then hauls ass like he's in a damn *Fast and Furious* movie until it's time to do it again. And thanks to him driving like a maniac, we make it from Farrelli's to Kyle's driveway in 16 minutes instead of 20.

"And remember that skanky-ass Piper Cummings girl who fucked and sucked damn near half the guys at school?" Tucker asks as we grab our backpacks from the backseat. The entire ride here, all he's talked about is which girls are gonna be at the lake party.

I grin at him on my way over to grab the pizza boxes from the passenger seat. "How can I *possibly* forget *the Cummings Dumpster* when she was all every guy talked about?"

"Valid point."

When I look over my shoulder to hand off the pizza, I see Tucker already walking backward toward the front door. Because that's Tucker for you. Mr. Inconsiderate. Rather than bitch about it, I grab the bag of fries and wings from the floor and shut the door with a hip bump. "She's coming tonight too? I thought college usually starts before high school. Figured she'd be gone by now."

"Nah, *she's* not coming," he says, opening the front door, which Kyle always leaves unlocked whenever we're coming over. "*But...* her little sister, Skylar, is friends with Nate Mahoney's little brother. And Nate said Nick told him that Skylar's gonna be at the lake tonight!" He stomps on the floor to summon the guys from the basement, like he always does. "So I'm thinkin' about passing up this guaranteed hook-up with Sarah K and shooting my shot at Skylar before she follows in her sister's footsteps and gets run through by the football and lacrosse teams."

I squint at him. "Wait, isn't Skylar gonna be a freshman this year?"

Tucker grins. "*And your point?* Rumor has it Piper racked up, like, six bodies before the end of her freshman year—many of which were upperclassmen. And legend has it that their older sister, Harper, started early and dated up too. It's hereditary with those Cummings girls, and I wanna be the first one in, not the tenth or fiftieth." He snickers. "Besides, I'm, like, three months away from being eighteen. As long as it's consensual and we're both in high school, who gives a fuck?"

"*Technically,* she won't be a high schooler until next week."

"*Technically,* fuck you!" He cracks up, and I just snicker. "And *technically,* she'll still be the same age next week that she is today, so... double fuck you!"

I half-laugh as the basement door groans open. "Well, good luck tryna hook up with Lil' Cummings, brotato. I'm gonna stick to girls *over* the age of consent."

"You ain't gonna stick to *shit*, Danny Boy!" Tucker fires back. "Because a dude who's never fucked a bitch—or even kissed one—ain't got shit to *stick to*!" He laughs like a psycho.

More laughter comes from my left, and I turn to see Kyle rounding the corner with the chubby ginger trailing behind him. "Oh damn, Tuck!" Kyle says, whipping back his sandy brown hair as he's handing me a Coors Light. "What'd Danny Boy say to deserve that verbal ass-whoopin'?"

Tucker grins wider and cocks a thumb at me. "Bro gave me a whole-ass lecture about *age of consent* because I said I wanted to bone Piper Cumming's soon-to-be freshman sister," he says, grabbing a beer from Gavin. "So I put the virgin in his place!"

"Whatever," I sigh, cracking open the can. "Things are gonna change tonight."

Tucker obnoxiously gulps his beer, then pats me hard on the back. "For your sake, bro, I hope so. Because senior year will be over before you know it, and the last thing you wanna do is roll into college as a fuckin' loser-ass virgin!" He raises his brows and shoots me a look full of judgment and fake concern.

"He's right," Kyle says, nodding and staring at me with those icy blue eyes. "So—" He lifts my beer to my mouth and tips it up. "—let's get you sufficiently fucked up during this pregame so you're nice and relaxed when it's time to rizz up Morgan."

"Chug! Chug! Chug!" the guys chant as I struggle to down the cold brew.

Near the end of the can, beer starts running down my chin. When I swallow the last mouthful, the guys erupt in cheers. The demonic burp that follows gets them howling even louder.

"Good shit, Danny Boy!" Gavin says, holding out a vape. "Now hit this THC goodness and get a nice crossfade goin'."

I shake my head. "Nah. I'm just gonna stick to beer. Remember last time I got crossfaded?"

The guys snicker.

"Yeah," Kyle says, "you got so fucked up you couldn't even form words."

"And you couldn't get off the couch for, like, three or four hours," Gavin adds.

Everyone laughs.

"Exactly," I say. "And I kinda need to be able to form words if I'm gonna talk to Morgan later."

Gavin bobbles his head. "Valid point." He takes a long pull from the vape. "More for us."

"Nah," Tucker says. "Fuck that! You gotta take *at least* two hits. Just enough to feel good, but not enough to fuck you all the way up." He swats my back. "C'mon!" He punches my arm. "C'mon!"

"*Fine,*" I grumble. "Depending on how much I drink, I'll smoke a little before we leave."

"Yeeeeah!" they all cheer.

"Oh," Kyle mumbles with a mouth full of pizza. "And speaking of being too fucked up to form words." He swallows loudly. "That Becca Dalio chick—the one who makes TikToks about living with a Uteroboscis—"

"Lemme guess," Tucker interrupts. "You finally got your brother to subscribe to her OnlyFans for you?"

Kyle grins. "No… Why would I do that when half her stuff's leaked all over the internet?"

He's not wrong. The day Becca announced she'd made an OnlyFans to show the world how much milky womb-worm slime was constantly gushing out of her—and what it looked like when one of those pink, phallic worms pushed its head through her cervix during orgasm—all four of us spent hours scouring the internet for leaks. By the end of the day, we finally found them on one of the usual sites. And damn… it was the most glorious thing I'd ever seen.

So glorious that regular porn doesn't really do it for me anymore. I just keep replaying the same five videos of her that I downloaded.

"True," Tucker mutters.

"Anyways…" Kyle groans. "Me and Gavin were just watching her recent posts—"

"You and Gavin watched her OnlyFans together?" Tucker snickers. "Hold up! Did you jerk each other off too?" He flashes a troll grin.

"The *fuck*?!" Kyle shoves him. "No! We were watching her recent *TikTok* post!"

"Sure, sure," Tucker says with a smirk. "Now we know why it took y'all so long to come upstairs just now!"

Kyle shakes his head. "You're a fuckin' tard…"

Tucker does that stupid *heh-heh-heh* laugh.

"As I was sayin'," Kyle continues, "she made another vlog about what happens if she doesn't let a dude finish in her for a few hours. The compounds those worms pump into her blood had her so high after two hours that she was slurring her words and could barely keep her eyes open."

"Oh shit…" I mutter. "Didn't a bunch of girls die from overdosing on the Uteroboscis opioids?"

"Yeah," Kyle says. "But the ones who died had multiple worms. I think she only has one?" He looks to Gavin, who nods.

"I know that," I say. "But the paper from the chick who discovered the Uteroboscises said the high and arousal keep getting more intense the bigger they get. So she could still overdose once it's big enough to produce the same concentration as two or three worms."

Tucker fake-coughs. "Nerd—keh-*hugh*!"

"Fuck off," I groan.

Tucker smirks and then looks at Kyle. "Did she say how big it is now?"

Kyle shrugs, then glances at Gavin. "I think she said her last sonogram put it at close to a foot long?"

"Yup," Gavin mumbles with a mouthful of fries. "Or just a few inches shy of a foot-long. Or maybe a little over."

"Oh fuck," Tucker and I say at the same time.

"That means it's probably outputting the same amount of drugs as two six-inch worms," I mutter.

"Bro," Tucker says, throwing an arm around me and Gavin. "I hope one of the chicks—or multiple girls—from school caught one during that Florida outbreak. That'd make it real easy for Danny Boy and Big Red Herring here to lose their virginities." He grins. "All you'd have to do is hang around a girl with a womb-worm and wait for the high to turn her feral. Then boom! She'd pounce on one of you, rip your pants off, and ride you bareback to sweet oblivion without you even having to speak a word!"

Gavin grins. "God, that'd be incredible."

"Mmhmm," I hum, nodding and picturing Morgan.

"And the best part," Kyle adds, "since the slime kills viruses, bacteria, and *sperm*, you wouldn't have to worry about STDs or about knockin' her up!"

Tucker snickers. "Only thing y'all *would* have to worry about is not finishing immediately," he says. "And since it's hard enough as it is to last in regular ol' wet pussy without a condom, I imagine it'd be damn near impossible for virgins like yourselves to last very long in one gushing slime that's more slippery than K-Y Jelly. Hell, I don't think I'd last long either."

Kyle snickers. "Same!"

We all laugh.

"Urrgh," I groan. "We'd still have to worry about one of those worms jamming a proboscis into our piss holes and laying eggs."

"I mean," Tucker says through clenched teeth, "nothing bad happens to dudes when the larvae hatch. So I'd say it's worth the risk."

"*Very* worth the risk," Gavin says with a wicked smirk.

Kyle nods. "Exactly! And if you're worried about that, all you'd hafta do is not let the chick finish. Either that or just pull out right before she does, then just stick it back in after it retracts! Simple as that!"

"And we all know the *pull-out* method works," Gavin adds. "Because we've all seen the Becca Dalio video where she and her male *co-star* demonstrated the proper technique."

"Multiple times," Kyle says with a grin.

"True," I mutter, picturing that white, noodle-like proboscis sticking out of her and wriggling in the air. It was as horrific as it was hot.

"Yo," Tucker says. "You know what I just thought of?"

"What?" we all ask.

"If neither of you gets laid this year," Tucker says, "we can fly y'all out to wherever Becca lives—or fly out to where some other bitch with a Uteroboscis lives—and just ask to meet up. Boom! Guaranteed trip to Pound Town! Because there's no way their worms will let them say no to the *seed* they so desperately need!" He waggles his eyebrows.

"Word!" Kyle says mid-laugh. "Considering that those poor skanks need to get nutted in, like, once or twice per hour to make the high and horniness go away, they'd probably *beg you* to *help them out*." He makes air quotes during that part he emphasized.

"Shit," Gavin says, "they'd probably offer to pay *us* to help them achieve sweet relief."

"Yo, seriously!" Tucker says.

Everyone cracks up.

"Shit," I mutter, turning to Gavin. "Maybe Kyle should use his pop's credit card to book us tickets to Florida tonight. Then we can try to link up with Becca or one of those chicks from Saint Augustine who *birthed* baby Uteroboscises all over that Target back in May. That way, we don't have to spend all year hoping some girl puts out."

"I'm down!" Gavin says, chuckling after.

"Let's be honest, *Daniel*," Tucker says. "The real reason you're talking about flying to Florida tonight isn't because you wanna get laid and finally lose your V-card. It's because all those stories about people disappearing around here have you too chicken-shit to wanna hike to the lake." He grins fiendishly and starts jabbing me in the arm.

"Nuh-uh!" I fire back, trying to swat away his punches.

"It's all good, Danny Boy," Kyle says. "Not gonna lie, I'm a little freaked out too. Especially after hearing Mr. Crawford—my neighbor—went missing."

Tucker lets out an exasperated sigh. "Ah shit… I swear to God, Kyle, if you dare fuckin' say you're bailing out—"

"Nah," Kyle says, shaking his head. "I ain't no punk bitch! And I know nothing's gonna happen to us if we stay together and stay alert." He pulls out a folding knife from his pocket. "Plus, I've got this if some cult member pops out and tries some shit!"

"That's what I'm talkin' about, bro!" Tucker says, nodding and grinning.

I snort. "Kinda hard to stay alert when we're gonna be drunk and high during the hike, and then completely shitfaced on the way back."

"Dude!" Tucker shouts. "Shut your negative-ass up, Danny!" He shoves me from the left.

Yeah, Danny!" Kyle adds, shoving me from the other side. "Shut the fuck up and stop being such a fucking buzzkill!"

"Myeah!" Gavin mumbles, his mouth stuffed with pizza this time. "Shuh-thuh-fuhh-uhh!" He swallows. "Fuckin buzzkill!"

They all laugh, then keep taking turns pushing and jabbing me.

"Quit it!" I growl, shrugging free and slipping out of the middle. "Fuck! I fuckin' hate you guys sometimes!"

"We hate you too, brotha," Tucker says with a wicked grin. "But, like… in a brotherly-love kinda way."

"*Whatever*," I groan, grabbing another beer from the fridge. I crack it open and glare at them while I chug.

"That's how you do it, Danny Boy," Tucker says. "Get nice and drunk so you don't have a fuckin' anxiety attack during the hike."

Still chugging, I flip him off.

Kyle's phone chimes as I'm setting the can down and reaching for a chicken wing with my free hand. "Oh shit," he says.

"Who is it?" Tucker asks, leaning over and trying to get a look at the screen.

Kyle grins. "Snapchat from Ashley Pemberton."

Instead of showing Tucker, he angles the phone toward me. It's a picture of two skinny white girls in bikinis with the lake behind them. My gaze immediately snaps down to their camel toes, which is something that happens whenever I see a chick dressed in leggings, swimwear, or lingerie. It's a problem I've had ever since puberty hit. Then again, I think it's a problem all guys have these days now that girls on TikTok and Insta purposefully pull their pants up all tight for attention and likes.

Oh my damn, I think, finally looking up at their faces.

The girl on the left is a pretty redhead in a yellow bikini—Ashley Pemberton. And the shorter blonde in pink?

Holy shit, I think as a huge smile spreads across my face. *Morgan Gallagher.*

In a bikini!

It's even better than I imagined…

As I'm giving her another once-over, I notice the caption.

Where u boys at? Morgan's drunk-ass won't stop asking about Danny 😊

"Holy fuck," I mutter, grinning even harder.

"Yeah," Kyle says, "*oh shit* is right."

"Oh shit, *what?*" Tucker shouts, craning his neck to get a look.

Kyle turns to him and Gavin, angling the phone to them. "Boys, Morgan's drunk and asking where Danny Boy's at! Which means we need to eat fast and get our bro to her ASAP so he doesn't miss out on this *Code Pink!*"

Everyone lets out a loud, collective "Ooooooh!"

Everyone except me.

Because I started shoving fries into my mouth before Kyle even finished talking.

CHAPTER 3:
THE HIKE

KYLE TURNER
Friday, August 26th

Like pretty much every wooded area in northwestern Washington, this forest is so densely packed with tall-ass trees that, no matter how sunny it is, the canopy keeps things below shady—like it's always on the verge of evening. And now that the sun's lower in the sky, it's getting harder to make out shapes in the distance. Which is a problem, because it'd be real fuckin' nice if I was able to see if someone or *something* is stalking us long before whatever it is gets close enough to be a problem.

I've been so busy searching for movement in the distance that I keep forgetting to check the trees for arrows carved into the bark. If I wasn't so fucking high and drunk, it wouldn't be so hard to juggle threat detection and navigation. It'd also be a helluva lot easier to stick to the trail if there was an actual one to follow. The closest thing to a trail on this 2-ish-mile route between home and the lake is a narrow, patchy dirt path that weaves through the gaps in trees and undergrowth. It was formed naturally from years of people hiking from my neighborhood to the different lakes out this way. But there are so many branches that splinter off the path, being on a dirt path doesn't mean you're on the right one. Also, all the trails tend to fade into the greenery the deeper in the woods you go. And then it completely vanishes halfway to Yelm Lake. That's because most people from my area tend to just hike out to Fiander Lake, like I used to with my parents back in the day. You know, before they started abandoning me all the time to travel.

Had I just used my compass, Yelm Lake would've been a straight shot southwest from Fox Ridge. But now that we're this deep in the woods with no real point of reference, the only way to navigate is by the tree carvings and the ribbons tied to branches. Most of those markers existed long before we started hiking out here, made by kids who were in high school while we were probably still in middle school. But we added a few and initialed them on our first hike back from the lake the summer after freshman year. And by we, I mean me, Tucker, and Gavin. It wasn't until the beginning of junior year that Danny moved here from Portland, Oregon. So his first hike to the lake wasn't until we brought him out here earlier this summer.

Out of our crew, I've logged the most hours in these woods. Which is why I'm always the one to lead the way.

Except I'm not sure we're still going the right way anymore…

It's been a while since I've seen an arrow or any familiar landmarks, I think, scanning the trees ahead. *Shit. Maybe I missed a few while I was checking for threats…*

Rustling in the bushes to my right makes me turn with a quick snap. And when it sounds like it's getting closer, I slow down.

"Dude!" Tucker says, shoving me from behind. "Quit freakin' out every time you hear a fuckin' squirrel scurryin' in the bushes!"

"I'm not freakin' out!" I snap, taking a long step over a protruding root. "I'm just making sure it's not a bear or some shit. Tryna keep us alive! Like a good squad leader should!"

"Nah," Tucker says with a grin. "You *are* freakin' out! Just like Danny is back there!" He chuckles.

"Nuh-uh! Am not!" I shout over whatever Danny says.

"Are too! And you know how I know you are? Because—in all the times we've hiked through these woods—you've never froze and hunched over and went all *stealth mode* every time a leaf moved in the distance! So, admit it. You're being a bitch-boy just like Danny because you're thinking about Mr. Crawford and all the other people who vanished around here, aren'tcha?"

"I'm not a fucking bitch-boy!" Danny shouts from the rear of the pack. "I'm here, aren't I?"

Tucker snicker-snorts. "Yeah, but I bet you're one more snapped twig away from running home!"

"Fuck you, Tuck!" Danny shouts.

"Play tough all you want," Tucker fires back. "I know you and Kyle are scared shitless right now."

I shake my head. "Nah. I ain't scared. It's just… being this high and drunk while out in the woods just has me a little more paranoid than usual. That's all," I say coolly.

Tucker snickers as he walks up alongside me. "You say that like you've never hiked these woods while this fucked up before. You're only paranoid because you think someone or something is gonna do to us whatever happened to Jake Landau and Mr. Crawford."

"Whatever," I grumble, speeding up.

"A non-answer means I'm right!"

I growl through a huff. "A non-answer means I'm not gonna waste my breath trying to convince you, Tucker."

I hate to admit it, but he's right. As much as I've smoked and drank since freshman year, my tolerance is too high for the six beers and several hits of THC dabs to have me this jumpy. I'd never confess this to the guys, but the news of those recent disappearances has had me freaking out over this hike and lake party all week. But it wasn't until I heard my former teacher—my neighbor—went missing that I started brainstorming ways to avoid hiking through the very woods he likely disappeared in. Had it not been for Ashley Pemberton's text from last night that hinted she was finally gonna let me smash at this lake party, I probably would've faked having food poisoning. Well, the prospect of getting laid by one of the hottest girls in Yelm High was a big part of me not chickening out, but it wasn't the only motivator. The main reason I didn't bail was that I didn't want to get roasted by the guys.

Why? Because I've had enough sex to be okay with not getting laid tonight. But what I can't handle is being tortured all year by my best bros...

"Fuck," Tucker grumbles from behind me.

"What?" I ask.

He huffs. "Nate texted a picture with a message saying, *'she's here, and dressed like an OnlyFans bop.'* But this shit ain't loadin'! And the message I sent asking him who won't send!"

"We never get signal this deep in the woods," I mutter, checking my phone right as my service goes from 1 bar to none.

"Umm," Danny groans from the back of the pack. "I haven't seen any arrows or tree ribbons in a while. You sure we're not lost, Kyle?"

Shit, he noticed... And if he was paying attention this whole time, that means we haven't passed any in a while. Which means my high-ass might've gotten us lost.

"Yeah," Gavin chimes in. "I was gonna say the same thing. Because it feels like we've been hiking forever."

I snicker, my gaze snapping from the *path* ahead to the phone I'm lifting to chest level. "We've only been hiking for a little over thirty-five minutes, so we're basically, like, halfway there. It only feels like we've been hiking forever because you're high as shit—"

"And because anything over ten steps feels like forever to your fat ass!" Tucker interrupts.

Everyone but Gavin cracks up.

"Urrrgh," the ginger grumbles. "You're such an asshole!"

"And I've been an asshole since the fifth grade," Tucker says, "yet you've been hanging out with me ever since."

"For some reason," Gavin mutters.

"He's not wrong," I mutter.

"Who knows," Gavin continues, "maybe that'll change when the school year starts. New year, new friends."

"Pssh!" Tucker blows. "Yeah, right…"

"Hey, look," I say, pointing at the arrow carved into the tree on our left. It's not one of ours since our initials aren't below it, which means we've wandered off-track to someone else's path, either a little further north or south. "See? We're goin' the right way! Now trust your boy to get us to the lake the way I always do!"

A gust of wind blows toward us as I'm saying that.

A beat later, Tucker sniffs dramatically behind me. "Ughh! I wish we could trust our boy to put on deodorant! Because you smell musty as all fuck!"

"What?!" I smell it as soon as I inhale through my nose—something that reminds me of skunk and sweaty armpits that haven't been washed in days. "Nuh-uh?!" I lift my right arm and start sniffing my pit.

"Damn," Gavin says. "If that's you, Kyle, you smell like the boys' locker room after gym."

"Dude, that's not me!" I say, holding up my arm on my way over to Tucker. "Sniff test me, bro!"

He scrunches his face. "Hell nah! Get your funky-ass away from me!"

"Dude, c'mon!"

Tucker sighs. "Fine. But only because you're my best bro…" He leans in and takes a whiff. "Oh shit. It's not him!"

"Told ya!" I say, lowering my arm.

"Thank *gahhd*," Gavin says. "Because if that was you, Ashley wouldn't get within twenty-feet of your ass, and every girl at the lake would avoid us all day!"

"Blehhh!" I gag. "That musty-ass smell's getting' stronger!"

"Mm-hmm," Danny hums. "And since the wind's not blowing anymore, that means we're getting closer to it."

"Well," Tucker says, scanning the area, "now I'm kinda curious to find out where that stank's comin' from. Because whatever that is smells too rank to be a skunk."

"Uhhh," Danny groans. "We evolved to detect stinky smells as a warning for us to avoid the origin of said stinky smells. So trying to find the source of that funk is *the opposite* of what biology says we should do instinctually."

"Thanks for the lesson, nerd," Tucker says.

"I'm with Danny," I say. "Besides, the smell might stick to our clothes if we get close to it."

"You right," Tucker says, following behind me.

A few yards later, the stench gets stronger. So strong that it makes me cough.

"Fuck!" Gavin shouts a few yards later. "This musk is straight-up chokin' me!"

"Yeah it is," I croak, looking around in search of a gap in the brush. Unfortunately, the only clear route that doesn't require a machete is the one we're on. "Maybe we should double back and go wide right?"

"Nah, fuck that," Tucker says. "It'll just take us longer to get to the damn lake if we double back."

"Mm-hmm," Danny hums. "Especially if the detour leads to a big slope or steep-ass hill or bushes too thick to pass through.

Detouring now would just lead to us having to come back this way anyway. Or lead to us getting lost."

"I got my compass," I say, "so we wouldn't get lost if we did detour."

Danny winces and bobbles his head side-to-side. "I mean… A compass only works if you got a map. Which we don't have. So, sure, we'd be able to navigate to a main road or a neighborhood. But without knowing *exactly* where we are, a compass wouldn't magically guide us straight to the lake or take us directly back to your place."

I sigh. "True, true… Alright, we'll just stick to the path then."

"Good!" Tucker says as he begins walking. "Pussy awaits! So let's get movin'!" He gives me a shove right as I'm turning around, making me trip over my own foot.

"Bruh!" I groan mid-stumble.

"Sorry, bro," he says, slinging his arm around me. "But we gotta make up for all the time you wasted standing around just now! Because if we get to the lake and I see someone rizzin' up my target, I'm gonna kick your ass for making me late."

"Dude," I say, shrugging him off me. "Stop calling girls your *target*. Sounds rapey as all fuck."

"Seriously," Danny says from behind us.

Tucker just does a 'heh-heh-heh' laugh in response. He then takes a sort of deep breath—the way one does before giving a long-winded response—but then just exhales and starts sniffing again.

At the same time, this sweet and floral smell cuts through the funk as though some girl just spritzed perfume a few feet ahead of us.

"Mmm-uhh," Tucker sighs in relief. "That smells so fuckin' good!" He tips his chin up and starts rapidly sniffing like a dog, turning his head right to left as he does.

"Yeah it does," I reply, my mouth flooding with saliva. Without even thinking about it, I start doing what he's doing—desperately trying to track down the source with my nose.

Danny and Gavin are sniffing just as rapidly and hard behind us.

With each step we take, that amazing fragrance gradually gets more potent, and that musty smell fades at the same rate. The next thing I know, I'm mindlessly drifting to the left—to where the scent is strongest.

This urge… I feel like I need to get where that smell is coming from.

It's like what Danny said earlier about instincts. Avoid funky smell, get to the sweet smell…

I look back at the guys. Just like me, they're all hugging the left side of this narrow corridor through the trees and foliage, each of them smiling subtly with this glazed-over look in their eyes.

"Dayum," Gavin says softly. "Smells kinda like sugar cookies!"

"And fruit," I whisper. "Like… maybe mango or somethin'?"

"Agreed," Danny says. "Like both of those mixed with vanilla and a really good-smelling flower."

"Yes to all those things," Tucker says. Then he snickers. "And of course Big Red's fat ass said sugar cookies!" He cracks up.

"Shut the fuck up!" Gavin shouts over our laughter.

The gloriously sweet smell gets even stronger a few steps later, drowning out the mustiness so much that it's barely noticeable. At the same time, I suddenly start feeling higher and drunker and dizzier. I'm starting to feel more blissful too. And it all just keeps getting more intense the more I breathe this stuff in.

No… I'm not just feeling more intoxicated, I'm also starting to buzz like I shotgunned an energy drink. And my body is, like, humming the way that only happens when I have too many strong edibles. My schlong swells a bit right after that thought crosses my mind, and I'm suddenly overcome with that same urge I get whenever a porn video reaches the good part. *Wait… why am I starting to feel hella turned on right now? Da fuck?*

"Uhh," I groan, looking over my shoulder at the guys while still marching forward. "Anybody else startin' to feel—"

"Like they just snorted Adderall after eating a whole bag of weed gummies?" Tucker blurts out with a grin. "Because *yeah*."

"Same," the rest of us harmonize.

"Uhhhh," Danny groans. "Is anyone else concerned that we all began feeling more altered *after* we started smelling this sweet, flowery scent despite not having any weed or beer in the last forty-minutes?"

"Lil bit," I mutter.

The instant I finish speaking, I suck in a deep breath—because I'm addicted to it. Only this time, the air has suddenly become so thick with this heavenly aroma that it feels like I'm snorting a fluffy cloud of it. And in the middle of that long breath, my dong somehow goes from semi-hard to fully bricked for no reason at all.

What the fuck, I think, urgently tucking my boner behind my waistband before anybody sees. *I wasn't even thinking about any girls… So why does it feel like my life depends on me rubbing one out right now?*

"Geez," Danny croaks. "It's gettin' kinda hard to breathe."

"Yeah it is," Tucker says, breathing heavily like he's aroused instead of winded. "Which means the source of this godly smell must be real close…" As he resumes sniffing rapidly, he begins dragging his feet to the left instead of toward me.

Where's he… When I turn around, I see him hurrying over to the wall of chest-high bushes.

Upon reaching the tall shrubs, Tucker tippy-toes, cranes his neck, and starts frantically looking around.

Weirdly enough, I feel compelled to do the same thing. Like some primal urge is commanding me to find the source of this fragrance by any means necessary. But I will myself to keep walking down the naturally formed path through the greenery, albeit at a much slower pace than before. Slower because it's like my body is stalling me, trying to keep me from straying away from what's beckoning me.

"*Dude!*" Danny says as Tucker disappears into a gap in the wall of ferns. "We should be running *away* from the intoxicating aroma, not walking toward it."

"Seriously," I mutter, my gaze wandering from Tucker to the leafless trees beyond the ferns and bushes he's walking toward. When I start looking up, I see in the corner of my right eye that all the trees toward the clearing where the path is leading are also missing leaves. "Hey, Danny…"

"Yeah?"

I point at what I'm staring at. "Isn't it too soon for the leaves to be falling?"

"Yeah… it is," he almost whispers. "Something's gotta be wrong for those to be shedding this early… And what's even more concerning is some of those are evergreens, which shouldn't be losing their—"

"Holy fucking shit!" Tucker blurts out.

Danny and I turn toward his direction at the same time. There's a wall of tall bushes between us and Tucker, but I catch a glimpse of him through the gaps. He's sidestepping between this tree and the foliage to his right—moving into an area that's a little further down in the direction we were heading, but several yards off to the left of this path. No sooner than I set my sights on him, he disappears behind another foliage wall.

"What?" we both shout.

"I—I…" Tucker snickers, and then he starts giggling. "I—I can't explain it. Y'all just need to come see this shit right the fuck now!"

CHAPTER 4:
THAT LOOKS LIKE A...

KYLE TURNER
Friday, August 26th

Gavin, being the closest, charges into the brush first. I'm right behind him with Danny at my heels. At the end of the leafy corridor, Big Red makes a right toward this cedar tree with a wide trunk that's partially obscuring Tucker's backside.

As soon as Gavin slips between that and the bushes a few feet to the right of it, he does a bit of a stutter step and rapidly shakes his head. "Ayo!" A snicker follows. "Bruh, what the fuck!" Now he starts cracking up.

"I know, right?" Tucker says mid-laugh.

Curiosity compels me to speed up. And as I'm approaching the gap Gavin just went through, my foot catches on a tree root, which sends my drunk-ass stumbling toward the bush. The plants rustle loudly as I come barreling through the narrow passage like a charging bear.

"Gah," I groan in response to the branch that just whacked my cheek.

A clearing the size of my parents' bathroom is what I stumble into. Even with all that commotion I just made, Tucker and Gavin don't turn to look at me. They're too busy giggling at and taking pictures of whatever's in the center of this patch of dirt.

As I begin making my way toward Gavin, I take a breath and immediately start feeling like I'm suffocating. That sweet aroma is so thick in this spot that it feels like I'm in a chamber filled with vaporized honey and minimal oxygen.

Holy shit, I think, smiling from the buzz rushing through me.

The overwhelming arousal makes me grit my teeth right after.

Gotta nut. I imagine doing the one-handed activity I do before bed most nights. *Now! Right now!*

It isn't until I'm passing behind Tucker that I see something bizarre through the gap between them—something that stops me dead in my tracks. "What the fuck…" I say in awe.

Danny runs right into my backpack a split-second after. "Dafuq you stop like that fo…" His words trail off as he comes to a stop on my right side—when he sees what has us all speechless. "Oh, that's whole-ass dick-mushroom!"

Tucker cracks up while taking another picture of it. "My first thought was alien dildo staff, but I think your description is better, Danny Boy…"

"Somehow, both are perfect descriptions," I mutter, slowly scanning it from bottom to top.

Growing perfectly straight up out of a mound of what looks like freshly upturned soil is this white fungal stalk—like the ones that portabella mushrooms have but 2-fingers wide and stretched to about 2-inches long. Instead of having a mushroom cap, though, what's growing out the top of this stalk *literally* looks like a beige dildo with some thick-ass petals hanging out the bottom of it like a skirt, hence Danny and Tucker's descriptions. Like, the top rounded part looks *exactly* like a glans with a urethra-like opening right in the center, and its 6- or 7-inch shaft is covered in waxy *skin* with these veins running along the length of it. Like, *actual* veins that are way more realistic than the ones dildos have. And as if that isn't freaky enough, growing out from the base of the shaft—like, growing down from the part where a real schlong would be connected to the crotch—and hanging down around the fungal-stalk-thing like a peeled banana are five beige *petals* that are the exact shape and thickness of starfish arms. Well, the outer side is beige like the rest of it, but the underside? It looks like raw beef but bright red, and it's glistening like it's coated in slime.

Slime. Lube.

Use it as lube to—I picture myself carrying out the act of self-love that I so desperately need to do right now.

"That's gotta be fake…" I say, turning to Danny. "Right? Like, someone from our school decided to play a prank by taking some weird alien dildo mounted to a white stick and burying it in the ground alongside the route to the lake… *Right?*"

Tucker nods slowly. "That was my first thought too," he mutters. "Because the soil looks like it was recently dug up and dumped back down here. But then I got closer and realized that sweet, vanilla, flowery smell was coming from this thing."

"Wait, is it really?!" I almost shout.

"Don't believe me?" He smirks. "Then just lean in and give that peen a sniff!" Tucker says.

"*Bruh…*" I groan.

He cracks up.

With a huff, I reluctantly lean in, stopping with my nose maybe a foot away from it. Danny and Gavin do the same on either side of me. The second I start inhaling, a heavy vapor of sweet floweriness floods my nostrils—one stronger than what I smelled when I first stepped foot in this little clearing. At the same time, I get crazy dizzy and hornier than I've ever been.

Gotta nut, I think, fighting the overwhelming urge to reach in my shorts. *Right now!*

Can't, the guys are here.

Say you gotta pee, then you can once you're hidden behind the trees!

If I don't nut now, you're going to lose your fuckin' mind and literally die.

All that goes through my mind in an instant—during the first few seconds of this inhale. But I just clench my jaw and ignore the primal command, still inhaling the entire time.

Towards the end of that same breath, my mouth floods with more saliva than I've ever produced at one time, and I have to slurp to stop from drooling.

The other guys make similar slurping noises beside me a beat after I do.

"Holy shit!" I blurt out while leaning away. "That smell *is* coming from this!"

"Which means it is some type of fungus," Danny mutters. "One that looks like a fungus but smells like a fruity flower… Or maybe it is a plant. Because I dunno if there are any fungi that smell like *this*."

"But it doesn't have chlorophyll," I say.

"Eh," Danny groans, not taking his eyes off the dong-shaped organism for a second. "Some plants don't have any. Saw a TikTok once about a pale, parasitic plant called a ghost pipe. They lost their chlorophyll because they evolved to feed off other plants using underground roots or mushroom networks or some shit."

In the corner of my eye, I see Tucker point at Danny's waist area. "Guys! Seeing this dick-mushroom got him hard!"

Danny yanks his shirt down over his crotch and spins away from us all in one quick, fluid motion. "No! That's not—"

"No wonder you've never hooked up with a chick!" Tucker teases. "You like peen!"

"Dude, I'm *not* gay!" Danny shouts.

"Oh, Daniel," Tucker says. "There's nothing wrong with being gay, brother."

Danny growls. "I know there's nothing wrong with it! But *I'm not*—"

"And I've got no problem with the rainbow flag community," Tucker talks over him. "So, if you just come out, I promise we'll still be bros no matter what! And I promise you'll still be on the CoD Squad!" He chuckles.

"*Dude!*" Danny shouts. "I don't have a problem with them either. *But. I'm. Not. Gay.* I just randomly got bricked up way *before* any of us saw this… dong-shroom. It just happened right around the time this thing's aroma started getting really strong."

"Yooo!" Gavin howls. "Dong-shroom is canon!" He always says something is canon when he wants it to be a part of our group's established lore or a part of our vocab.

And this should definitely be a part of our canon. But instead of agreeing with him, I sigh. "Alright, you know what? Danny's not lyin'. This might be T.M.I., but I also got bricked up right when the smell started getting super strong too."

"Uhhh…" Gavin groans with a wince of a smirk. "Since we're being honest… Same…"

Danny gives me a faint smile. "Thanks for backing me up, dude," he says, holding out his fist for a pound.

I bump my knuckles against his. "You got it, brotha!"

Now he fist-bumps Gavin.

Tucker laughs in the middle of that. "Thanks for admittin' that, fellas! I randomly got hard too when the smell started getting' strong, so I was just tryna get someone else to admit it first to make sure it wasn't just me."

"You dick," Danny says.

"No," Tucker says, pointing at the dildo-shaped mushroom. "*It* dick!"

We all crack up.

"Okay…" Danny mutters after we all settle down. "Okay… So… this… *thing* is secreting some sort of pheromones that make humans high and horny the way Uteroboscises do to girls, yet we're *still* standing a few feet away from it and staring at it like that's not a huge fucking red flag? Like, should we not be running the fuck away from here *immediately*?"

Tucker snickers. "Umm… *Valid point.* We definitely should be—"

"Agreed," Gavin and I interrupt.

"And…" Tucker continues, "I think the reason we're not is because this shit we're inhaling has us feeling better than alcohol or weed or any drug ever has or ever could."

I nod. "That's without a doubt why. I feel—" A sleepy smile creeps across my face. "—so good right now." An involuntary laugh escapes me.

"Same," Gavin almost whispers, smiling the same way I am. "Feels like I can't walk away."

Danny sighs and starts backing away. "All the more reason we *should* go before we figure out why this thing evolved to intoxicate humans, lure us in, and make us aroused to the max."

"Mm-hmm!" I hum, slowly backing away only to stop a foot later.

"Or…" Tucker says, taking a step towards the dong-shroom. "Better idea… Wait for it… We pull it out of the ground and take it with us to the lake!"

Danny rapidly shakes his head. "Uhhhh. Touching it and keeping it around us is the exact *opposite* of what we should do!"

"Yeah," I groan. "The fuck would you wanna take an organic dildo with you to the lake?"

Tucker snickers. "Because of what our genius bro, Danny, said a bit ago."

"Umm," Danny groans. "And which of my dire warnings could've possibly convinced you that taking this with us is a good idea?"

Tucker grins harder. "Alright, here me out… You said this thing uses its scent to make humans horny the way Uteroboscises do to chicks, *right?* So…" He gestures toward us with a twirl of his hand.

Gavin's face lights up. "If we take it with us to the lake, all the drunk girls near us will get crazy horny and feel compelled to hook up without us having to put in any effort!"

"Bah-bah-bah-bah-bingo!" Tucker cheers the way Star-Lord did in *Avengers: Infinity War.*

Danny bobbles his head side-to-side, his expression going from concerned to partially smiling. "That idea is as genius as it is terrible."

"Thanks!" Tucker says with a shit-eating grin. "And since taking this plan will get us all laid for sure…" He slowly reaches for it.

"Dude, *don't* touch it!" Danny shouts.

Tucker's left hand wraps around the thing's veiny shaft while his right hand grabs the fungal stalk coming out of the dirt. "GAHHH!" he yelps a split-second later, snatching his hands away and scrambling back. "Holy fucking shit!"

The rest of us jump.

"What?!" I shout.

"What happened?" the others say at the same time.

"It's warm! And the—the skin around the shaft moved the way real dick skin moves around a boner! And it fucking twitched in my hand!" Tucker shouts, speaking a mile a minute.

"Nuh-uh!" I say. "You're fuckin' with us."

"Dude!" Tucker shouts, looking genuinely distressed. "I fucking swear on my life, on our brotherhood, and on my parents' lives that I'm not lyin'! Go on, touch and see for yourself!"

I shake my head. "Nah! I ain't touchin' some dong-shaped fungus!"

"Bro, just do it!" Tucker says. "And you don't have to touch the dick-shaped part. The starfish-arm-shaped petal things are warm and twitched too!"

"Oh shit," Danny mutters, pointing at it. "Look, it's oozing sap or something…"

I turn and stare in awe at this golden bead of syrupiness that's oozing from the urethra-like hole at the top. "Oh shit, it is…"

Danny snickers. "Tucker, you made the dong-shroom precum with one tug! Good job, buddy!"

"You really know how to please a guy, huh?" I tease next.

Tucker barks out a laugh. "Shut your asses up and touch the damn thing so that y'all know I'm not lying! *Please.*"

"Fuck it," Gavin says, taking a step forward. Rather than touch the dong-shaped part, he reaches for one of the thick, starfish-arm-shaped petals. And after pausing for a moment, he presses his finger against it. "Oh fuck, it *is* warm!"

"Told ya!" Tucker shouts.

"*How?*" Danny says, looking up at the sky. "There's not even any sunlight shining down here. Probably hasn't been any shining in this spot for hours…"

I let out a long sigh. "Alright…" Ever so slowly, I reach for the petal-thing to the right of the one Gavin touched.

Heat greets my pointer finger the instant I touch it—a heat that rivals the temperature of human flesh. At the same time, Gav runs a finger down the shaft, and the damn thing gently spasms against my digit.

"Oh fuck!" I shout, snatching my hand away. "It's warm! And it twitched!"

"And the waxy skin does shift around the shaft!" Gavin adds.

"Like I said!" Tucker shouts as a thicker bead of honey-like slime oozes out of the tip.

"This is so fucked!" I mutter while backing away.

Tucker turns to him. "Hey, science nerd. Do you know of any plants or mushroom-fungi-things that are warm to the touch?"

"*None…*" Danny replies. "But there are plants that react to touch."

"Venus flytraps, right?" I blurt out.

He nods. "Yeah, those and sundew vines or whatever they're called. And they're both carnivorous plants that lure in bugs and small animals with *sweet odors*, trap them, and digest them. Which means we should probably leave that shit right where it is before it's sap melts our skin. Or before some hidden part of it pops up out the dirt and grabs us. And now that I think about it, that freshly upturned soil beneath it makes me think something might actually pop out the ground if it's stimulated enough."

Without missing a beat, we all take several steps back.

"Danny's right," I say, looking around. Off to the right, I spot a narrow gap between the tall bushes that looks like it leads toward the clearing our original path was leading us to. "We should go. *Now.*" I start walking while looking back at the guys.

Tucker pouts. "But… but… we all get laid if we take this thing with us," he says in a whiny kid voice.

I picture myself fucking Ashley.

Gotta get laid!

No, the lake's too far. Go behind those bushes and—I picture myself doing what I do when I watch porn—*and then go!* That exact thought has been constantly running through my mind since I sniffed the dong-shroom.

That thought, like the others, doesn't feel like my own.

"We'll just have to get laid the old-fashioned way," I say, walking toward it. "C'mon, we can get back to the path though here." It takes all my willpower to start walking away.

"Right behind ya!" Danny says, his hurried footfalls crunching leaves and branches behind me.

"Let's go, Tuck," Gavin says, marching behind Danny. "We can't get laid if you get us killed!"

Tucker lets out an exasperated sigh. "Fine-*nuhh*. But when you and Danny end up being forty-year-old virgins, just remember you could've had some guaranteed pussy today if not for Nerd McGee scaring us out of my genius idea!"

This dirt path through the ferns and tall bushes is so narrow that leaves brush my arms and legs with every step. Maybe around halfway through it, I start noticing that a lot of the bushes around here have lost a good portion of their leaves, just like the trees ahead. A branch snaps beneath my foot a moment later.

Immediately after, something rustles in the underbrush to my left.

"Holy fuck," I whisper, looking for whatever that was while moving as stealthily as possible.

"Calm your tiddies, Kyle!" Tucker shouts from the back of the pack. "It sounded small. Like a rabbit or some shit."

"Umm," Danny groans. "Is it just me, or is that musty smell coming back?"

"Yeah," I whisper, still staring off to the left. During my next step, something squishes beneath my sneaker—something spongey, not something mushy like mud. It's so bizarre that I immediately freeze and shudder. "What the…" My gaze slowly wanders down.

Beneath my shoe is something resembling lumpy pork meat that's yellowish-tan, coated in a slimy sheen, and webbed with bulging veins. It's a thick biomass of some kind that's completely covering the ground from where my foot is all the way to where this path disappears behind the brush. It isn't until I start scanning the area that I realize this shit isn't just blanketing the path. It's also growing out to the left and right of it too, covering the lower half of the leafless bushes and the base of the tree trunks within its vicinity.

"OH-WHAT-THE-FUCK!" I shout, frantically scrambling backward.

My backpack crashes right into Danny.

"Guhhfff!!" he grunts, palming my shoulder and stopping me from backing off this biomass. "What the hell—"

Then I hear someone crash into Danny. "Dude!" Gavin shouts.

Danny abruptly stumbles right back into me with some force—like Gavin just pushed him—and the impact makes my right foot slide across the slick, meaty surface. With my arms flailing, I quickly step forward with my other foot to keep from going down.

"Fucking move! Fucking move!" I scream while hurriedly backing up to my left this time, my sneakers sliding across the fleshy slab with each drag of my feet. "Go back! Go back!"

"What happened?!" Danny and Gavin shout.

"Fuck's goin' on?" Tucker yells at the same time.

When my sneakers finally hit dirt, I don't stop—I keep scrambling backwards. My backpack crashing into a tall bush is what finally stops me. At the same time, something that feels like a rubber ball hits the base of my calf and wet branches poke me just below that. Whatever it is, I don't pay it any mind. I'm too captivated by the horror ahead.

"Oh, what the fuck..." Danny mutters as I sidle up beside him.

Now that I'm back on regular ol' soil, I take a moment scan whatever fuck it was I just stepped on. It's then that I realize it's much thinner toward the edge—thin as a cheese slice compared to the steak-thick spot I stepped on—with tan tendrils stretching out across the soil in a zigzag pattern.

"Ayo…" Tucker mutters. "That shit's gross as all fuck!"

Gavin dry-heaves. "Seeing this while inhaling that musky-ass stench has me on the verge of pukin'!"

"What the fuck is that?" I pant out. "What did I just fuckin' step on?!"

"I dunno…" Danny almost whispers while backing away. He then points at the edge of the biomass nearest us. "But these zigzaggy tendrils stretching out from the edge of it? Looks like how slime molds branch outward from the main part of it…"

I let out a shaky breath, shivering as I do. "Do slime molds have *veins*? Because this pork-looking shit has thick-ass veins toward the edge of the path!"

Danny looks where I'm pointing. "Oh fuck! No, they—they don't!"

"Whatever this shit is," Gavin pipes up, "I think this is where that musty smell has been coming from."

"Mm-hmm," I hum. "And I think it's also what's causing all these trees and plants to lose their leaves. Because everything it's growing on or near is dying."

"I think you're right," Danny says, taking a picture of it. "Well, whatever this is…" He turns and faces the way we came. "We need to get as far away from it as fast as we fuckin' can! So move your asses!"

"Say no more, fam!" Tuck says, turning and jogging off the way we came.

As soon as Danny starts moving, I take a step, only for something to immediately pull at the skin between my left calf and ankle. "Ahh!" I groan, putting my foot back down.

"What?" Danny says, skidding to a stop.

"Something's just—" I gasp when I see this giant, beige, spiked asparagus-looking thing that's stuck to my leg.

The fleshy bulb at the top looks exactly like a pinecone that's about the size of a baseball. As for the stalk, it's maybe 8 inches long and about as thick as 2 of my fingers. And then there are the black quills sticking out all over the stalk—rubbery-looking things, each tipped with an orange, gelatinous ball. Those protrusions are what's stuck to my skin…

What's even more concerning than finding out that there's a hellish asparagus stuck to my leg is realizing that it's not sticking out of the soil like a normal plant. Instead, this thing is seamlessly growing out of another part of that same meaty biomass I stepped on earlier—a section that was hidden beneath the dead leaves of these dying plants…

"Oh!" Danny yelps. "The fuck's on your leg, dude?!"

"I—I dunno!" I stutter, reaching down for it with my left hand.

Grabbing the pinecone-shaped bulb feels like gripping a rubber ball wrapped in thick skin. And I'm so freaked out by how fleshy the scales feel that it takes a second to register how warm it is.

It's the same temperature as the dong-shroom! Maybe a little warmer.

As soon as I try pulling it away from my leg, the gelatinous balls at the end of the quills pull my skin like Crazy Glue that's long since dried. "AHHHH-HA-OWW-chuh-hurrgh!"

"What?!" the guys shout.

"What happened?" Danny continues.

I pull harder, but it feels like my skin's about to rip off. It hurts so fucking much that I immediately stop. "Oh fuck!" I look up at him with wide eyes. "It's—it's stuck to my fucking leg!" I croak in the breathiest, most panicked voice. "I—I can't get it off! It fucking hurts too much when I try pulling it off!"

The guys all stare at me with terror in their eyes. I've known Gavin and Tucker since Kindergarten, but I've never seen them this scared before.

"What the fuck do we do?" Tucker asks.

I just look back at the thing stuck to me. "I—I dunno! But someone needs to fucking help me get this thing off my leg! Now! Please!"

As Danny steps toward me, a tickling sensation spreads outward from where the orange-ball-things are touching my flesh, and I reflexively look down at my leg. "What the fuck," I mutter.

Feels like something's crawling on or in my skin… But I can't see anything from this angle.

Panic surges through me like a bolt of lightning.

The next thing I know, I'm trembling, hyperventilating, and staring at this thing with unblinking eyes.

CHAPTER 5:
SQUAWK

KYLE TURNER
Friday, August 26th

Danny squats beside me and then starts examining whatever's adhered to my leg. "Oh fuck…" he mutters before I can ask if he sees what's causing this tickling sensation. "Shit…"

"What?!" I bark.

He huffs. "Good news is… it's not stuck *in you* like thorns. It's more so… these orange globs are, like, stuck *on* your leg…"

"How's that good news?!" I shout.

He looks up at me and shrugs. "Better on you than *in you*, right?"

I bobble my head.

"That's what she said?" Tucker jokes. "Wait. No. That's what *he* said!"

"Not the time, Tuck!" I shout.

Danny looks back down at it. "Alright, so… I think… we need to rip it off before it starts digesting you or some shit."

My eyes go wide. "What the fuck do you mean *before it starts digesting*?!"

"Remember what I said about the sundew plant earlier?"

"Vaguely…"

"Well, it has sticky beads at the ends of its needlelike leaves that trap the bugs. And since this is way bigger than that plant, it's reasonable to assume it evolved to catch prey the size of a raccoon instead of insects. Which is why we gotta rip it off *before* it digests your leg. You know… if that's what it's tryna do. But we have to do it without touching the sticky orange stuff on the ends of the black spikes."

"Oh fuck…" I resume hyperventilating mid-sentence. Right as I do, this wooziness hits me out of nowhere, making me feel the way Nyquil does when it starts kicking in. "I can't, bro. I don't think I can even pull it hard enough from this angle. You're gonna have to do it! Please!"

Danny lets out an exasperated sigh. "Okay, okay! Uhh… Hold on a sec…" He urgently shrugs off his backpack and then unzips it. After rifling around inside for a bit, he pulls out a spare shirt. "Just in case I'm wrong about the quills being the only sticky part," he says while wrapping the shirt around his hand.

"The fleshy pinecone part didn't stick to me when I grabbed it, if that's what you're worried about."

"Figured… But I just don't wanna touch it at all." Danny carefully grabs its bulb. "Oh fuck! This thing's kinda hot too!"

"Yeah," I groan. "Forgot to warn ya…"

"Ugh!" Gavin gags. "What. Thee. Fuhhhh-kugh."

"It's warm, *and* it's almost the same color as the dong-shroom?" Tucker says. "They've gotta be related."

"I was thinkin' the same thing," Danny says. "Well, I was thinking they're connected to each other, not related. Like—"

"Hey!" I bark. "How 'bout we save the analysis for *after* you've gotten this man-eating plant-fuck off me?! Kay?!"

Danny looks from Tucker to the organism he's holding. "Yeah, okay. Sorry… Guess I'm just stalling because I don't wanna hurt you."

"If you don't save me by hurting me, it'll turn me into goo. So do it, bro! Fucking now!"

Danny gulps hard. "Okay… On the count of three. Alright?"

"Okay, okay," I pant out. "Fucking go!"

"One…" he says quietly.

I shut my eyes and clench my jaw.

"Two…"

Searing hot pain radiates from between my calf and ankle.

"GAHHHHH!" I roar as my leg reflexively kicks away from the hell-asparagus. "Fuck! That shit hurt like a bitch!" I suck in air through my teeth. "Fuck! Is it—is it bad? I'm scared to look."

"Nah, it's not bad," Danny says while reaching back into his bag. "Just a little bit of skin is missin'."

Wincing, I twist my left leg outward and look down. Just like Danny said, the wounds aren't as bad as they feel—there are about 6 shallow holes, and only a few of them are bleeding. Two of them, though, are oozing some weird-looking white pus.

"Goddamn!" I growl. "Anyone got Band-Aids?"

"Nope," Gavin and Tucker say.

Danny shakes his head. "The one thing I didn't pack, unfortunately. But here…" He holds out an unopened bottle of water. "At least rinse it off."

"Better than nothin'," I say, taking it from him. The water stings as soon as it hits the wounds, making me wince. "Ahh fffff-uhh-kurrrghh!"

Now that the blood's been washed away, I kick my leg back and grab my ankle so I can get a closer look. That's when I notice these little hairs sticking out of the wounds.

How the fuck did it rip off enough skin to leave a divot but not rip out my hairs with it? I angle my leg to the light a bit more. *Wait, these strands sticking out of the wounds are darker than my hairs… Black instead of sandy brown… And they're thinner…* My gaze drifts back to the pus oozing out around one of the black fibers like a popped pimple. *And why didn't that pus wash away with the blood?*

"You good?" Danny asks.

I let my leg drop. "Yeah, I was just checking—"

"Oh shit…" Tucker says from a few feet. When I look up, I see him peering over the bushes on the side that the pinecone stalk is on. "This meaty slime mold or whatever the fuck it is stretches out another ten or more yards! Oh fuck! And there's, like, a long strip of it growing *directly* toward where we just came from—toward where that dong-shroom is!"

"Wait, for real?!" Danny shouts, hurrying over to him. "Because that's exactly what I was thinking we'd see if we checked back there!"

"Well, you thought right, D!" Tucker says.

Danny stops beside him and then peers over the bushes. "Holy fuck… He wasn't lyin'…"

Tucker scoffs. "Why would I lie about that?"

"Because," Gavin says as he's sidling up beside him, "all you do is troll us and shit."

"Mm-hmm," I say, coming to a stop beside Danny and setting my sights on what they're staring at.

Tuck snickers. "You right."

"The question now is," Danny continues, "is this meaty biomass growing *out* from some underground part of the dong-shroom? Or is this shit growing *toward* the dong-shroom to, like, connect to it? Because one of those has to be true if the *only part* of the… *meat mass* that's growing in a perfectly straight strip happens to be growing *directly* toward—or from—the direction of the dong-shroom."

"Only one way to find out," Tucker says, heading back the way we came.

"What does *that* mean?" Danny shouts, chasing after him as me and Gavin are following suit.

Tucker looks back at us with a grin. "It means I'm gonna dig up the soil beneath the dong-shroom to see if they're connected underground!"

I snort. "So now the guy who was just rushing me to get us to the lake wants to waste time investigating this biomass from hell that tried to eat my fucking leg?"

"Yeah," Tucker says. "Because as gross as all this shit is, it's pretty fuckin' cool and fascinating! And I wanna see if Danny Boy is right!"

"No," Danny says, "you wanna see if I'm *wrong*. Because if it's not connected underground, you're gonna dig up the dong-shroom and take it to the lake."

Tucker looks back at us again, grinning even harder than before. "*Maybe*... Maybe not..."

"Fuck that!" Danny says.

"Ah, c'mon!" Tucker says as we reach the small clearing where the dong-shroom is. "It'll only take a few seconds if you fools grab some big sticks and help me dig!" He snaps a branch off a nearby tree.

"Fuck it," Gavin says, picking up a branch from the ground. "I'm let's do this! For *science*!"

"That's the spirit!" Tucker says, already scraping soil away from the side closest to the meat mass.

Breathing in this organism's sweet vapor again doesn't just calm me down, it erodes whatever hesitation I had about this dumb idea. "You know what?" I say, grabbing a branch. "I'm curious too."

"Psshh," Danny scoffs from a few feet back. "I'll just chill back here so we all don't get squad-wiped at once."

"Knew you would, pussy!" Tucker shouts.

With three of us scraping away soil from beneath the dong-shroom, it doesn't take long to uncover something beige and fleshy connected to the bottom of this thing's stalk.

"Dear God," Danny gasps.

Tucker gags. "Me thinks Danny was right!"

We keep digging until we've exposed a patch about the size of my backpack. Then we stop. But no one says anything. We just stare.

The dong-shroom's white stalk is fused to a mass almost identical in texture to the meat-mat we stepped on earlier, and it has the exact same black roots growing out of it. Where they differ is that this thing is beige instead of yellowish-tan, and it's not all slimy. Also, it looks way lumpier than what I stepped on.

"Similar fleshy tissue…" Danny mutters while backing away. "Identical roots… There's no way it's not connected to that biomass genetically or physically. And if it's not physically connected to it yet, it will be once the biomass reaches this spot."

"Fucking wild," I whisper, wincing from the burning wounds on my leg.

"Uhh," Tucker groans, turning to us. "Anyone else feel weird staring at this while they're hard?"

"Yeah…" We all say.

Tucker pokes it with his stick, and it jiggles like the belly of some obese creature. "Blurrgh!" we all retch while backing away.

"Fuck!" Tucker shouts. "Felt like I poked a pig belly! What the fuck!"

I huff. "Still wanna take this dong-shroom, Tuck?"

He tosses his stick. "Hell fuckin' no!"

Everyone laughs nervously.

"Good," I say, dropping my stick. "Then let's fucking go!"

I lead the way back out to the trail we were on before that heavenly smell lured us off track. Not long after making a left onto it, my leg wounds suddenly go from burning to itching.

Fuck, I haven't wanted to scratch myself this bad since I got that poison ivy rash…

A few yards later, as the sweet scent is being drowned out by the musty stench, the trail banks right. Then the path through the corridor of head-high ferns curves back to the left maybe 5 yards later—curving toward that clearing with all the leafless trees. As we're rounding that bend, I start noticing every plant on the left side of this path is bare.

Don't tell me…

My gaze drops, and there it is—the same meat mass from earlier is all over. It's plastered across the ground and covering the lower half of the plants, and hundreds of tendrils are creeping onto the edge of this trail.

No way, I think, scanning the border to see how far it goes.

It isn't until the path straightens out that I get my answer.

The ground ahead vanishes beneath a mat of fleshy corruption that stretches several feet past the wall of dense foliage and trees to our right. And dead ahead, just a few feet from me, stands another spiked asparagus-looking stalk that's much bigger than that first one. This one's maybe 2- or-3-foot-tall. Its pinecone bulb is twice as big, the stalk is as thick as my wrist, and the black quills jutting out from it are as long and thick as chopsticks.

"Guh-guh—guys?" I mutter, pointing at the sight ahead.

"Oh fuck," Danny whispers. "The path… it's—and there's another pinecone stalk thing!"

"What the fuhhhhk," Tucker and Gavin harmonize as he's saying that.

Just as I'm thinking the stalk ahead is massive compared to the one that stuck to my leg earlier, I turn left and gasp at the hellish sight.

Dozens upon *dozens* of pinecone stalks are scattered across the biomass-covered clearing, each one thicker and taller than the one we just saw. Most of them look around 5 feet tall. The ones along the edges are a bit shorter and more spread out, but there are some clusters randomly scattered throughout the peripheries—like the group of 6 near where we're standing. But toward the center, they're even denser. In some spots, those spiked stalks are crowded so close together that it'd be near impossible to side-step between them without brushing past them.

I don't know acreage and shit, but this clearing is about the size of my backyard—which is bigger than the ones in most neighborhoods—and the slime-coated meat mass covers every inch of it. What's even worse is that it doesn't stop there. It stretches past the clearing's edge, and there are spiked stalks scattered between the trees as far as I can see.

A layer of frozen, lumpy peanut butter glazed with syrup—that's what this slimy biomass makes me think of.

As I slowly turn to the right, something in the center—past all the stalks—catches my eye.

"Holy fucking shit-balls…" I mutter, my body tensing as my heart starts racing.

Seeing all those giant, sticky, potentially carnivorous spiked stalks isn't what has me fucked up right now…

It's not the black T-shirt stuck to a stalk nearest us, or the men's cargo pants dangling from one further down that has me hella worried…

The fact that the towering trees near the center of the clearing have veiny hell-meat stretching 10 feet up their trunks isn't even what has me stunned into silence.

It's what's sitting in the dead center of the clearing that has me too terrified to breathe or blink.

A person…

Someone with long brown hair, sitting upright in a fetal position, their chin tucked just behind their knees…

A petite person whose entire body is covered in the meaty biomass, except for the hair coming out the top of her—or his—head.

The most horrific part about the sight is the way the corrupted body blends seamlessly into the biomass covering the ground, making it look like the sitting corpse is growing out of it the same way the spiked stalks do.

"Fuck!" I say even louder, slowly lifting my hand and pointing at it. "Guys… What the fuck am I looking at right now?"

"OHH FUCK!" Danny yelps.

"Dear God," Gavin mutters.

"Please—please tell me that's not a body!" Danny croaks.

On my way over toward where the path becomes meat mass, I pull out my phone, open the camera app, and hit record.

"Holy fucking shit, bro!" Tucker shouts. "That's definitely a person!"

I stop an inch from the biomass and zoom in on the corrupted corpse. That's when I spot a purple backpack resting against a tree a few feet back and to the right of the body. "I—I think it's a girl!"

"How the fuck can you tell?" Tucker whispers.

"Long hair with bangs, a petite body, and—not to sound perverted—but I see side boob."

Gavin looks at my screen. "There *is* side boob!"

Tucker sighs in relief. "Glad it's a chick…"

"Umm," Danny hums. "*Why?*"

"Well," Tucker says, "because I'm still fully bricked-up from that dong-shroom's sweet pheromone fragrance, and I'd feel weird if this mutated body I'm staring at while hard was a dude instead of a chick."

Gavin snickers. "Good to know I'm not the only one whose soldier is still at full attention while staring at the most horrific thing I've ever seen." He chuckles nervously. "I was startin' to get worried that it hasn't gone down yet."

I just nod. Because I'm still recording, and I don't want my verbal admission documented in the video.

"Same," Danny mutters. "Probably because that sweet smell is stronger here than it was on the path between there and this area."

"Maybe there's another dong-shroom nearby," Gavin says.

"Uhh," Tucker groans. "You… You guys think she's alive?"

Danny snickers. "What kinda dumb fucking question is that?"

"Yeah," I chime in. "Every inch of her skin, *including* her nose, is covered in the meat mass. So, I fucking doubt she can breathe."

"Hey!" Tucker shouts. "You alive?!"

The biomass-encased girl doesn't move. She doesn't speak.

"*See?*" I say, still recording. "She's dead."

"Rest in peace," Danny mutters, holding up his phone like he's about to take a video or picture.

"Or…" Tucker says, looking around the ground. "Or maybe she can't hear because her fucking ears are covered." He picks up a couple of rocks.

Since it's obvious what he's about to do, I turn the camera back to the girl's body.

"*Dude…*" Danny sighs out. "Don't tell me you're gonna pelt that poor girl's corpse with rocks."

"If you're alive," Tucker shouts, cocking his arm back. "Sorry if this hurts! And if you're dead, sorry for desecrating your corpse!" With a grunt, he launches a rock at her.

It flies in a perfect arc and then drops, hitting her right in the shoulder.

"Mwuhh-uhh!" is the feminine yet also kinda deep squawk that comes from her direction. It's a sound that both fills me with crippling dread and gives me this bizarre urge run over and help her.

Wait, she's alive?

Thinking of a girl while in this pheromone-induced state of arousal immediately makes me imagine boning some really hot brunette.

Get to her. Quick. Cut that biomass off her body. If you do, she'll let you hit it as a reward for you saving her—that all comes to me both as a thought and as a vivid montage that flashes in my mind.

"No way..." Danny says as I'm thinking that.

"Wait..." Gavin gasps.

"She's fucking alive!" Tucker says.

"No..." Danny says. "That sounded more like a raven imitating a girl's cry for help!"

I snicker more out of nervousness than humor. "Actually, that's exactly what it sounded like. But that squawk-ass sound came from near the ground right where she is, not from up in the trees or in the bushes further back."

"Well," Tucker says, cocking his hand back once more. "Let's see if it happens again." He throws a slightly bigger rock.

I watch on my phone screen as this stone hits her right on the top of the head.

Another feminine "Mwuhh!" squawk comes from that direction. But this time, her left hand spasms.

"Ayo!" I shout. "Am I the only one who saw—"

"Her hand move?" Danny says before I can finish. Then he nods. "No... I saw it too."

"Me too," Gavin and Tucker say.

She needs saving.

Go save her—it's an urge, not a thought.

I picture carrying a cute brunette back toward home.

I imagine her getting all turned on as we're passing where the dong-shroom's fragrance is strongest.

Then I start fantasizing about her riding me cowgirl right there on the trail.

Save her.

Tucker turns to me. "Please tell me you recorded that!"

I nod slowly, staring back at him with wide, unblinking eyes. I'm looking at him like that because I'm still in a trance—still stuck in that fantasy.

"I recorded it," Danny whispers. "But… I don't get it. Like, *how?* How is she moving and making sounds with her face covered in that shit?"

I shrug. "I dunno… Maybe… Maybe her mouth isn't covered?"

Tucker scoffs and arches a brow. "How about we just go over and help her instead of debating how the poor girl is still alive?!"

"I was about to say the same damn thing," I say while reaching for my pocket.

Danny's eyes go wide. "I'm all for saving her, but how the fuck do we do that?"

I hold up my folding knife. "I go over there and cut that meat mass off her."

Danny's eyes bulge even more. "No…"

"The fuck you mean, *no?*" Tucker snarls. "Real men save women and girls!"

Danny shakes his head. "No, I wanna save her. But it's just—"

"It's just that you're a pussy!" Tucker interrupts, shoving him playfully.

"It's not that I'm scared!" Danny shouts, pointing at where the beige cargo pants and the shirt are stuck to their respective pinecone stalks. "I'm just takin' into account that some dude clearly stripped to get free of those spiky-ass stalks while on his way to save her, but *didn't* save her!"

"Maybe he didn't have a knife," I say, unfolding mine.

"Or…" Gavin chimes in. "Or maybe those clothes were there *before* she ended up like that."

"True," I say.

Danny lets out a sharp huff. "*Or* maybe he *did* venture out there to help her, only to realize she couldn't be saved. And maybe she's still here because he wasn't able to get help. Like, what if those spiky stalks digested him and he got absorbed by the biomass? Or what if he died on the way back to civilization because the digestive enzymes from those things kept liquifying him long after he pulled them off?"

Hearing that gets my heart racing. "Those are good points too…" I mutter, looking down at the itchy wounds on my leg.

It's itchy instead of burning like it should be… Is my leg dissolving?

"Danny," Tucker says. "If it were you who were trapped in a fleshy biomass and knew people were nearby, would you want them to try and help you ASAP, or would you want them to fucking leave you there to go get help because they were too chickenshit to do the right thing?"

Danny bobbles his head side-to-side. "I mean, I'd obviously want to be helped right away, but—"

"And that's *exactly* why we can't do nothing!" Tucker says.

I nod. "Especially when we don't know how long she'll last in there. Like, what if we go get help and then she dies during the time it takes for help to arrive? Then her death would be *on us*. And I can't live with myself if she dies because we did nothing."

"Me either," Tucker says.

"Same," Gavin says.

Danny lets out a long sigh. "You're right… But I ain't stepping foot on that meat mass or weaving through those spiked stalks!"

"None of you are," I say, taking off my backpack. "Because I'm goin' *alone*." My bag hits the ground with a thud.

"Nah, fuck that!" Gavin says, unslinging his bookbag too. "No bro rolls solo!"

"Damn straight!" Tucker says, doing the same.

I shake my head. "Nah. Y'all need to stay here."

"Nuh-uh, bro——" Gavin starts to say.

"Whatever you're gonna say, Gav," I bark. "Fuck that! Because if we all go and get got by those sticky-ass, man-catching stalks, there will be no one to save us or get help. But if I go alone and something happens, one of you can go get help while the two who stay behind can save me. And it'll probably take two people to save me, given how many stalks are out there."

Gavin shakes his head. "I don't give a fuck what you say. I'm goin' with you in case another one of those stalks sticks to you somewhere you can't reach."

"*No*," I almost growl. "*You're staying, bro.*"

Tucker turns to him. "I think he's only saying that because he knows your fat-ass won't fit through the gaps in the pinecone stalks!" He snickers.

Gavin holds up a fist. "I swear to God, if you make one more fat joke…"

Tucker raises his hands in surrender. "Chill, bro! I was just jokin'!"

"It's not because of your weight, Gavin," I say, placing a hand on his shoulder. "I don't want either of you to go. Because you both drank and smoked *way more* than I did. And because you've both been strugglin' to walk in a straight line this entire hike. So it's safer for my drunk-ass to go alone."

Tucker bobbles his head and snickers. "You know what? Valid point."

Gavin nods. "Alright. *Fine.* We'll hang back 'til you need help."

I hold my knife in reverse grip, turn around, and start walking toward the meat mass. "I ain't gonna need no help!"

"Not gon lie," Gav says. "That was badass!"

"Wait a minute…" Tucker blurts out. "I bet this fucker wants to go alone because he's thinking she'll fuck him for being the one who saves her!"

He and Gavin start laughing.

A smile creeps across my face, so I don't turn around. "Nuh-uh!" I stop an inch from the edge of the biomass and start looking for the best route through the spiked stalks. "That's not why!"

"Bruh," Tucker groans. "You know how I know you want to? Because that's part of the reason why I want to!" He chuckles. "Can't stop thinking about it. About getting to her."

"Uhh," Gav groans. "Same, actually." Now he starts laughing.

"You know…" Danny chimes in. "Alcohol and weed lower inhibition—they make people more likely to take risks. And I think that dong-shroom's pheromonal fragrance does the same thing. I think it's making our drunk and high asses even less risk-averse than we already were, while also making us so insanely horny we'd do something stupid to get laid—like running into a biological death trap to save some chick who's probably beyond saving." He shoots me a look.

I turn and shake my head. "Nah. I wanna save her *because she needs help*!" With that, I face front and take a step forward.

My entire body shudders the moment the meat mass squishes beneath my right sneaker.

"MWUHHH!" the girl groans at the same time, making me freeze immediately.

"The fuck…" I mutter, turning around with a quick snap and staring at the guys who are staring back at me in absolute horror.

"She squawked as soon as you stepped on the meat mass!" Danny shouts.

I nod. "Yeah… Almost like she… sensed me touch it…"

"Take another step and see if it happens again!" Gavin shouts.

I turn and place my left foot onto the flesh-covered ground with just as much force as the first step, but nothing happens this time.

Tucker snickers. "Maybe that was just her tellin' you to hurry your ass up!" he says as I'm slowly sliding my right foot forward.

This meaty surface is so slick that, to keep from falling, I have to shuffle forward instead of taking regular steps. Just like I did the one time the ground froze over a few winters ago. "Unfortunately for her, this is as fast as I can go without eating shit!"

Steak…

Feels like I'm moving across a wrestling mat made of steaks.

Feels like I'm shuffling across a giant's abdomen that's oversaturated in lube…

Now that I'm a few feet from the edge, it dawns on me that the *veins* bulging out of this biomass resemble the vascular lines on a jacked dude's forearms. But further ahead, I spot a bunch of veins that are growing out of and lying across the biomass like squiggly garden hoses wrapped in skin—like giant, purplish earthworms with their heads and tails fused to this organism's tissue. It's only when it comes time to step over one of those fleshy cords or the leathery black roots that I lift my feet.

Dear God, I think, staring at the spread-out cluster of spiked stalks I'm approaching. *They're almost my height… And those stalks are damn near the girth of my forearm…*

The gap between them is nearly as wide as Tucker's Honda Civic is long, so I won't have to sidestep to get through.

"Stop, Kyle!" Danny shouts as I'm about to pass between the stalks.

"Gwaah-uhh!" the biomass-encased girl bleat-moans at the same time, quieter than the last few times.

I start turning left. "Wha—" I freeze as soon as I see that the stalk a few feet away is now bent toward me with its pinecone bulb pointed at my fucking face! It's still over 6 inches away, but the sight freaks me the fuck out nonetheless.

"The stalks!" Danny shouts a beat after I lock onto it. "They're reaching for you like tentacles!"

I glance right and jump when I see that the one on that side is also angled directly at me. The two closest to me are *pointing* at me, but the ones further away remain upright.

"Oh, what the fuck!" I shout, my vision pulsing in sync with my throttling heart.

Tentacles… These things are tentacles masquerading as plant-like stalks.

"I think they can feel when you're close to striking range!" Danny shouts.

"This is so fucked!" Gavin shouts.

"Dude, you gotta come back!" Danny yells.

That sweet smell coats my nostrils.

Get to her. Save her. Hook up with her.

"Nah!" I say, continuing forward. "All I gotta do is stay out of their reach."

"Fine," Danny snaps. "But before you go any further, let me get you some big sticks so you can push them away if you need to! And you're gonna need to when you get to where the stalks are closer together!"

I turn around as he's disappearing behind a tree and the leafless bushes in front of it. "Good thinking, bro!"

Nearly a minute later, he reappears with two big-ass branches. Thick, long ones. "These should work!" he shouts, chucking the first one toward me.

It lands a few feet from me.

"Good throw!" I say, watching the second one flying in almost the same path.

This one lands a few inches from the first. As soon as I pick them up, sliminess smears across my fingers.

"Ugh… Gross…" I whisper. Now I look up at him. "Thanks, Danny Boy!"

He nods. "You got it, brotha!"

Using the long branches like walking sticks, I resume shuffling forward. My heart was beating crazy fast before, but now it's pounding harder than it ever has in my entire life.

Why am I doing this?

It doesn't take much introspection to figure it out.

Because you feel compelled to.

The same urge that got me to go off-trail and gravitate toward the source of that sweet and flowery odor is what's pulling me toward *her.* When I accidentally stepped on the meat mass earlier, all I wanted was to get as far away from it as possible. But now that I've seen her—now that I know she's alive—I don't care that this fungus or whatever has pulsing veins and sticky tentacles that are trying to grab and digest me.

Every cell in my body is screaming at me to hurry up and save her. That's what's making me brave enough to keep shuffling across the most horrific organism anyone's ever seen.

I mean, I'm still scared for my life. But I'm also… *excited?*

Yeah, I'm excited. It's the same level of excitement I felt back in the 9th grade when Chrissy, my first girlfriend, texted me to hurry over because her parents were gone for a few hours. That text came a week after she'd admitted she was finally ready to do the deed. I was a virgin back then, so I immediately started hauling ass. I grabbed my bike and pedaled faster than I ever had in my life. Thankfully, she didn't change her mind about going all the way.

Get to her, save her—that thought's been looping through my head ever since the biomass-encased girl squawked and twitched.

Get laid—that intrusive thought always follows immediately after.

The closer I get to her, the more that heavenly dong-shroom fragrance overpowers the musty stench of the meat mass. And the stronger that scent gets, the more often those intrusive thoughts pop into my mind.

With each step I take, the urge to reach her as fast as possible gets more intense, making me increasingly more anxious. And I'm not really an anxious guy, unless it's the minutes before a big lacrosse game.

Danny might be right, I think, shuffling straight toward the pinecone stalk with the cargo pants hanging from it. *That sweet, flowery smell is mind-controlling me. It's making me take this dumb fucking risk. It's luring me right toward where the stalks are densest because it wants to eat me. Just like a bug to a sundew or a Venus flytrap…*

But unlike a bug, you're aware you're being manipulated into going toward danger. And yet you're still moving forward anyway…

"Dafuq are you walking towards the tentacle thing for?" Danny shouts.

"Because," I say, stopping about 6 feet from the 5-foot-something stalk. "I wanna see if there's a wallet in one of the pockets while I'm out here."

Now I jab the meat mass with the stick in my right hand, hitting it a few feet from the base of the stalk. But it doesn't bend toward me.

"Fucking be careful!" Gavin shouts.

"I will!" I shout back, shuffling forward to where I just poked.

This time, I prod it a bit closer to the base, but nothing happens. So instead, I lift my foot and stomp hard onto the spongy surface.

Without missing a beat, the tentacle swings right toward me—faster than the others—and stops inches from my thigh right as I'm jerking my leg back.

"Holy fuck!" I shout, dropping my right stick and grabbing the pants at the farthest point from the rubbery black quills. Now that I've got it, I let the other stick fall.

"That was fucking close!" Tucker shouts.

My left hand trembles as I reach for the article of clothing. Since the right pant leg of these cargo pants is what's stuck to the stalk's quills, I'm not at risk of brushing past them when I reach into the bulging back pocket.

"Okay, nice and slow, Kyle," I whisper, gripping the free pant leg with my left hand while reaching into the pocket with the other.

"Anything?" Tucker shouts.

"Yup!" I say, holding up the wallet.

While taking a deep breath, I pat the other pockets. There's nothing in any of them, though. So I let go and take a step back. As I do, the tentacle slowly leans away and straightens back up a bit.

So fucking weird and unsettling, I think, looking from the stalk to the wallet that I've just opened.

My eyes widen the instant I read the name on the license. And when I look over at the picture, my heart jackhammers against my chest.

"Holy shit," I whisper so low that I can barely even hear myself. "I don't believe it."

It's him…

CHAPTER 6:
SLICE

KYLE TURNER
Friday, August 26ᵗʰ

The shock—the panic—has me frozen and trembling.

I'm so stunned that it takes a good couple of seconds for me to finally open my mouth. "Guh—guys!" I stutter, my eyes still glued to this license's picture as I'm slowly turning around.

"What?!" they all holler back.

"This license…" I look up at them with wide, unblinking eyes. "These clothes… They're Mr. Crawford's!"

"No fucking way!" Danny shouts, staring back at me in shock.

"Are you bullshitting us, Kyle?" Tucker asks.

"*Dude*!" I bark. "I wouldn't lie about shit like this!"

Tucker makes a come here motion with his hand. "Toss it over!"

I throw the wallet as hard as I can.

Thankfully, it lands, like, a foot past him instead of going in the bushes. The others huddle around him as he's picking it up.

"Holy fuck!" Tucker shouts. "It *is* his!"

Danny looks up at me with an even more horrified expression, his face paler than usual. "I guess that means this… meat mass is what's behind these disappearances…"

"Which means…" I mutter, turning back toward the biomass-encased girl. "Which means she's probably one of the two chicks who went missing this summer."

"So that's either Savanna Lockhart," Danny says, "or that twenty-something-year-old girl from Seattle. Julie… whatever her last name was."

I pick up my sticks. "Well, Savanna was a brunette," I say as I resume shuffling forward. "And this girl's hair is the same color… You remember what color the other girl's hair was?"

"Uhhh…" Danny groans. "Pretty sure she was a redhead?"

"Then this has to be Savanna!" I shout. Saying her name immediately gets me imagining myself plowing that recent high school grad.

"Savanna was a hottie!" Tucker shouts. "We definitely gotta save her!"

I shake my head. "I was gonna save her whether or not she was attractive," I say, more so for her to hear than for him to. "Because it's the right thing to do."

"Wait," Tucker blurts out. "If this biomass *is* responsible for *all* the disappearances, then where are the other bodies? Shouldn't there be a bunch of other squawking meat statues all around here?"

"Good question," Danny says. "Maybe they all got away and died from some sickness caused by coming into contact with those tentacles…"

Hearing that freaks me out so bad that my stomach churns. Bad timing, considering that I'm side-stepping between two tentacles that are bending towards me—stalks that are closer together than the last pair I passed. As soon as I'm clear of them, I stop and look down at my leg.

Oh, good. It's not red or infected-looking.

Something too dark to belong to me catches my eye.

Wait…

I focus in on these dark strands that are stretching from the center of two wounds to a few millimeters past the edges.

The fuck is that? Dried blood?

No… Looks like ingrown hairs.

But my hair isn't that dark…

"Or," Gavin chimes in, "maybe there's another meaty fungus with tentacles somewhere else in the woods that got them!"

I tear my eyes away from my leg and resume shuffling forward. *Worry about it once you're back on regular ground*, I tell myself while stepping over a cluster of thorny black roots.

"Yeah," Danny says. "Because it's highly unlikely that there's just one of these organisms in this area. Or in the world, for that matter."

"Or maybe there is just the one," Tucker counters. "Think about it. Somethin' this fucked-up and incomprehensibly bizarre would've been all over the internet by now if people knew it existed."

Danny nods. "Good point."

At the same time I step onto a bulging vein, it swells slowly and then contracts a bit quicker—pulsing like a heartbeat.

A split-second later, a softer "Gwuh-uhh!" comes from the biomass-encased girl.

I jump, and my stomach flips. *What the fuck… That happened right when I stepped on the vein…*

That's when something dawns on me.

Wait… Why does she keep making that same squawking noise over and over instead of making different sounds or saying something?

"Savanna's tellin' you to hurry again, bro!" Tucker shouts during that thought. "Poor thing is probably horny like we are! And if she is, she desperately needs you to free her on the quick so she can get some dick!"

"Dude!" I shout back as I'm approaching the cluster of more tightly packed tentacles that are surrounding her. "Have some respect! She can probably hear us!"

"Sorry, Savanna!" Tucker shouts. "I'm drunk and high as fuck, so please forgive me!" He laughs like a psycho.

"Speaking of being horny—" I start to say.

"I don't like where this is going," Danny says.

"Nah, it's not like that," I continue. "I was just gonna say, that same sweet smell from the dong-shroom is getting stronger the closer I get to her!"

"Well then," Tucker says. "That explains why things *down there* have been hard as stone this entire time," Tucker says.

"Umm," Danny hums. "Here's a thought… What if that's not a girl at all?"

"Whatchu mean?!" Tuck fires back.

"I mean," Danny continues, "what if it's just a girl-shaped mass that evolved to grow into a humanoid, feminine shape for the sole purpose of tricking horny guys into helping *it*."

The thought sends shivers through me.

If he's right, that'd explain why she's not talking… Even though I feel like that makes the most sense, I keep shuffling forward through the next gap between stalks.

That almost instinctual urge is what's driving me to keep going. It's so intense now that I'm unbearably anxious—anxious to the point that I feel like I might have a heart attack if I don't scream at the top of my lungs and start sprinting toward her. It's that mixed with this deep sense of dread that I'll legit die if I don't rub one out ASAP.

Get to her. Save her.

What pops into my head right after that thought is me and Savanna Lockhart going it like adult film stars in a hardcore video.

The vivid fantasy makes me throb so hard it hurts a little.

Save her, then you two can fuck and end each other's maddening arousal…

It's not until I reach the tentacles encircling her that I notice something bizarre. The spiked stalks closest to this girl are all between 3 feet and 6 feet away from her, and they're more densely packed together here than they are elsewhere.

It's like they're protecting her.

Or like they're waiting for prey to get within a couple of feet of her.

"Hmm," I hum, stopping about 6 feet out and scanning the circle of death for a way through.

Behind her and to the right, there's this big-ass tree. Not only are there no tentacles between it and her, but there's also a decently wide gap between those man-catchers a few feet to the right of that.

To the right, it is, I think, shuffling over there.

A few feet from the tentacles' striking range, I switch my grip on the sticks, holding them like swords—holding them high and a little more than shoulder width a part.

"Okay," I whisper, slowly sliding my right foot forward.

Nothing happens, so I keep scooting.

Both tentacles whip toward me in a flash, but the smooth parts between bulbs and the spikes slam into my sticks and come to a dead stop.

All those years of lacrosse came in handy.

"Bad ass!" Tucker shouts.

"Holy fuck! These things are strong!" I shout, my arms shaking as I push back against what feels like two limbs that are nearly as strong as Tucker's.

"Are you fucking around?" Danny asks. "Or are those things that powerful?"

"Guhh!" I sigh in relief right when I slip past the spiky appendages. "They're strong as fuck! No lie!"

The guys say some shit I can't hear in the middle of me shuffling up to the next pair. These 2 tentacles swing at me from further away than the last set. But I react fast enough, fending them off by whacking them at the same spot above the quills.

The same thing happens with the final pair of stalks.

"Phew," I blow out right when I reach the spot between her and the tree.

"Good shit, Kyle!" Gavin yells as the boys erupt into a cacophony of howls and applause.

I drop my right stick and then hold my fist high in the air. And as soon as I start lowering my arm, I turn to the girl. "Hey," I say while circling around to her left side. "Can you hear me?"

"GWUHH!" she squawks louder than ever before as every tentacle in my periphery bends towards me.

I start turning in a slow circle only to find that it's not just the nearby ones. Every stalk in the clearing and beyond is pointing at me like some hellish monster's fingers.

Every. Single. One.

"Oh, what the fuck…" I mutter, tensing up as my body shivers violently.

Something's wrong…

"Kyle!" Danny shouts. "What the fuck did you do?! All the tentacles are, like, pointing at you!"

"I see that!" I shout back, finally taking a step forward. "And I didn't do shit! I just talked to her while moving forward a bit!"

She doesn't react to me yelling or my movement this time.

"I—I think you should get the fuck out of there!" Danny stutters.

"Yeah, dude!" Gavin says. "Come back!"

"Nah, I'm good!" I shout back, stopping right in front of her.

My eyes are immediately drawn to the top of her head. Where her hair parts, there's no white skin—just the same yellowish-tan flesh as what makes up the meat mass.

"Hello?" I say to her. "Sa—Savanna? You hear me?"

No sound comes from her.

"Julie?" I pause. "Is your name Julie?"

Still nothing.

During my next breath, that familiar sweet and floral smell hits me. It's just as thick and heavy here as it was by the dong-shroom.

Is there another one of those things between your legs, or is that smell just coming from you?

I slowly drop into a squat, lean right, and peer through the triangle-shaped gap formed beneath the bend of her leg. That's when I see something freaky growing out from where her vagina should be. A fleshy, red *flower* with 5 finger-sized petals that are shaped like starfish arms. And in the center of that flower-looking growth is a slit between two plump folds, with a tiny opening right where a birth canal should be.

"Gah!" I yelp, springing up. "What the fuck kinda mutated pussy shit is that?!"

"What is it?!" Gavin shouts.

"What happened?!" Danny asks right after.

"Nuh—nothing!" I suck in a deep breath and immediately feel dizzier. Hornier. More altered in the best way.

Fuck, I think, my head swirling and my body swaying, a smile creeping across my face. It takes extreme focus to not topple over. *Her cooch-petals look exactly like the underside of the dong-shroom. Same vibrant red color. Same texture. Same smell...*

A dick-shaped fungus sticking out the ground is one thing. But a flesh-flower growing out the cooch of a girl trapped in the same biomass?

That's just fucked.

For some reason, I picture myself touching it.

I imagine slipping a finger in there only to discover that flesh-flower's passage is just as deep, soft, and slick as the real thing.

Then a weird fantasy pops into my head—I visualize me going at it with a version of Savanna who's normal everywhere except for the part of her *down there* that's got meaty petals growing out of it.

Midway into that fantasy, she suddenly goes from looking like how she did back in school to looking like she does now.

"Urrgh," I groan, rapidly shaking my head as though that'll dislodge the fucked-up thought.

Sorry for thinking that, I try to telepathically tell her. *I promise I won't violate you like that, Savanna—or whoever you are. Tucker definitely would finger your flower if he was here instead, though. So I'm glad I'm the one who came.*

"Bro!" Tucker shouts. "What the fuck are you doing?! Bein' a perv and checkin' out her no-no hole?" He laughs like a maniac.

"What?!" I spring up and turn toward him. "No! Saw something weird down there, so I was checkin' it out."

"Something weirder than the shit covering her body?" he asks.

"Actually… Yeah!"

"What'd you see?"

"It's impossible to explain! I'll take a video."

"Alright!" he shouts.

"Before you do that," Danny yells out next, "check her bookbag! There might be an ID in there! Or something else to identify her."

"Ooh!" I shout, turning back the way I came. "Good call!"

The bag that's resting strap-side down against the biomass-covered tree trunk is a purple JanSport. Fleshy tendrils have grown onto all the parts in contact with the meat mass, but it looks like they just crept up a few inches onto it before stopping.

Guess it doesn't grow on fabric? That's what crosses my mind as I'm squatting and reaching for the zipper.

When I get the bookbag open, I find one of those rectangular girl wallets on top of a lavender insulated water bottle. The speed with which I snatch it out, undo the button latch, and flick it open makes me feel like I'm racing to get a cure out of it or some shit.

My jaw drops and my eyes bulge the instant I see the picture on this driver's license. I don't need to check the name since I know her face well, but I glance over at it anyway. Just to make sure.

"Holy shit!" I shout, springing up from a squatted position.

"What?! Who is it?!" the guys shout, not at all in sync.

I hold up the lavender wallet even though there's no way they can see it from way over there. "It's fucking Savanna Lockhart!"

"Holy shit-fuck-balls, dude!" Tucker screams.

"I can't believe this," Danny says a beat later. "That's two of the six missing people who've come in contact with this biomass."

"Fucking wild!" I shout, easing back onto my haunches.

I place the wallet back in her bag and zip it up. That way, people will know we're not lying about her identity if I fail to cut her free of this shit.

The moment I start making my way back to her, I let out a long sigh.

"Okay…" I whisper, reaching for the top of Savanna's head, my hand shaking harder than someone with a bad case of Parkinson's. "Savanna… If you feel this, make a sound."

Her hair feels perfectly normal. But right when my palm fully cups her head—right when I feel the squish of her freakishly spongey-feeling scalp and the heat emanating from it—

"GWAAAHH-UHHHH!" she squawks loud as all fuck.

"GEEYAH!" I shout, jerking my hand back.

It rattles me so bad that it takes me a few beats to notice the wide, horizontal, oval opening where a mouth should be. No sooner than I stare into that dark hole, it starts slowly closing. But not before I catch a glimpse of her teeth—straight and mostly white with some plaque—and something moving just behind the bottom row that's too beige and lumpy to possibly be a tongue.

That hellish wail of hers ends right when her corrupted lips come together.

"What's happenin' over there?!" Danny shouts.

"Her mouth!" I shout back. "It opened during that squawk! And she's got teeth! Human teeth! It's definitely a person trapped inside! Not a growth mimicking a human!"

The guys start murmuring as I'm pulling out my knife, but I can't make out what they're saying. All I can hear is my heart thumping in my skull.

"Okay," I whisper, dropping back into a squat. "I'm gonna cut you free, Savanna…" I unfold the knife. "If I cut too deep, just yell or move, and I'll stop. Okay?"

There's no response.

I hover the blade near her cheek. A moment later, I bring it down to her bicep. Then I lift it back to her cheek right after.

Maybe I should cut along her arm first. That way, I can figure out how deep to slice first. Last thing I wanna do is butcher this poor girl's face and scar her for life…

Touching the sharp edge of my steel to the fungal tissue covering her arm feels exactly the same way as pressing a knife to a steak does. And feeling that makes my hand tremble even harder than it already was.

Nice and slow, I remind myself as I begin slicing downward.

The yellowish-tan *skin* splits like an overcooked slab of pork, and the sight makes my stomach churn.

"GWUHHH!" she squawks in my fucking ear.

That makes me jump. "Fuckin' hell," I whisper to her. "Can you please stop doing that, Savanna?!"

She remains silent during the next slice. But I don't. Sawing into this tough fungus meat feels so gross that I can't help gagging quietly every other second and groaning in between each dry-heave.

Another squawk comes during the third cut, and the arm I'm cutting into spasms hard during her inhuman cry.

That happens again during the fifth slice, but she spasms even harder this time.

Shit, I'm starting to cut pretty deep now… Where the fuck is her skin? Is this biomass just that thick?

Amber-colored snottiness oozes out of the incision as that thought comes to an end.

"Ugh!" I yelp, jerking my hand back.

"What's happening?" Danny shouts.

What the fuck is that? I take a closer look. *That's not blood… It… It looks like that same syrupy slime that the meat mass is coated in…*

It's not super thick, but it's viscous enough that it takes a while to flow out of the gash and start running down her arm. Eventually, it thins enough for something a different color from the tissue to become visible at the deepest point. Not flesh. Something white.

Is that…

I hesitantly bring the tip of my blade toward it and tap the metal against it.

CLACK—the same sound a metal knife or fork makes when it's tapped against a chicken leg bone.

"Oh fuck!" I shout, spasming and accidentally slicing toward her elbow.

"GWUUHHHH!" she cries out at the same time, her arm awkwardly flailing and swatting the knife out of my hand.

"EE-YAHHH!" is the sound I make as I throw myself backward to keep from being grabbed.

My back slams into the spongy meat mass, and I hit it with so much momentum that I skid across its slick surface.

Then something firm and warm crashes down onto my left forearm right as I'm slowing to a stop.

"Kyle!" the guys scream at the same time I lock onto the tentacle rapidly coiling around my arm, its rubbery spines bending and stabbing into my skin as it does.

I've landed about 3 feet from the base of this 5-footer that's squeezing my arm with the force of a boa constrictor.

"Oh fuck-fuck-fuck!" I shout, grabbing the pinecone-shaped bulb and pulling with all my might.

"Holy shit! Holy shit!" the guys clamor.

No matter how hard I pull, the tentacle doesn't budge.

"I can't get it off! Guys, I—I can't get it off!" I scream so hard that my voice cracks.

"Pull harder, bro!" Tucker shouts. "You're strong as fuck! You got this!"

"I'm pullin' as hard as I can!" I yell back. "But it's like arm-wrestling fucking Captain America!"

"Are you serious right now?!"

I groan from how hard I'm straining to pry this thing off my limb. "I wouldn't lie about that, Tuck!"

It isn't until I stop trying to pull it off that I feel it—the tentacle pulsating against my arm, slow and subtle. It's not just its tubular stalk, but the black quill-things too. The rubbery spikes… they're throbbing faster—quick little twitches—and there's this weird tickling sensation underneath my skin. Feels like something's crawling out of those things and going into me.

No, more like something is flowing into me…

"What the fuck…" I whisper, my body shaking harder than it ever has before.

What the fuck is this thing doing to me?!

An intense wave of drowsiness comes over me out of nowhere as that thought leaves my mind.

Wait… why do I feel so woozy all the sudden?

"What do we do! What do we do!" Gavin shouts over the others.

"Cut it off, Kyle!" Danny shouts. "Get your knife and cut it!"

Right, my knife, I think as I begin looking around for it.

It's nowhere to be found. So I start patting the slick biomass with my free hand while frantically scanning the area.

Where the fuck is it?

I replay Savanna knocking it out of my hand. Then I remember it flying off to the right.

That's when I look a little farther out and catch a glint in the corner of my eye. Groaning, I twist and sit up as far as I can. And there it is—10 feet away, nestled against a pulsating vein that's inches from the base of another tentacle.

"Ah shiiiiit-*tuh*!" I roar. "It's—it's outta reach!" The most intense sleepiness I've ever felt hits me the moment that last word leaves my mouth, and my eyelids start fluttering the way they do when I'm about to pass out. It feels like I double-dosed NyQuil after smoking way too much weed.

"Fuck!" Tucker shouts. "C'mon! We gotta get the knife and help him!"

"I'm sorry, but I'm *not* goin' out there!" Danny shouts.

"Yes the fuck you are!" Tucker screams back. "It'll take all of us working together to get through them tentacles without getting got!"

An argument breaks out, but even with all the shouting, I can barely hear them. I'm too busy trying to pull this thing off me—too locked in on the tickling coming from where the quills are pressed into my flesh. A crawling sensation that's getting worse by the second.

Something is definitely moving under my skin, I think, letting go of the bulb and lifting my arm as much as I can.

I stop breathing the instant I see them.

Just beneath each bit of skin in contact with the quills' orange globs are centimeter-long black fibers—zigzagging lines that look like little lightning bolts tattooed into my flesh.

Wait…

I think back to the weird 'hairs' I found sticking out of the leg wounds I got from that first little stalk.

So that wasn't my hair…

I twist my body as much as I can so I can look back at the guys, wincing as the tentacle tightens and pulls my arm. That's when I realize all the other spiky stalks have gone back to standing straight again.

"Guys!" I scream, my voice cracking as a sudden wave of drowsiness hits. "You—you gotta get over here! Now! *Please!*"

"What's wrong?!" Gavin shouts.

"There are black roots growing into my arm!"

Tucker's face scrunches up. "The fuck do you mean roots are growing into your arm?"

"I mean, *there are black fibers growing out of these quills that are moving beneath my fucking skin!*" I damn near screech. "And I think this tentacle is pumping a tranquilizer into me! Because I'm getting crazy sleepy all the sudden! So *please* get over here and help me before I pass out and never wake up again! *Hurry! Please!*"

Tucker turns to Danny and says something I can't hear.

But Gavin doesn't hesitate. He just shrugs off his backpack and charges forward. "Hold on, Kyle! I'm coming, bro!"

CHAPTER 7:
HURRY!

DANNY HOLLAND
Friday, August 26ᵗʰ

"Wait!" I shout just as Gavin's about to step onto the nightmare flesh.

He freezes with his foot hovering inches above it. "Huh?" Gav groans while spinning around. "*What?!*"

Tucker grabs my shirt with both hands. "We've got no time to wait, bitch-boy! Kyle needs help *now!*"

I huff. "I'm not bein' a bitch! I stopped him to *remind him* he needs sticks before he goes out there—to fend off them tentacle-shits!"

Tucker releases me. "Oh, right. Good call."

"Phew," Gavin sighs in relief. "Yeah. Thanks for the reminder, Danny. That adrenaline hit, and I completely forgot about that."

"I know," I mutter as we make our way to the tree line. "Good thing I have your back."

"Seriously."

"Guys!" Kyle calls out weakly. "Hurry… I feel like I'm 'bout to… blackout."

"We'll start headin' over in a sec, bro!" Gavin shouts. "Just gotta get some sticks first!"

"He doesn't sound good," I whisper to Tucker.

"Nah," Tucker says. "He doesn't."

"Hey, Kyle!" I call out.

"Yeah?!" he yells back.

"Talking will help you stay awake!" I continue. "So—uhh—talk to us! Umm… Tell us what happened? Like, what scared you enough to jump back toward the tentacles?"

"When I cut into her arm," Kyle says weakly, "I kept slicing deeper into the biomass in search of skin… then I hit bone."

"Like you cut too deep?!" I ask.

"*Nah*… Like, everything from the top layer of skin all the way down to where the muscle ends was the same shit as the meat mass! No skin. No muscle. No blood! Just that fungal biomass. Then bone."

A shiver runs through me. "Oh dear God…"

If all her flesh mutated into that shit… she's definitely dead.

"Got one!" Gavin says, holding up a long branch that seems thick enough to withstand the force of those tentacles. Hopefully.

"So the squawk—" I say loud enough for Kyle to hear.

"Wasn't her!" Kyle cuts in, sounding weaker than before. "It was—but it wasn't. I think the biomass, like, hijacked her vocal cords! To bait prey with distress sounds. That's why she squawked whenever I stepped on the edge and random spots along the way!"

But how? As I'm turning to Tucker, he looks at me with the same horrified expression I have. *How can a fungus activate and control a corpse's vocal cords?*

Unless she's not fully a corpse…

"That is so fucked!" Gavin says.

"Yeah it is…" I mutter. "Which means, even if you didn't hit her with that rock—"

"She still would've made that sassy-ass crow noise the second one of us stepped on that shit," Tucker says. "And Kyle still would've went out there to try and save her after hearing her."

I spot another good stick right after he finishes speaking. "Gav!" I shout, picking it up and holding it out to him.

"Ooh! Good shit!" Gavin says, rushing over.

As I'm rising from my haunches, my still-stiff glizzy slips from beneath my waistband. So I turn away and quickly tuck it back where it was. Because the last thing I need is my bros seeing me pitching a tent.

Being hard this long fucking sucks, I think while turning to face Gavin. *Especially because it's kinda starting to hurt…*

Gavin skids to a stop a few feet from me, snatches the branch out of my hand like it's a baton, and then takes off. "On the way, Kyle!"

"Hurry!" Kyle almost slurs, sounding like he's already half asleep. "I… I don't feel so good. Feels like… I've been roofied or some shit."

"Gav!" Tucker shouts out. "Wait for us! The best way to get through them tentacles is if two of us fend them off while the other passes through!"

"No time!" Gavin shouts. "He's being fucking sedated—or worse! And you saw how long it took him to cross that slippery shit! I gotta get to him. *Now!*" With that, he steps onto the meat mass.

"UGWUHHH-UH!" Savanna squawk-moans at the same time, sounding louder than all the other times she—or *it*—made that noise.

Unfortunately, because it kinda sounds like a moan, I immediately imagine it's a porn star who made that sound. Which makes me picture myself banging Savanna.

I hate that my brain goes there every time I hear that dinosaur-ass mating call.

It's the sweet smell in the air, not some fucked-up mutated-girl kink, Danny, I tell myself while watching Gavin shuffle across the fungal meat.

No more feminine crow noises follow during that time.

Interesting…

Every time someone steps on the edge of that thing for the first time in a while, the corpse makes that sound, I think, picking up another suitable branch. *But she doesn't squawk again right after that… Not until someone steps near the tentacles or on certain spots toward the center…*

It seems like this fungus-thing makes Savanna's corpse cry out whenever there's pressure on the edge so it can convince people she's alive and needs help. To lure them toward the center where they'll be easier to catch. Then it makes the sound again to distract prey right before the tentacles strike. Or to keep baiting them in closer to her.

It's almost like the biomass absorbed her into itself and turned her into an organ that it can use to make distress sounds with. The thought makes me shudder and hyperventilate. *Maybe it needed human vocal cords because its intoxicating fragrance wasn't enough to catch the prey it wants.*

"Here!" Tucker says, holding out one of his 3 thick sticks in front of my face. "Let's go!"

I grab it, then he turns and hauls ass.

You shouldn't go out there, I think, following behind him. *They can save him without you…* As that thought trails off, I realize that Kyle doesn't have his backpack on. Neither does Gavin. *Maybe I should take mine off so I won't have something sticking out that the tentacles can grab…*

Worst-case scenarios run through my head.

What happens if we get stuck out there with no water?

What if I need something from in here while we're out there?

Fuck it. I'll keep it on. If it gets snagged on a stalk, I'll ditch it.

Just like Kyle did, and like Gavin is doing right now, we shift to holding our sticks ski poles—like walking sticks—when we're a few feet away. Tucker halts inches from where the tan tendrils at the edge meet uncorrupted soil. Then he takes a deep breath, lifts his foot, and slowly sets it down onto the fleshy organism.

"*Ugh-huh-ugh*," he stutter-groans, shivering dramatically. "It's like steppin' on a wrestling mat made of fucking steak!"

Savanna didn't squawk just now… Maybe because Gavin is already walking across it… Maybe it can't process that much input?

"Fuck!" Tucker shouts, snapping me out of my trance. "It's hella slippery, dude! Be careful!"

"Oh—k-kay," I stutter while slowly lowering my foot. It sinks beneath my sneaker like a gel-filled pad. "Blurrgh… Fuck, this is gross!"

"Right?" Tucker says, shuffling forward some more. He comes to a stop a few feet later and then shudders again. "Ughh-blerrgh-ruhh! It's even thicker over here!"

Shuffling up to where he is feels like moving up a slight incline. And it's way more muscular here than the edge felt. "Gughhh…" I dry-heave. "Fuck… It really does feel like a gym mat made of steaks."

"Told ya! Maybe we should be calling this a meat-mat instead of a meat mass!"

"Yeah," I mutter. "It's canon."

"Meat-mat is now canon!" Gavin yells from up ahead.

Tucker turns to me and gives me a nod. "It's canon." After facing forward, he takes a deep breath and then lets out a long-ass sigh. "Alright, stay close to me so I can make sure nothin' happens to you."

I nod. "I won't let anything happen to you either, broski."

We shuffle side-by-side at the same pace until we reach a thick cord-vein that's tangled with black, thorny roots.

"Fuckin' hell," I grumble as we're stepping over it in sync.

Our feet land at the same time, but only he slips. "Oh fuckin-shit-fuck!" Tucker shouts, slamming his sticks down. He steadies himself right as I'm an inch away from grabbing him.

"You good?"

He nods. "I'm good, Danny Boy."

We sigh in relief and then resume shuffling, keeping our eyes locked onto the hellish flesh beneath us the entire time.

"Hey…" Tucker says quietly.

"Yeah?"

"This is kinda personal, but uhh… You know what's got me fucked up right now, bro?"

"What?"

He sighs. "That I'm still rock-hard, constantly thinking about havin' sex, and fighting the urge to tug the ol' elephant trunk—all while being grossed the fuck out by this meat-mat that smells like swamp ass, and while being terrified that Kyle might die. And I'm scared that something bad might happen to us too."

I snicker. Then I shake my head. "Funny, I was thinkin' the exact same thing. It's this fucking sweet, pheromone shit. It's got us more horny and high than scared. Because *that's what it wants.*"

"I know… But it still has me all sorts of conflicted… And the urge to get behind the bushes and rub one out just keeps getting worse the closer we get to… *her.*"

"Mm-hmm," I hum while stepping over a bulging vein. "Now that you've got that off your chest, can you please stop talking about how horny you are and how bad you wanna jack it, bro?"

He chuckles. "Sorry. These pheromones got me feelin' extra honest."

"It's all good. Besides, it's not like you're not always sayin' shit like that when you're drun—"

"UGWUHH-UHH-UH!" Savanna squawk-moans.

My gaze snaps from the meat-mat to where Gavin is sidestepping between the first pair of tentacles Kyle passed through, holding his branches like swords instead of walking sticks.

"Dude!" I shout. "Slow down and wait for us!"

"Nah, I'm good!" Gavin yells mid-shuffle. "I'll keep going until I lose a stick or some shit. If that happens, then I'll wait for y'all!"

"Guysssss…" Kyle slurs. "Hurry! Pleathh!"

"I'm halfway there, bro!" Gavin says.

"I don't…" Kyle's words trail off. "I doan-think… I can… stay-wake… mussh longer." That all came out in a breathless jumble.

That's when Gavin goes from shuffling to speed-walking without lifting his feet too high.

I get why he's hauling ass like this. Even though they've all known each other since kindergarten, he and Kyle were always closer. Because they were best friends right from the start, and Tucker didn't really start hanging with them for real and getting close to them until around fourth or fifth grade.

They're all bros. But Gavin and Kyle? They're *brothers*. They're more like brothers than any blood brothers I know. Kyle is legit closer to Gav than he is to his actual older brother.

And real brothers? They'd risk their lives for each other without hesitation.

"You're goin' to fast, Gav!" I shout.

"Nah! You two are going too slow!" he yells, still going the same speed.

"He ain't gon' listen, dude," Tucker says. "We gotta hurry and catch up to him before his drunk ass gets got!" He quickens his pace.

But I don't.

In the time it takes me to blink, Gavin goes from stepping over a tangled mess of black roots to his left foot catching on them.

"GAHH!" he yelps as his right foot skids forward, forcing him into a partial split.

"GAVIN!" Tucker and I shout.

As his body twists in the direction that his foot's sliding, he falls backward, right toward a tentacle. Then he crashes down onto it, the spiked stalk lining up almost perfectly with his spine before he hits the meat-mat with a wet thud.

"GWUHH-AHH-UHHH!" Savanna's corpse cries out as the tentacle curls against the left side of Gavin's neck, pressing the pinecone bulb against his cheek.

"AHHHH"! Gavin roars.

"OH FUCK!" Tucker shouts, racing toward that first pair of stalks Kyle passed through. He's shuffling so fast that it looks like he's speed-skating.

But I just freeze.

I just stand there watching my thrashing friend frantically try to pull up his shirt. His efforts are futile, though. Because the hem is stuck to the quills near the stalk's base, and the ones right beneath the bulb are glued to his neck.

"FUCK!" Gav screams, grabbing the bulb with his left hand. Of course, it doesn't budge when he tries pulling it off him. "FUCK! HELP! It's stuck to my neck! It's fuckin' stuck to my neck!"

"We're coming!" Tucker shouts, glancing to his left, only to find I'm not beside him. He stops so abruptly that he skids a bit. Then he whirls around and glares at me. "Danny, come the fuck on!"

Still staring at Gavin with unblinking eyes, I shake my head. "No... I—I'm not goin' any further."

Tucker growls, and then he starts coming at me with the same speed he was moving toward Gavin. "Yes the fuck you are!"

I slowly back away, slipping a bit as I do. "Nuh-no! We're drunk and high as fuck, so we—we should go get help! *Real help*! Or else we're all gonna get got by these tentacles!"

As the gap between us is about to close, he drops his right stick. "Your bros need you," he snarls, grabbing my arm, "and you wanna pussy out on us?! No fuckin' way! We need Kyle's knife to save them, and I'm gonna need your help to get it! Now come the fuck on!" He tugs me, and my sneakers slide across the biomass.

"Chill!" I shout, leaning back and widening my stance to brace myself. "I'm gonna fuckin' fall!"

He yanks again. "I'll stop once you start movin'!"

I jerk my arm away from him, but fail to break free. "I'm not goin' any further!"

His features harden into a scowl. "When you were a new kid at school with no friends, we took you in—we invited you to sit with us at lunch that first day of junior year so you wouldn't have to eat alone. Then we accepted you into our brotherhood! And we've had your back ever since! Now act like you're our brother, Danny!" He tugs even harder, and I almost fall.

I drop my sticks and grab his arm. "Stop!" I shout, trying to wrestle him off of me.

"Man the fuck up!" He yanks me even harder, and I start slipping—I slide into a partial split.

"FUCKING STOP!" I shout, reflexively shoving him in the chest with one hand while the arm he's holding flails upward.

His grip finally slips as we both stumble and slide backward.

The next thing I know, I'm falling back.

Then, as my ass crashes onto flabbiness, I let out a loud "GUGHH!"

"Whoa-ahh!" Tucker screams while flailing and stumbling back, heading straight towards 3 spiky stalks.

He topples over sideways a split-second later, and then he lands on his right hip and elbow.

WHACK—the nearest tentacle slams down onto the left side of his skull, instantly curling across his forehead with the bulb end bending toward his right cheek. The second hell-asparagus slams onto the meat-mat with a wet thud, the pinecone-shaped end of it landing just inches from his mouth.

"GYEEAHH! My eye!" he screams, reaching for the nightmarish thing coiled around his head. His right hand grabs the bulb, but the other slaps down onto the quills. "OWW-WUHH! OH-FUHHHK! There's a spike in my fuckin' eye!"

"Oh fuck!" Gavin croaks out mid-sob.

"Tucker!" I shout, scrambling onto all fours. My left hand lands on a pulsating vein, and the other slaps against dense *muscle*. Both sensations nearly make me puke. Or maybe it's the guilt that's got my stomach churning. "The quills! Get your hand off the quills!"

Tucker tries lifting his left hand, but his palm and fingers don't peel away from the sticky tips. "FUCKING SHIT, DANNY!" he snarls, trashing even harder. He kicks like a kid throwing a tantrum, and when his sneaker hits the meat-mat near the base of that third tentacle—

"GWAHH-UHH!" Savanna cries out at the same time that the stalk whips down onto his left shin.

"NOOO!" he screams as it's coiling against his calf. "GAHHHH! No-huh-huh-ho-wuhhhh!" That's how he sobs as I'm coming to a stop a foot away.

"Holy fuck…" I mutter, my eyes widening and my body tensing when I see the quill in his right eye.

The little orange bead covering its tip is glued against the outer corner of his eyeball, stuck right against where his brown iris borders the white part. And even though his eyelids are stuck to it too, they're still open wide enough for his pupil to be visible.

My gaze wanders from that horrific sight to all the bent quills pressing against his forehead and cheek, and then to the spikes that vanish into his dark hair.

I let out a shaky breath. "Tuck—Tucker… I'm so sorry—"

"Danny, what the fuck!" he snarls through a sob, spitting everywhere.

Tears blur my eyes. "I'm—I'm so sorry, dude!"

"Sorry?! Sorry's not gonna keep me from losing a fucking eye, dipshit! I'm—I'm probably gonna fucking die because you decided to fucking push me towards a cluster of death-tentacles instead of just coming with me and helping me save the guys!"

Tears spill down my face. "I… I didn't mean to, Tucker! I was about to fall because you wouldn't stop pulling me! I was just tryna get you to stop pulling me!"

"You didn't have to shove me *that hard,* though, you dumb-fuck!" he screams.

"I'm sorry, bro! I'm so fucking sorry!"

"Don't call me bro, *Daniel,*" he snarls. "You don't ever get to call me bro after what you just did!"

"But I didn't mean—"

"Hey!" he barks so loud that I jump. "How 'bout you shut the fuck up, go get the *fuckin'* knife, and cut us all free before I lose my fucking eye, you pussy-ass piece of shit!"

"Yeah," Gavin groans, sounding much weaker than before. "And hurry, Danny! Feels like… I'm 'boutta… pass out. And Kyle… he's not responding anymore… He's not movin'… I think he's… unconscious…"

"Oh shit…" Tucker mutters, his voice cracking. "Go, Danny! Fucking now!"

I snap out of my trance, looking from him to where my sticks fell. "Ah—alright!" I say, scrambling toward them.

The second I grab the branches, I start moving toward Gavin, shuffling as fast as he was before he fell. Barely a few seconds later, Tucker starts sobbing and sniveling. And hearing that makes me cry even harder.

I'm so fuckin' sorry, dude… I'll make this right. I'll get the knife and save y'all before it's too late. I promise.

I'm so guilty over what happened that I can barely look at Gavin as I pass. I just glance at him, staring just long enough to see him wiping tears away with a trembling hand.

"Hurry…" he whispers as I'm looking away. "I'm… about-tuh… pass out…"

"I'm hurrying!" I croak, looking back at him as his eyelids are shutting. "Just hang on! I'll be back soon."

I imagine him falling asleep and never waking up again…

I imagine reaching Kyle only to discover that he's cold and has no pulse.

I visualize getting back to Tucker and finding him dead too.

Dead because of me…

The guilt is so overwhelming that my stomach sours.

Salty stuff floods my mouth.

And then…

"BLURRGH!" I puke to my left as I skid to a stop.

Watching all that half-digested food splatter across the gross-ass meat-mat—and tasting it as it does—makes me vomit again.

And again.

And again.

CHAPTER 8:
BLOSSOMING

TUCKER WILLIAMS
Friday, August 26th

The way I'm sobbing, whimpering, and making that pathetic hiccup sound whenever I try to breathe—I haven't cried this fucking hard since I was 8 or 9. On the day I crashed my bike while going full speed and lost a whole lot of knee and hand skin.

But, like, how can I not cry over what's happening right now?

Having alien-ass tentacle-things squeezing my head and leg harder than I used to rear-naked choke kids during my jiujitsu competition days is traumatizing enough on its own. But the fact that these things are injecting shit into my veins to tranquilize me so it can turn me into what it turned Savanna into? That'd be enough to make even the toughest dudes bawl their eyes out.

And on top of all that shit, this fucking rubbery spike that's basically Crazy-Glued to my fucking eyeball burns and hurts like shit. And now it's itching. Not just on the surface, but a bit deeper. Feels like something is slowly crawling into it.

Wait, it's not just my eye… That crawling feeling is happening everywhere the spiky things are touching me…

What Kyle said shortly before he passed out pops into my head.

*Roots… He said black roots were growing into his arm from the spikes'
tips.*

That's what I'm feeling in my eye…

I'm about to go blind all because…

My brain replays Danny shoving me toward the tentacles, and
rage swells within me. So much rage.

So much rage that I'm suddenly overheating.

Danny, you pussy-ass bitch… I'm gonna lose my eye because of you!

I'm gonna die because of you!

That's what I *want* to shout at him. But instead, I just let out
this raw, animal-like roar while picturing myself beating the shit out
of him. Then that beastly scream tapers off, turning back into more
crying.

Never in my life have I wanted to kill another person before.
But now that I might go blind in one eye because of that little
bitch? Now that I might die and turn into what Savanna did, all
because of him?

I wanna kill Danny for that…

I legit to beat him to death with my bare hands…

*No… I wanna beat him half to death, and I wanna then push him onto
a cluster of tentacles. And then I wanna jam one of these fuckin rubber spike
things in his eye so he can suffer whatever fate I do…*

But then I think about him saving me before I go blind, and
that murderous rage simmers down. I mean, I'd still kick his ass for
what he did, but I probably won't end his life if I don't end up
losing my eye. And if, by some miracle, I survive this without any
permanent disfiguration, there's a smaller chance that I maybe
might forgive him.

But that's a hard maybe…

A wave of drowsiness hits me out of nowhere—one that's
more intense than what I've experienced even after getting stoned
out of my mind while blackout drunk. And at the same time, the

tickling sensation just below the surface of my eye turns into this sharp stinging.

"GAHH!" I flinch, squeezing my eyes shut only for it to hurt worse.

You gotta get this thing off right the fuck now. I squeeze the stalk with the hand already stuck to it, and then I grab the bulb with my right hand. *C'mon, Tucker. You can do this…*

Even though trying to peel my hand off the quills earlier hurt too much to bear—even though ripping this thing off my head will without a doubt be worse—I pull anyway.

And as soon as my skin starts stretching, I stop.

You gotta do this, I think, wincing. *No matter how bad it hurts!*

"GRRRR-MMMM!" I growl as I begin pulling this thing away from my cheek with more strength.

Fuck… It's like tryin' to pry away the arm of someone twice my strength.

Slowly, the bulb lifts. The sticky globs stretch my skin with it. It hurts. Bad. Then worse.

But I keep pulling. Until searing-hot pain flares from the right side of my face and the corner of my eye.

"GAHH! GURR-HAH-HURGH!" I cry out, releasing the tentacle at the same time.

And then I break down again.

When my obnoxious sobbing finally fades into quiet whimpering, all I hear is someone puking their guts out. It's not coming from the direction I'm facing—from where Gavin is. It's coming from over by Kyle. I strain my head back against the tentacle around my skull until my tear-blurred vision finds Danny near where I last saw him. After blinking away the tears, I see that he's doubled over, hands on his thighs. A second later, vomit pours out of his mouth, splattering onto the pile at his feet. Based on the volume of grossness already there, he must've been throwing up for a while. Guess I just didn't hear it over my loud-ass crying.

"Danny, what the fuck!" I shout, my voice cracking like it used to during puberty. "We don't have time to wait for you to finish puking! Get up and get the fucking knife before this shit puts me to sleep too!"

"I'm tryi—blurrrrrgh!" he pukes again. "I tryin'!"

"Stop trying, and *fucking go*! For fuck's sake, man! We're all dyin', and you're over there taking your sweet-ass time getting what you need to save us!"

"I'm sorry, Tucker!" He hurls again. Then he gasps as soon as vomit stops pouring out his mouth. "But… it's kinda hard to walk without slippin'—" He gasps again. "—when you're puking this hard!" Danny vomits again.

"God dammit!" I mutter, slowly angling my head back down.

My eyes damn near bulge out of my head when I see the bulb that's inches from my face—the one at the end of the tentacle that's still lying flat on the meat-mat, for some reason.

Wait… it's closer than it was when it first slammed down…

Not only is it closer, but it looks different too. Those beige, fleshy scales that give it its pinecone look? They've fanned open like a blooming flower, and hundreds of black, almost plastic-looking threads are poking straight out from between them.

"What the fuck," I whisper, watching in horror as the strands slowly lengthen.

These strings… they're growing right toward my mouth…

Right as that thought crosses my mind, the tentacle subtly drifts to the right, shaking ever so slightly as it does. It's trembling like the arm of someone struggling to grasp something that's just a little too far away.

Closer… It's getting closer… It's…

"Danny!" I shout as my head suddenly swirls with the most intense wave of drowsiness yet.

"Yeah?" he croaks back.

"The tentacle layin' in front of my face—it's reachin-for-meh." That comes out in a slur.

"What?! Whaddya mean?!"

Suddenly, my right eye gets crazy blurry. At the same time, that pinching, tickling sensation shifts deeper, like something thin is tunneling toward the center of my eyeball.

No matter how much I blink, that blurriness won't go away. Instead, it just keeps getting worse.

Blind…

Am I going blind?

Please don't let me be going blind!

"Isss-fuckin' stretchin' towarssss my face!" I mumble. "And my eye… I—I think I'm goin' blind, man…" Another surge of drowsiness hits, and my eyelids droop. "Arrgh fuck! Jusss—jussss hurry, you fucker… Move your ass…"

"Kay! I'm going!" His voice sounds like it's a football field away all the sudden.

I try opening my eyes to see how far he's moved, but I can't. No matter how hard I try, I can't.

A split-second later, it suddenly becomes impossible to form a thought.

Then everything starts going numb, and it feels like I'm sinking into the ground.

CHAPTER 9:
BEFORE YOU PASS OUT

DANNY HOLLAND
Friday, August 26th

Hearing Tucker say he was going blind sent so much adrenaline surging through me that my nausea subsided. And now that I'm done puking my guts out, I'm shuffling almost twice as fast across this meat-mat as I was earlier, following the same route Kyle did. But I still have kind of a long way to go, though.

The closer I get, the stronger that sweet, floral smell becomes. Every breath makes me feel more intoxicated. More aroused.

The closer I get, the stronger the urge to get to where Kyle is—no, the stronger the urge to get to the female corpse puppet…

I sidestep through the first set of close-ish tentacles without even needing to fend them off with my sticks.

At the next set, where the gap is tighter, I raise one branch like a sword and hold the other in a reverse grip, then stomp hard between the hell-stalks.

Savanna squawk-moans at the same time the tentacles crash against my sticks with the force of karate chops. They're so powerful, my arms tremble as I push back against them.

"Holy fuck," I groan, staring at the one on my right—staring at where I hit it between the bulb and the quills.

These things are damn near as strong as Tucker and Kyle, I think, glancing left. My eyes go wide when I realize my reverse-grip branch struck lower, right into the quills.

"Fuck!" I shout, watching the appendage wrap around it. Without missing a beat, I swiftly long-step between the stalks. And once I'm clear, I yank both sticks back—but the left one doesn't budge. "Fucking shit!" After two more useless tugs, I let it go, screaming as I do.

What am I gonna do now? I need two branches to get through the rest of these things… My gaze wanders to the one I'm still holding. *Wait… If I break this in half, the pieces should be long enough to fight off the tentacles…* Now I look ahead, over to Kyle's sticks. *Then I can just use his on the way out…*

I lay the wood down, step on the middle of it, and then start bending it.

SNAP!

Not exactly half, I think, picking up the slime-coated pieces. *But close enough.*

When I reach the dense stalk cluster around Kyle and Savanna, I veer right like he did, heading toward the widest gap.

Now that I'm this close to *her*, that sweet smell is just as strong as it was at this same distance from the dong-shroom. It's dizzying. Intoxicating. It's fucking me up so much that I have to pause.

Before I took that first step onto the meat-mat, all I cared about was getting to Kyle safely. But now that I'm this close to Savanna, survival and rescuing my friends barely crosses my mind. And my guilt—I barely remember why I felt so guilty in the first place.

The only thing I can think about now is how badly I want to drop my pants and maniacally tug away at the part of me that looks like a Uteroboscis—doing that to the thought of me smashing

Savanna Lockhart instead of Morgan. The mere thought has me feeling like I'm one stroke from reaching completion.

I rapidly shake my head, forcing myself to visualize what I need to do instead. *Focus. Focus.* Now I look back up at the spiky stalks ahead.

"Okay, okay…" I mutter, raising the sticks.

Here we go… Now I stomp in between the pair of death-appendages.

"UH-GWURHHH!" corpse-Savanna wails as both tentacles slam against my sticks with a *THOOK.*

This time, my branches hit clean—right under the bulbs and just above the top ring of quills. The tentacles bear down against the sticks, my arms once again trembling against the force. As I'm stepping forward, the right stalk suddenly swings left—almost deliberately—quickly sliding across my branch, my hand, my wrist. It happens so fast, I don't react until the spikes' tips are already dragging against my forearm.

"GAHH!" I scream, throwing myself back towards the tree right before it can fully coil around my limb. At the same time that my ass hits the spongy surface, I grab the pinecone bulb, stopping it from snaking around me more than it already has. "No-no-no-no!" I whimper through clenched teeth, pulling with everything I've got.

Surprisingly, it starts to bend. But the instant my skin starts stretching—burning—I hesitate. Then, in the blink of an eye, it tightens around my arm like a fucking snake.

"Oh God… No… No…"

What do I do? What do I do?

Still gripping the bulb, I scan for Kyle's knife and spot it immediately—5- or 6-feet to my left, at the base of a tentacle stalk. Too far to reach even if my stick wasn't snapped in half.

"FUCK!" I scream.

That's when I feel it…

The stalk throbbing against my arm like a tubular, slow-beating heart.

These rubbery quills rapidly twitching against me…

Itchiness spreading beneath my skin…

"Roots," I mutter.

Kyle said black roots were growing under… The thought evaporates when I see them—black, hair-thin, barely millimeter-long fibers just beneath the epidermis, stretching out from where the orange globs are glued to me.

"Oh fuck!" I shout, turning to Kyle with a quick snap.

It's his arm that I lock onto. Even from here, I can see the black roots zigzagging beneath his flesh, each one a few inches long. And somehow, that's not even the worst part. Growing around where the quills' tips are pressed against his skin, there are these tan, gooey globs that look like a meat-mat tissue in the center and off-white frosting toward the edges.

Wait…

My eyes snap over to corpse-puppet Savanna. Then they dart back to his arm.

His skin is turning into the same shit that's covering her…

Oh fuck… I need to get this off me. Now.

I start looking back and forth like a maniac, scanning for something—*anything*—to get this tentacle off my arm. Right as I do, I suddenly go from buzzing with adrenaline to feeling sedated as fuck.

It's drugging you. Like it drugged them…

Get this thing off before you pass out!

The branch I dropped catches my eye. Specifically, the jagged, pointy end that formed when I snapped it in half.

Without missing a beat, I release the bulb and throw my body forward, stretching my arm as far as I can.

"GRUHH!" I growl as the tightening tentacle pulls my limb back at a weird angle, twisting my arm hard enough to make my shoulder hurt. "GAHHH! C'mon!"

My fingers finally hit the stick, and I sigh in relief once I start dragging it toward me.

Another wave of drowsiness hits as I'm leaning forward and placing my arm flat against the meat-mat.

"RAHHH!" I roar, driving the jagged end into the stalk like a stake meant for a vampire's heart.

It stabs right through a gap between the quills stuck to me and the ones that aren't. Brown goo and something white that resembles mayo oozes out around the wood.

"GWUHH-AH-UHHH!" Savanna moan-wails at the same time that all the tentacles in my peripheries snap toward me.

"GRRRR!" I growl, stabbing it again. "GRR! GRRR! GRAHH-GRMMM!" With each feral grunt, I stab into it again.

And again.

And again.

It's on the sixth stab that the section clamped to my arm finally tears away.

"Oh fuck," I sigh out while urgently sitting up.

Even though it's completely severed, it's still pulsating against me. But I ignore it and just climb to my feet, holding my arm far away from my body so the goo doesn't drip on me.

"Kyle!" I call out weakly, swaying from a sudden bout of wooziness. I slap a hand against the biomass-covered tree in time to steady myself, and it sounds like a bare ass just got spanked. "KYLE!"

He doesn't stir. But when I get closer, I see his chest rise.

"Oh thank God…" I whisper.

When my gaze shifts from his chest to his right arm, I stop dead in my tracks. Those same beige tendrils from the edge of the meat-mat are also creeping up every inch of skin in contact with the biomass.

"Oh no…"

It's absorbing him!

I glance from Kyle to the sticks on the other side of him. Then I turn right, looking at the narrow gap between his feet and the corpse-puppet. "Fuck…"

I don't wanna get near her…

The moment I start tiptoeing over, I shudder and let out a shaky breath.

"GWUUH-AH-UH-UHH!" Savanna groans as I'm passing between them, making me jump and slip a bit.

Another wave of drowsiness hits right when my fingers touch the first of Kyle's branches.

Why am I feeling more sedated? I glance at the end still clung to my arm. *Is the bulb what's secreting the sedative into me? Or is whatever it pumped into me earlier just taking a while to kick in?*

The second I grab the other stick, I turn and start toward the knife. But I only take two steps before stopping at the sight of Kyle's left leg. Those same gummy globs growing on his arm are speckled along the side of his calf too, spreading over the wounds he got when I ripped that first little stalk off him. And beneath his skin are more black fibers, each one an inch or 2 long.

Wait… The roots and the biomass tissue are still growing, even though I pulled that thing off him almost an hour ago? Then that means… My eyes drift to my arm. *Longer… The roots are a few millimeters longer already.*

"Oh fuck!"

I need to get this the fuck off me, I think, grabbing the bulb. *Now!*

A mix of panic and drowsiness sends me crashing to my knees.

And then I need to cut out the infected skin…

I take a moment to look at just how many quills are stuck to me.

Oh God, this is gonna hurt so bad…

The longer you wait, the more it spreads. And the more it spreads, the more skin you'll have to cut away.

I take a slow, deep breath.

On three…

"One…" I exhale deeply, then take another deep breath. "Two…" My lungs get emptied and refilled once more. "Three- AHHHH!" I scream as I yank this stalk with all I've got.

That battle cry crescendos into a roar when the quills start tearing free in rapid succession, ripping chunks and strips of flesh away with them. And as soon as the last rubbery spike leaves my arm, I toss that severed tentacle way off in the opposite direction that I came from.

Liquid warmth pours down to my wrist. Blood drips onto the meat-mat. I don't even look at my arm. Because I can tell from the white-hot pain that it's bad. And because I don't want to look down and find out that the roots are still in me.

"OH FUCK-KUGH-HURRRGH!" I growl, looking over at Kyle through barely open eyes.

Kyle didn't even stir from that loud-ass scream. Not good. I look over at the others. *Damn. None of them woke up from that…*

You need to hurry, Danny.

Growling, I pick up the branches and try to stand. But then I crash right back down to my knees.

Get the fucking knife. Cut the roots and infected skin out of your arm before it's too late.

It takes everything I have to stand up.

My wobbly legs buckle beneath me with each step I take toward my objective.

About 6 feet out from the tentacle, I drop into a squat and hold out my right stick an inch away from the base of the bulb.

A little lower, I think, adjusting it down to right above the quills.

Now that I'm confident my measurements are correct, jab the ground near the base with the other branch.

"GWUUH-OOH-UH!" Savanna wails right as the stalk swings downward.

It slams into my stick—harder than the last few did. Or maybe I'm just weaker.

"Fuck," I groan, shoving it back while raking for the knife with the left stick.

Its tip hits the handle on the first try, and then I manage to drag it an inch or so toward me.

A little more… I rake it a little bit closer. *Almost there…*

It takes a few more attempts to drag it out of the tentacle's range.

"GRAH!" I grunt, kicking off the meat-mat while simultaneously throwing myself backward.

The stalk thwacks down inches from my feet a split-second before my back even hits the meat-mat.

"Phew…" I sigh out, grabbing the knife.

Now for the hard part…

On my way over to the tree, I get crazy sleepy. Then my eyelids droop the way they do when I'm extremely exhausted and about to pass out.

No… not yet.

My legs buckle when I'm a foot away, and I crash onto my knees.

"Urrgh," I groan, crawling forward.

Why do I feel this drugged even though I got the tentacle off after only a minute or two?

As I maneuver into a sitting position, I think about how much I drank. About the two hits of that weed vape I took after swearing I wouldn't.

Sedatives hit harder when you're already fucked up, I remind myself as I lean back against the meat-covered trunk.

I straighten my legs, and the second that warm, spongy, slime-coated surface touches my calves, I think of the tendrils creeping onto Kyle's flesh.

Wait… I need something between me and this shit. Just in case I black out.

I'm so sluggish, it takes forever to get my backpack off. My towel and my spare shirt are what I pull out. I lay the towel lengthwise at the base of the tree, sling my backpack back on, then lean against the trunk. Now I drape my shirt over my head. That way, if I black out and slump back, I won't touch it.

By the time I'm done, the wooziness is worse.

"Okay…" I whisper, finally looking at my arm.

There's a little bit of mayo-looking goo oozing from a few wounds. There aren't many black fibers near the gashes. I'm guessing most must've ripped away with the quills. Or maybe I just can't see them under all the blood.

The edges of the globs on Kyle's arm are off-white and gooey-looking. So that white shit must turn into that biomass tissue…

"Errgh," I groan, bringing the knife to the first spot. "Fuck…"

If you don't cut it out, what happened to Savanna happens to you… And becoming a squawking corpse-puppet who's probably trapped in a vegetative state will be way worse than slicing off your own skin…

I press the blade flat against the healthy skin, millimeters from the glob. Then I blow out three sharp breaths.

"GAHHHH!" I scream, slicing forward and flaying a chunk of skin free.

A beat later, my eyelids sag.

No… Not yet, I think, forcing them back open. *Two more to go…*

"GAAHH!" I roar, cutting off the next small patch.

I scream again during the last slice.

"GRRUH-HUH-HUH-HUH-URRH!" is how I cry right after.

You did it… Now… to free… Kyle…

I set the knife off to the side, and then plant my hands flat against the towel-covered surface in what feels like slow-motion. Right as I'm about to shift onto my hip, my limbs go weak and my eyelids flutter shut.

Come on, Danny…

No matter how hard I try, I can't reopen my eyes.

Fight it…

My head suddenly hangs forward. It's too heavy to lift back up.

Get up.

Numbness spreads all over me as my consciousness slips away.

CHAPTER 10:
WORSE THAN HELL

TUCKER WILLIAMS
Friday, August 26th

Something tickling between my lips, all over my tongue, and along the inside of my cheeks—that's what I feel as I wake up from the deepest sleep of my life. In the next instant, before my eyelids even start to rise, I become aware of other things—something pulsating around the top of my head, something subtly throbbing beneath my right hand, and more slow pulses coming from the weirdly spongy surface I'm lying right-side-down on.

My left eye shoots open. At first, all I see is a blurred forest, an orange glow behind the treetops, and a dark-blue sky above.

My other eye doesn't open as wide. The eyelids are stuck together near the outer corner, and even though I feel that it's open about halfway, there's nothing there but darkness. Just darkness, and a faint crawling sensation deep inside my right eye.

Suddenly, it all comes back to me. Danny pushed me, and I fell onto the biomass. Then a quill went into my eye as a tentacle wrapped around my head.

Blind… The realization makes me whimper. My one good eye squeezes shut as I break into shaky sobs. *I'm blind in one eye!*

"Dan—" I stop when something that feels like a wad of hair brushes my tongue, lips, and the inside of my cheeks.

A sharp gasp rips out of me as I open my mouth wide and start blinking my good eye hard to clear the tears. The moment I try curling my tongue back away from the hairs, whatever's between my lips goes taut and yanks it forward.

What the fuck…

When the blurriness finally clears, I start hyperventilating and trembling…

The tentacle stalk lying in front of my face—the one that slammed down after the other wrapped around my head—is closer now. Longer. Its pinecone-shaped bulb has fanned open, fleshy scales spread wide. Long, black, plastic-looking fibers spill out from between them, along with a thicker black stem in the center. And that entire tangled mass leads straight into my mouth.

"AHHHH!" I scream as I try to lean away, but the stringy things tighten and yank at my mouth's interior, instantly stopping me.

I reach for it with my left hand and try to sit up, but something tugs back at my hand, the right side of my head, and my arm. The sensation instantly makes me think of being stuck to a glue trap.

"DANNY!" I scream.

No response.

"GRAAAHHH!" I roar, lifting my head and turning toward Kyle and Savanna, straining against whatever's tugging at my cheek.

That's when I see Danny sitting slumped against the meat-covered tree, head hanging, arms limp at his sides.

"DANNY! WAKE UP, YOU SON-OF-A-BITCH!" It comes out as a garbled mumble since I can't really move my tongue. "WAKE THE FUCK UP RIGHT NOW AND HELP ME!"

He doesn't budge…

Shit… Something must've happened to him while I was out…

My gaze snaps over to Kyle. He's still lying backside-down where he fell.

And he's still out cold...

As the thing on my face pulls my head back to where it was, I glance toward Gavin. He's unconscious too.

"Oh fughk," I slur around the plasticky roots as I get crazy sleepy out of nowhere.

Everyone's unconscious, I think, sobbing as my left eyelid slowly falls shut. *No one knows where we are...*

We're all gonna die here...

I picture Savanna's biomass-encased body.

We're all turning into what she did.

Out of nowhere, unbearable pain flares deep behind my right eyeball.

"ARRRGHH!" I cry out.

Rapid flashes light up my blinded eye. But when I squint with my good one, there's nothing happening in front of me.

"What the fuhhgh," I mutter, my left eyelid slowly drooping shut even though I'm fighting to keep it open.

A few beats later, the flashes get worse. The phantom visuals twist into amorphous, strobing blobs—lumpy shadows edged with faint light, swirling and expanding and shrinking all at once.

Oh God, I think as the drowsiness intensifies, dragging me back to the verge of another blackout.

That's when the tickling at the back of my tongue creeps to my throat.

"Gehk-gehh-hahh!" I gag. "No..." I try to open my good eye, but my eyelid won't budge. "HE-ALP!"

Hell. This is hell...

No, this is worse than hell...

This can't be how I die!

"DANNY!" I scream as loud as humanly possible.

Warm numbness rapidly spreads from my face and head down my arms. Then to my legs.

The choking sensation fades, but I can still hear myself gagging…

My consciousness starts slipping, and I get that falling feeling. But it feels like it's just my head that's being pulled down into an endless pit.

Then my ears start ringing. It's faint at first. But then it suddenly gets louder.

And louder.

Until there's an abrupt silence and everything goes black.

Everything but those pulsing, swirling shadows with glowing edges.

And then…

CHAPTER 11:
WHERE IT ENDS

DANNY HOLLAND
Friday, August 26th

From somewhere beyond the darkness, a male voice screams my name.

Waking up feels like rising through thick soup while my body is slowly materializing from scalp to toes.

My eyelids are too heavy to lift—so heavy that they feel glued shut…

My head is hanging forward, which is probably why my neck is aching like crazy. But I don't have the strength to adjust my position.

My mouth is so dry that *thirsty* would be an understatement…

My torso… it's upright, leaning back against something instead of lying on a bed or couch…

My left arm rests on my lap. The other lies limp beside me, on top of some kind of fabric covering something lumpy and warm…

My morning wood… it's painfully stiff and straining against my boxers…

My legs… they're straight out in front of me, too numb to move, pressed against the same cotton-feeling fabric as my right arm…

My body… it's cold even though the air on my skin is warm. My shirt clings to me like those times I woke up all sick and feverish, drenched in a cold sweat.

During my first deep inhale, my nostrils fill with a gloriously sweet fragrance layered with a subtler dankness.

"Urrgh-ughh," I groan, slowly lifting my head and forcing my eyes into a squint.

Instead of my living room or bedroom, I see a blurred forest—a green-and-brown smear of canopy against a dusk sky, with tans and browns below.

The last thing I remember is hiking to Yelm Lake, I think, blinking hard, trying to clear away the blurriness. *I must've passed out drunk on the walk back.*

It takes making my eyes tear up and blinking a few more times before my vision finally clears.

"Whuhh?" I groan when I see the alien world before me.

No. It's a forest where the entire ground and the bottom halves of the trees are coated in veiny, yellowish-tan biomass that has dozens of tall, quilled stalks rising out of it.

"What the…"

My gaze then wanders down, and I find that I'm sitting on my navy-blue towel. As I'm looking to the right, I spot these yellowish-tan tendrils that have grown onto the edge of it. Same by my feet. Same to the left.

"What the fuhh…"

Before I can finish the word, it all comes back to me in a rapid burst of flashes…

Hiking through the woods to Yelm Lake for the party…

The musty smell in the air…

The sweet fragrance that aroused us and lured us to a dildo-shaped fungus…

The blanket of fungal meat creeping across the ground nearby…

Ripping off the tiny, fleshy stalk that stuck to Kyle's calf…

The trail disappearing under a mat of the same steak-thick biomass I'm staring at now…

A meat-mass-encased girl—Savanna Lockhart—squawking in the center of a corrupted clearing when Tucker hit her with rocks or whenever we stepped on certain parts of the meat-mat…

Kyle rushing to save her, only to fall and get grabbed by a tentacle like the ones in front of me…

Gavin sprinting across the slimy mat to save him, then watching him slip and fall back-first onto another stalk…

What happened to Tucker because of me…

The events leading up to me sitting on this towel…

Filleting off my own flesh in slices as thin as a paperback cover to stop the infection from turning me into what Savanna became…

My arm, I think, looking down and to the right.

Instead of bleeding wounds or scabs, I see the same beige, frosting-like growth rising from my flayed cuts like pimples, black fibers poking from their centers—and beneath my skin, the black roots have grown another centimeter or two.

"No…"

I cut those fungal-glob things off… Why are they back?

My eyes snap over to the knife, and I contemplate slicing away more skin.

But then I think to myself—*If it's grown this much in the hour or however long I was out, Kyle's gotta be much worse. I need to cut him free first… I gotta save him and then save the others first.*

"Kyle!" I shout, leaning forward and pulling the shirt off my head.

No response.

All I hear is a horrendously sticky, wet tearing sound behind me as my backpack peels away from the tree. I look over my shoulder, and then I watch in horror as the biomass tendrils latched onto my bag stretch and snap like overstretched taffy.

"Blrurrghhh," I groan, retching after.

Glad I kept my bookbag on… And glad I had enough sense to use it, that shirt, and this towel as a barrier between me and this shit that's trying to absorb me.

"Gavin!" I shout even louder while maneuvering onto my knees.

"OORUHH-GWUHH-UHH!" the corpse puppet wails as my bag finally rips from the flesh-covered tree.

Hearing that ghastly sound out of nowhere makes me jump, shiver, and scream out an "Eeee-yuhhh!"

That sounded different than its earlier wails.

"Gavin!" I call again, in case that thing's cry drowned him out. He doesn't answer.

During my rise, I suck in a deep breath. "TUCKER!" I scream even louder, my legs shaking and buckling beneath me. "GAVIN!"

Nothing.

They're all still unconscious… But I'm awake?

I think back to how Kyle didn't pass out when that first little stalk latched onto his leg. Then I replay me ripping the one off my own arm a few minutes after it grabbed me.

I'm awake because I got that thing off me fast enough… which means they might wake up once I cut the tentacles off them too…

Whatever hope I had dies when I see Kyle.

"Oh fughh-k…" I croak-gag.

Last time I saw him, tendrils were just starting to stretch up the flesh touching the meat-mat.

But now? A tan sheet of biomass—thick as a slice of cheese—has crept 2 or 3 inches up his arm, leg, torso, and the back of his head. A membrane has swallowed every inch of skin still in contact with it, and the edge of it almost looks like it's blending into him.

"Fuck-fuck-fuck!" I croak as I begin speed-shuffling across the slippery, muscly surface.

A few feet away, I stop and look down at the tentacle wrapped around his left forearm, making sure it's not about to spring up and grab me.

"Dear God…" I mutter when I see just how much worse his arm is compared to where the meat-mat alone has grown onto him.

The little gooey tan globs that used to be around the quill tips—like off-white frosting the size of pencil erasers—have fused into one continuous membrane. It looks exactly like the biomass, covering maybe six or seven inches of his forearm and three inches across. The black quills embedded in it blend seamlessly into the growth, just like the roots in the meat-mat. And where the edge meets uncorrupted skin, tan frosting-like tendrils bristle with tiny spikes made of paste.

This is so fucked, I think, staring down with wide, unblinking eyes. *This is so royally fucked…* I scan the stalk from its bulb to where it's fused to his flesh, searching for a place to cut. *No. It might spring up and attack me.* My gaze drops to the base. *I'll cut it there first. Then I'll deal with the rest.*

First, I wrap my shirt around the arm I'll be reaching out with. Just in case. Next, I brace a branch straight up in front of me, one end pressed firmly into the meat-mat—a defensive measure for the event that it detaches and swings at me. And when I'm confident it won't attack, I drop to my haunches and let out a long breath.

"One… Two…"

On three, I swing the blade into the base of the stalk, then I start sawing back and forth like a maniac.

Right as amber mucus and white, creamy stuff start oozing from the gash, a low, feminine growl rumbles from the corpse puppet to my right. Then Savanna lets out a blood-curdling, "GWUH-RUHHH-UHH-UH!"

At the same time, Kyle's body spasms. "Gahh-ha-ahh!" he cries weakly.

"Kyle!" I shout, still feverishly slicing at the stalk. "Relax, I'm cutting you free, brother!"

"Da-Danny?!"

"Yeah, it's me, bro!"

Groaning and sobbing, he tries to sit up, but the membrane fused to the back of his skull snaps him back down like a rubber sheet that's too elastic to rip. "It… hurts! What're you doin' to me?!

"I'm not doin' anything to you!" I say breathlessly, speaking a mile-a-minute. "I'm just cuttin' this tentacle so I can get you out of here!"

"It hurtsss-SAHHH!" he screams out right as my final cut separates the stalk from the meat mass.

"What hurts, Kyle?" I pant out, staring in horror as amber syrupiness, mayo-like goo, and pink yogurt-looking shit start oozing from both severed ends.

"My…arm…" He tries lifting it, but the membrane tethering the rest of his limb to the mat yanks it back down. "You… cutting *my arm*… hurt!"

I shake my head. "I wasn't cuttin' your arm! I was cuttin' the tentacle stuck to it."

His bloodshot, half-open eyes stare in me at confusion. "The tent-ta-cull?" he croaks.

I point to the right. "One of those."

Kyle turns his head as far as he can. "Oh fuck…" Then he looks back at me, eyes filling with tears.

"Yeah… Those tentacles growing out of the meat-mat? You fell, and one grabbed your arm while you were trying to save that girl—Savanna."

His face scrunches up like it hurts to think. "Oh… Right…"

"Yeah… And those things pump some kind of sedative into its prey. That's why you're so out of it."

"Urgh," he groans, writhing and trying to sit up. "Feels like I'm stuck to the ground."

"Uhh… You are…"

"Whahh?!"

"I don't wanna freak you out, but… the biomass you're layin' on? It grew *onto you*. Like, it formed a sheet of tissue that wrapped against all the skin in contact with it, and then it fused to your flesh. So I gotta cut it away before you can stand up, okay?"

He starts trembling hard. "Oh fuck… Oh, what the fuck… What the fuck…"

I put a hand on his shoulder. "Hey. Just breathe and try to relax, bro. Okay?"

"Oh… kay…" he pants out.

Exhaling slowly, I bring the knife toward the membrane consuming the back of his skull. "Keep your head still, alright?"

"Okay… But… you gotta hurry, Danny… I don't feel so good… Feels like—" His eyelids droop shut only to open right back up. "Feels like I'm gonna pass out again."

"Alright," I say as I start slicing. "Gonna go as fast as I—"

"GYAHHH!" he screams, squeezing his eyes shut.

"GWUHH-UHH-UH!" Savanna squawks at the same time.

I yank the knife away. "What?!"

"Felt like you were cutting into my scalp!"

"Dude, I was inches away from your scalp!"

"You sure?"

I look down at the cut to double-check. "Yeah. I'm, like, an inch away, dude. I swear."

"Oh…"

The second I resume slicing, he screams. "GAHH! Stop!"

I yank the knife back again. "I'm not anywhere near your skin!"

"Feels like you are!"

Wait… My gaze drifts to the severed stalk's base. *He woke up screaming when I cut it, and the corpse puppet screamed at the same time… Then they both cried out again when I cut into the membrane on the side of his head… Does that mean… he somehow feels what she and the biomass feel?*

The thought gets me hyperventilating. "Alright, alright," I say, standing up. I start speed-shuffling, moving between his feet and *her body.*

"Where' you goin'?"

I drop into a squat near his right side. "Look down at your hand," I say, bringing the blade toward the membrane on his wrist.

"Grrrr," he groans, fighting against the fungal tissue pulling the left side of his head. Kyle's eyes widen when he sees it. "Oh God…"

"See how far the knife is from you?"

"Ye-yeah?" he croaks.

"Okay. Now watch me cut the membrane."

I slice back and forth in slow passes. A bit of hope swells within me when he doesn't scream.

But then, a beat later, his face contorts into a pained expression—right as amber slime and something that looks like blood start oozing out around the knife. "GAHHH! It feels like you're cutting me!"

"But you see I'm not, *right?*"

He nods as much as the membrane allows. "Yeah… I see that… Which is why…" His eyes start closing again. "Danny… I don't understand… why it feels like you're cutting me when you're not?! What the fuck is happening?!"

I wince. "Hold on…"

Using the knife and the end of the stick, I lift the credit-card-thick membrane I just cut and peel it upward.

"Ahh-ahhh," he groans as it starts to tear away from his arm with a horrendously sticky noise that sounds like open-mouth smacking.

"Sorry, just… bear with me, bro."

I keep pulling, and it keeps tearing.

The more I peel it, the harder it gets to strip away, and the louder Kyle screams in agony.

I don't stop until the tan, fungus-looking tissue transitions seamlessly into pink flesh. That's when more blood, brown slime, and white goop start oozing from the wound. Then more crimson gushes out a beat later. Looks like I hit a vein or some shit.

"Ehh-ugh," I groan, letting the flap fall.

"Wha-what?" he murmurs weakly.

"I uhh…" I take a slow breath, then exhale. "Don't freak out, but uhhh… You remember how Savanna made that weird squawking noise whenever you stepped on certain parts of the biomass?"

He cracks one eye open into a squint. "Ye-yeah?"

"Well, I think that's because this entire thing can *feel* pressure. Like it has nerves… And I think you're also feeling what Savanna and the meat-meat feels… Like its *nerves* somehow connected to yours when it grew onto you…"

His eyes snap open wide, and he rapidly shakes his head. "What?! No—"

"It's the only thing that makes sense… Because you woke up screaming *right when* I cut into the far end of the tentacle, and then you just felt pain when you *watched* me cut the tissue inches from your arm."

He whimpers as tears stream down his cheeks. "I don't—I don't understand…"

Seeing him cry makes me tear up. "Me either, bro… This shit makes no fucking sense. All I know is that the back of your head and the skin on your limbs touching the meat-mat are… basically fused to it—"

"Fused? What do you mean by fused?"

"I mean, like—that flap I pulled up? I saw where your skin was becoming biomass. And I couldn't tell where the membrane ended or where your flesh began… Like, it didn't grow onto you and then got glued to your skin—*it became your skin.*"

He retches. "Oh fuck… No…"

I shake my head. "I wish it wasn't true. But it is. And I don't think there's a way to cut you free without hurting you—or without you bleeding out. Because whenever I cut too deep, the membrane started bleeding like it was a part of you. Like, *bleeding a lot.*"

"Oh, gawd… No…" Kyle shakes his head, thrashing as much as his fleshy restraints allow. "No-no-no-no!"

"Kyle… Since I don't think I can cut you free without you bleeding out, I need to go get help. Like, *real help.* Doctors. EMTs. Scientists. Someone who can get you out of here without killing you. Okay?"

He nods as his eyes slowly shut. "Go, bro… Hurry…"

I nod. "Okay. I'm gonna haul ass back to your neighborhood, call for help as soon as I get signal, and then I'll lead them back here as quickly as I can! I promise!"

"Don't go to… my neighborhood," he mumbles without opening his eyes.

"Why not?"

"Go… north…" he whispers, barely moving his mouth. His eyes are fluttering like he's having a seizure. "Closest neighborhood is… straight north… Faster… get… signal… sooner…"

"Okay! I'll go north… Wait—where's your compass?"

He doesn't respond. So I shake him.

"Where's your compass, Kyle?!"

"Bookbag…"

I scan the immediate area, but I don't see it. Then something comes back to me.

Wait, he ditched it by the trail before he stepped onto the meat-mat.

"Alright," I say, patting his shoulder. "I'm heading out now. I'll be back soon, bro. I promise."

He nods while cracking one eye open into a squint. "Go…" The eye shuts again. "Hurry… I'm… 'bout to black out."

A shaky breath escapes me as I struggle to rise out of this squatted position. Right when I go to fold the knife, I freeze when I see brown goo and creamy white stuff smeared all over it.

That's what oozed out of my arm when I ripped the stalk off. The same stuff that turned into biomass while I was asleep… Assuming this is what's converting his flesh into that fungal tissue, I shouldn't touch it. Which means I need something to wipe it off with… The thought trails off when my sights set on the towel by the tree.

Halfway there, a wave of drowsiness hits. My legs go noodly and buckle, but I somehow make it all the way there without tipping over. It takes a few hard wipes to clean off the blade. After double checking to make sure I didn't miss a spot, I fold it and put it in my pocket.

"Okay," I sigh out, grabbing the two long sticks.

The moment I start moving again, my legs wobble and my head spins. Suddenly, I feel weaker. Colder. And I'm sweating like crazy even though it's fairly cool out here.

Guess the sedative isn't out of my system yet. Or maybe this fever's about to knock me out, like when I had the flu last year.

I stare at the tentacles between me and solid ground. With the way I feel right now, I know I'm too woozy to fend them off the way I did earlier.

If only I could cut them down instead…

Wait, I can.

I pull the knife back out, and then I stare at it for a few beats.

No... It'd be damn near impossible to hack them down while it's not wrapped around its prey. If only this knife was longer... Like... a machete...

Wait... My eyes drift to my stick. *Longer.*

What immediately pops into my head are those survival movie scenes where people tie their knife's handle to a branch, turning it into an improvised spear.

That's it!

Holding the hem of my shirt with my right hand, I use the knife to slice it into strips. Once I have four long ones, I work fast, tying the handle to the end of the longest branch.

"Alright," I whisper through a huff.

You got this, Danny, I think as my legs begin wobbling toward the pair of tentacles I passed through earlier—the intact one and the one I butchered to get free of it.

The severed one isn't an issue. But the other will get me if I try to skirt past it. So, I press the stick forward, pushing between the bulb and the first row of sticky quills. It pushes back—harder than before.

"Grrrr," I growl, fighting against its downward force as I'm bringing the knife-tipped stick towards its base.

It's not stronger, you're just weaker, I think, sawing through it as fast as I can.

"GWUUH-OORUHH!" Savanna cries out as white cream and brown goo ooze from the cut.

Kyle doesn't cry out along with her this time. Or maybe he did and I just couldn't hear him over her.

Since it's harder to generate force with the knife tied to a stick than it is when it's handheld, it takes nearly twice as long to sever this tentacle.

That's one down, I think, watching the squirming thing fall.

At the next pair—a set with a slightly wider gap—I use the same technique on the one to the left. Thankfully, it goes just as smoothly. So does the one to the right of it.

A few shuffle-steps later, I get crazy lightheaded out of nowhere. It's so bad that my legs buckle and I crash onto my knees. Thankfully, I've landed out of range of any tentacles.

"Fuck," I groan, struggling to get back up.

I'm getting weaker… And sleepier… Gotta hurry.

The next 2 stalks are far enough apart that I should be able to get by if I only cut one. The second I touch my stick beneath the pinecone bulb, it pushes down, and my arm gives out. Then, in a blur, the tentacle swipes down the branch and curls tightly around it.

"Fucking shit-fuck!" I groan, driving it back while sawing through the base with the knife-stick.

When it finally falls, it remains tightly coiled around my branch. I don't bother trying to pull it free. Because there are still two sticks by Gavin, and I'm only a few feet from him.

It's no surprise to see that he's in the same state Kyle was—a biomass membrane creeping over every inch of flesh touching the meat-mat, with a thicker fungal mass spreading out from where the tentacle is fused to the side of his neck.

"Gavin?" I call from a foot away.

He doesn't even twitch.

After picking up his sticks, I poke his arm.

No reaction.

"GAVIN!" I shout louder, jabbing his big belly.

Nothing happens.

The base of the stalk he fell on is pinned beneath his back. And since all that biomass tissue is tethering his head and sides down, I'll have to cut it all away before I can sever it. But he might bleed out if I do that…

Which means I'm gonna have to leave you like that.

"I don't know if you can hear me, Gav," I shout as I resume shuffling away, "but I'm gonna go get help, brother! Just hold on for a bit longer!"

By the time I'm within 5 feet of Tucker, I feel the same way I did right before blacking out earlier. *Why am I getting drowsy again? It's been hours since that stalk was on my arm...*

Is something else wrong? Or is this fever just that bad now?

Hurry, Danny... Get to the regular dirt-covered ground. Now.

At first, guilt makes me shuffle past Tucker without looking down at him. But then curiosity about his current state makes me glance back. The flesh beneath the tentacle curled around his head—and the one wrapped around his awkwardly bent left leg—is just as corrupted as Kyle's and Gavin's.

As I'm about to check out his eye, something else catches my attention.

There's a tentacle lying across the meat-mat with its bulb inches from his face. The fact that it's still lying there even though it never touched him isn't the weird part. What's got me fucked up is that those fleshy scales that give the bulb its pinecone look have peeled back toward its stalk like the petals of a bloomed flower, and a mass of black fibers jut out from between them, stretching right toward Tucker's face. And when I follow them to see where they go, I discover that the entire tangle disappears into his mouth.

That's when I hear it—a quiet, labored, raspy gasp... followed by gurgling.

"OH FUCK!" I shout.

He's choking!

My gaze snaps to his eyes.

His left eye is closed, but his right is held half-open by the quill embedded near the outer corner. Instead of biomass covering it, black fibers are woven into his bloodshot sclera like some hellish tattoo.

"Oh-oh *God…*" I mutter, retching.

I can't leave him like this, I think, dropping one of the two pieces of wood I just picked up.

With the branch that's still in my left hand, I pin down the top of the tentacle that's lying in front of his face. The blade at the end of the other stick chops into its base a beat later.

"GWUHHHH!" the corpse-puppet squawk-groans.

The tentacle spasms hard the instant I start sawing. At the same time, the corpse puppet wails again, and Kyle lets out a gurgly groan.

Oh shit, I think, slicing faster.

A few quick cuts later, the tentacle finally severs—and more distressed sounds rip out of Kyle and the corpse puppet at the same time.

Now for this, I think, bringing the blade to the roots coming out from between the bulb's scales.

Even though they're thin, they take longer than expected to cut.

It's like slicing through rubber-wrapped wires or some shit…

More fleshy threads snap with each pass of the knife. When the last one gives way, I reach down to pull them out of his mouth, only to freeze inches away.

I wish I had rubber gloves. Thinking about latex instantly makes me picture condoms. *Wait. I've got condoms!*

I dig into my pocket and pull one out. It takes a bit to stretch it over my hand and roll it down. Once the base ring gets to my wrist, I grab the thick fibers and pull.

"GEHHK!" Tucker gags.

I keep pulling, but they don't snap or dislodge. And even though he's rasping harder now, he still doesn't wake up.

"Fuck!" I shout, letting go.

The condom leaves my hand with a loud snap, and then I toss it away as far as I can—both out of frustration and to ensure it doesn't land near him. Because the last thing I want is people finding that rubber next to his body and thinking Tucker died doing some deviant shit.

He starts choking louder as I'm turning back to him. It's impossible not to cry from seeing him like this and hearing him suffering like this. I stare at the hairlike clump sticking out of his mouth for a few seconds, then shift my focus to the appendage wrapped around his head.

Guess I'll at least just take care of this before I go.

With the way it's wrapped around his head, there's no way for me to pin it down between the bulb and the spikes. So, I instead press down on the middle of the stalk and then touch the knife to the base of it.

I drag the knife back across it… then forward…

On the third pass, Tucker's body starts spasming like he's seizing. "GUHHHH! GUHHHH!" he wheezes.

"GWUHH-UUHHH!" corpse-puppet Savanna wails at the same time.

"GAHHHH!" Kyle shouts over them.

Gavin grunts and groans, twitching the way people do while having a nightmare.

My arm jerks the knife-stick back before I even think to stop. "OH FUCK!" I shout, stumbling back.

A beat after I stop cutting, Tucker goes still. The others stop wailing and twitching a split-second later.

When I resume sawing at the tentacle, it all happens again. But louder. And Tucker seizes more violently this time.

"Fucking hell!" I shout, pulling the blade away.

It's like cutting that thing was killing him or some shit… I blow out a shaky breath. *I've already fucked him up enough… I can't hurt him anymore. Not when whatever pain I inflict on that tentacle is hurting the others too…*

"Fuck!" I scream as I stagger away. "I'm sorry, Tucker… I'm so fucking sorry this happened to you because of me…"

The first pair of tentacle stalks we all passed between are the last ones blocking the way. This gap's wide as hell, so I don't need to cut anything to get by them.

The second my sneaker hits dirt, I blow out a long sigh of relief. About a foot from Kyle's backpack, my legs give out and I collapse to my knees.

"Oh-ho-ho-ho-uhhh-uhhh," I sob-laugh, doubling over and slapping my hands against the dirt.

As I dig my fingers into the soil just to make sure it's real, another wave of drowsiness crashes over me.

No time to rest, I think, forcing myself upright and grabbing Kyle's backpack.

Every time I crawled across the meat-mat or picked something up off its slime-coated surface, my hands got coated in that amber slickness. In the time it took to get here, it's coagulated into sticky, gelatinous clumps—a sort of jelly that's been making my skin itch.

That's why the first thing I do is yank out Kyle's towel and the vodka bottle he *borrowed* from his parents' stash. A corner of the linen gets soaked in alcohol, and then I scrub that shit off my hands and knees. I scrub until it hurts—until there's not a trace left.

Soon as I'm done, I soak the opposite corner of the towel and get to work wiping down the knife, being careful not to touch it.

Next, I rinse my arm wounds with the vodka.

"Grrrr," I growl, watching the blood wash away.

Gooey, tan, pus-like stuff bulges out of the gashes. *Fuck, they've grown a bit since I woke up… I've gotta cut it away.* My heavy eyelids start to droop. *Now.*

I feverishly remove the knife from the stick. Even though it's spotless, I pour more alcohol over the blade. Then I just stare at it.

What if it's not clean enough and I just end up reinfecting myself?

If only I had a fire source to sterilize it with…

Tucker's lighter pops into my head—the one he always keeps in his bag in case he needs to light up a blunt.

I dig through his bag and find it in the same pocket as the compass—the small pouch at the bottom.

It takes two tries to spark a flame. I pass it back and forth over the blade for so long that I almost doze off.

That should be good, I think, blowing on the sooty steel.

After giving it a few seconds to cool, I bring it to the first hellish *scab.*

One… Two…

"GAAAAHHHH!" I scream as I carve out a deeper, wider chunk of infected flesh than before.

Another quick swipe flays off another chunk.

Then I roar through the next cut.

By the end, I'm sniveling and snotty, woozy from the fever and the sight of all that blood.

It takes a bit to slow my breathing. When the hyperventilating ends, I take a big gulp of vodka. Then I gargle with it to get the vomit taste out my mouth. After that, I pour it all over my forearm.

"GYAAAHH-HAH-AH-AHHHH!" I scream through the burn—through the pain that nearly rivals what I felt while ripping that tentacle off earlier.

Gavin's spare shirt is what I wrap up my arm with. Now that first aid is complete, I finally drink some water. Even after chugging Kyle's bottle, I'm still insanely thirsty, so I pull out mine and take a couple more gulps. After stashing my bottle and Gavin's into my backpack, I slip the straps over my shoulders and struggle to my feet.

North is that way, I think, turning 90 degrees to the right from the path we came in on, toward the leafless brush and the meat-mat beyond it.

Either I head back into the biomass-covered clearing and go north, or I backtrack and try to find another way around.

Without missing a beat, I start hiking toward the dong-shroom, using my walking stick to stay upright.

The fever worsens with every step. My body gets weaker by the second.

A few minutes into the hike, it gets too dark for me to see.

Thank God I put in fresh batteries last night, I think, clicking on my flashlight.

It takes about 10 minutes to find a side trail branching north.

Maybe 5-minutes later, a dizzy spell hits. The next thing I know, my legs are buckling beneath me and I'm stumbling.

"GAHH!" I groan as my knees crash onto the dirt.

My flashlight rolls away a beat before my hands hit the ground. Of course, it stops way out of my reach.

No matter how hard I try, I can't push myself up. My arms just shake.

My muscles ache too much to move.

I'm too dizzy to stand even if I could.

Eventually, I give up and collapse belly-down onto the ground.

I just need to...

My eyelids fall shut in what feels like slow-motion.

... rest for a bit...

Almost immediately, I start drifting off.

Then I'll... keep... hiking...

One second, there's a weird warmth spreading across my body.

The next, everything goes numb at once, and my thoughts go silent.

CHAPTER 12:
MAYBE I SHOULD JUST…

KYLE TURNER
Some Time Later…

Drowning…

I'm drowning… Which makes no sense, considering I'm sitting upright with my knees clutched to my chest in the middle of a forest clearing…

I'm drowning but… from the inside out?

Yeah. I can feel it. Something thick is slowly flooding up my esophagus from my stomach. It's not like vomiting. It's more so that whatever's got my abdomen all bloated like a pregnant woman's is overflowing into my throat…

Then there's this unbearable pressure in my gut and bowels. It feels like my intestines are about to rupture, like an overfilled water balloon…

And speaking of my bowels, it also feels like I need to shit out an impossibly huge turd right now. It's definitely sticking out partway already, but no matter how hard I try, I can't push it the rest of the way…

When I finally look down, I realize I'm naked, and…

Wait… Why does it look like I have tits? And why's my hair so long and dark?

Out of nowhere, I start gagging. These things that feel like thin noodles start sweeping back and forth in the back of my throat, crawling up toward my uvula and tongue.

I try to scream, but all that comes out is a gargling sound…

Because the slime flooding up my throat has just begun filling my mouth. Salty, bitter, thick mucus stuff coats my tongue.

"GEHHK!" I gag, coughing out brown slime that splatters onto my knees.

Twice as much fills my mouth a beat later. Then I hurl, barfing up bowlfuls of maple-syrup-looking goo.

As I begin choking, I try thrashing, but I can't move… Not only is my body numb, but it also feels like my ass is anchored to the ground by… something.

Choking turns into suffocation…

My eyes roll into the back of my head as everything slowly fades into black…

I jolt awake with a sharp gasp, my eyes snapping open to a star-speckled night sky framed by leafless branches. As I spring up off this weirdly spongy ground, something tugs at the skin on the back of my head, neck, and arms the instant I'm about an inch off the ground. It doesn't hurt, though. It just feels… kinda numb?

"Uhhh…" I groan as the elastic-type shit stuck to me goes taut and stops me from sitting up any further. My body tenses at the resistance, which makes my morning wood throb so hard it hurts—like it's about to explode, overcooked-sausage style. "Whaaaa-uh…?" I try sitting up a little more, but my skin stretches like taffy. The sensation gets so weird and painful that I go limp— and then immediately get yanked back down onto my back. "Urrggh… Whaa-rrr-mmm…"

I try lifting my legs next. But something pulls at the skin on the back of my calves pretty much right away.

What's happening?

I'm delirious as hell—probably from this horrible fever that's got me cold, sweaty, and achy all over—and my brain feels soupy, like I chugged a bottle of vodka after eating 400-milligrams of edibles. I'm so out of it, I can barely remember how I got here, or why it feels like I'm stuck to a human-sized glue trap.

"Hrrrrng!" I groan as I try sitting up again, twisting my head toward my right arm to see what's holding me down.

I don't have to move far before I see it glistening in the faint moonlight…

A sheet of slime-coated, lumpy, lunch-meat-looking shit wrapped against both sides of my forearm and hand like a bandage. Tendrils stretch from its edges in places, while the tissue between them blends seamlessly into my skin, like it's part of me. Beyond that, the same slime-slick biomass stretches across the clearing as far as I can see.

That's when it starts coming back to me.

"No…" I whisper as I begin hyperventilating.

It's so much worse than it was when Danny tried cutting me free.

I turn my head left as fast as the biomass fused to the back of my skull and neck will allow. And when I see my left arm, my panic attack turns into a full-on tantrum.

"Oh fuhh-k…"

Just like my right arm, the membrane has wrapped around both sides of my limb. The tendrilled edges are only a few inches from meeting in the middle—maybe 3 inches from closing the gap.

And if that's not bad enough, all the flesh beneath where the severed tentacle is coiled around my forearm has transformed into that same biomass shit. Like, there's so much of it that the only normal skin left is a narrow strip along my bicep, between where a sleeve would be and the mutated tissue creeping over the bend of my elbow.

And my hand… every inch of it is covered, unlike the other one.

My arm… Oh, God, my whole arm has almost been turned!

All the sudden, I become aware of this tickling deep in the back of my neck—an almost deliberate crawling sensation, moving slowly up and down my spine.

Now that I'm focused on it, I realize the same thing is happening in my scalp near my ears, creeping toward the top middle of my head.

Feeling all that makes me think back to the pulling sensation I felt in the back of my head and neck when I tried sitting up earlier.

And then I picture myself completely encased in this biomass, like the girl I came here to save.

"Oh FUCK! AHHH! AHHHHH! Dah-nnn—Danny!" I scream out, thrashing with as much strength as my achy muscles can muster.

"GWAH-UHHH!" the meat statue before me squawks, scaring me so bad that I spasm.

"Oh, fuck…" It takes a second to catch my breath. "DANNY!"

Nothing but crickets this time.

"Tucker!"

Silence.

"Gavin!"

More crickets, and something rustles in the distance.

I scream their names over and over, but no one answers.

Dead… They're dead!

I shake my head as though that'll dislodge the morbid thought from my mind. *No… They're not dead… They can't be…* I think back to the hazy memory of Danny telling me he was going to get help. *He's probably just lost. Or he's already on the way back with help, and it's just taking him a while to find his way back here. Yeah, that's it.*

And the others… I look down at the severed stalk coiled around my arm. *I'm only awake because Danny cut this thing from the biomass. And if Gavin and Tucker aren't responding, that means he didn't do the same for them…*

I picture Danny leaving me, only to get immediately grabbed by a tentacle himself.

Unless he never made it to them…

Maybe he's being sedated and consumed too…

Maybe Tucker and Gavin died from being tranquilized for too long…

Maybe no one is coming to save you in time…

"HELP!" I scream, thrashing harder than before. "SOMEONE HELP-MEHH!" That comes out in a slur.

No matter how violently I struggle or how hard I try to sit up, the membrane between me and the meat mass doesn't tear. It just stretches, goes taut, and yanks me back down.

It doesn't take long for my achy muscles to start burning.

It doesn't take long for them to feel too weak to keep going.

And it doesn't take long for that overwhelming sleepy feeling to creep back in.

In the middle of my tantrum, I suddenly remember screaming in agony when Danny tried cutting this membrane off me. *This shit isn't just stuck to you. Your flesh is turning into it.*

Which means all you're doing is wasting energy.

"AHHHHHHHHH!" I scream at the top of my lungs. "HELP! SOMEONE HELP!"

No one answers. Because there's no one else out here this late at night.

No, there might be someone out here… Depending on what time it is, there might be a few kids hiking back from the lake party.

I keep screaming until my throat burns and my voice goes hoarse. When I finally stop, I break down sobbing, whimpering like a little bitch.

I'm gonna fuckin' die here… All my skin's gonna turn to that fungus shit, and I'm gonna die as a fucking mutated corpse-thing!

Another wave of drowsiness surges through me, and my eyelids immediately fall shut.

Wait… why does it feel like I'm still being sedated? Is it this fever? Or is the meat mass pumping the same shit into me that the tentacle was?

Fight it, I think, forcing my eyes open. *Gotta stay awake. I gotta stay awake in case someone walks by. I gotta stay up until Danny gets back with help. Because if I pass out again, I don't think I'll wake back up this time…*

And if my eyes stay shut for too long, I'll definitely fall asleep.

All you gotta do is keep that from happening.

My eyelids close right after that thought, and I instantly get sleepier.

"GRMM!" I groan, squinting as I squirm in a pathetic attempt to stay conscious.

Keep moving… Moving will keep you awake. You gotta keep moving for as long as you can.

I sit up a little and look down at my right arm.

Question is, how long do I have left before this shit fully covers my body?

I look up at the stars. *It's either been a few hours, or it's been over a day…*

If it's only been a few hours since I last saw Danny, I'll end up just like Savanna before noon. Or by evening at the latest…

But if it's been over twenty-four hours, that means I've got another full day to lie here and suffer…

I imagine Danny coming back with paramedics. Then I picture them numbing me and cutting me free.

Suddenly, something horrible pops into my head—I remember trying to cut Savanna free and discovering that her flesh had turned into biomass all the way down to the bone.

Wait…

Even if they separate me from this meat mass, they won't be able to get this shit off me without removing most of my skin and muscle!

I imagine going back to school with half my body covered in this yellowish-tan fungus. I imagine people staring in disgust, whispering and making fun of me as I walk the halls.

Then I imagine growing old alone, because no girl would ever want to be with someone like this.

Then a darker thought creeps into my mind.

That's only if my skin stops mutating once they cut me free…

"Hrrrng," I groan, lifting my head and turning toward the tentacle still wrapped around my left arm.

If the biomass is still growing after the stalk was severed, it's probably not gonna stop…

I visualize walking through school completely covered in this shit—looking like Savanna does now, but with eyes that aren't covered.

I'd rather die…

Still trembling and sniveling, I sink back down and let my eyes close.

Maybe I should just let go…

It only takes a few seconds before I start drifting off.

If you just go to sleep, you won't have to suffer… You'll just dream. And then you'll…

The thought dissolves as my body goes numb and all the rustling sounds around me grow muffled.

Then everything goes quiet.

And then there's nothing…

CHAPTER 13:
UNTIL DAWN

DANNY HOLLAND
Night

Lost. In the Woods. At night. With no flashlight…

Everything in this part of the forest looks the same in the faint moonlight, so I can't even tell if I've been walking in circles or not. To make matters worse, my phone's been dead for a while, so I have no idea how long I've been roaming like this. It feels like forever, though it could've just been a few hours. Which means it's either getting close to sunrise, or I've still got a long-ass wait until dawn…

"Help!" a young-ish-sounding dude shouts from somewhere off to my right.

I turn toward the sound. "Hello?!"

"Danny?!" he shouts.

That voice…

"*Gavin*?!" I shout back. "Is that you?!"

"Yeah! Help me, Danny! Please! You gotta get here! *Quick*!"

I'm already sprinting through the tall underbrush—I started hauling ass the second that 'help' left his mouth. "On the way!"

A thick wall of bushes and trees lies between us, so I have to weave through the gaps in the foliage. It doesn't take long to start wondering if I'm even going the right way.

"Gavin?!" I call out, coming to a stop.

Nothing but crickets.

"Gavin, you gotta keep talking so I can find you, bro!"

Still no response.

"Fffffuck…" I mutter, breaking into a jog in the same direction I was going before. "Gavin?!"

Twigs snapping and leaves crunching beneath my sneakers—that's all I hear.

"Gav!"

Nothing.

As I open my mouth to shout again, I hear this wet, ripping sound up ahead—like my mom tearing juicy roasted chicken off the bone. Only louder.

The fuck is that?

That gross-ass noise gets louder with each hurried step I take.

And as I'm slipping between two trees, I see something through the ferns ahead that makes me stop dead in my tracks…

That corpse puppet—Savanna—is trying to stand. She's gone from a seated fetal position to crouching on her hunches, a thin sheet of biomass stretched between her ass and the rest of it. Thick strands and flaps of fungus dangle beneath the parts tearing free.

The instant I lock onto her, the fleshy tissue rips apart with a series of wet snaps—*SPOP-SPOP-POP.*

Now she's rising, turning toward Gavin, who's still stuck backside-down on the biomass like that mouse I once found trapped on a glue board in our garage.

"Da—Danny!" Gavin shouts.

At the same time, the corpse-puppet's mouth opens inhumanly wide.

Her eyelids snap open with a wet, sticky, smacking noise.

Then she breaks into a sprint—running faster than I've ever seen anyone move. But the way she moves, all hunched and flailing, it's like watching something trying to imitate a human.

"AHHHHHHH!" Gavin screams.

The biomass-encased girl bolts across the meat-mat like it isn't slippery at all, her feet clapping against it with wet smacks that sound like hands speed-slapping raw steak.

"GEEEYAAAAHH!" Gavin cries as the gap rapidly closes.

Before I can even move, she pounces at him like a cheetah. The next thing I know, she's on him and biting into his fucking neck. Her teeth chomp into him so hard, I hear the squish from here.

"GAHHH-GEHK!" he gags, choking and gurgling on blood.

"Oh-ho-oh fuck," I whisper breathily.

Savanna's head snaps toward me, her eyes widening more than should be possible. And then she's already charging before I've even registered that she was rising.

"Oh, *fuhhhh!*" I scream, spinning and sprinting the way I came.

I'm running as fast as I can, but her wet, sticky footfalls sound twice as fast as mine.

Bushes rustle as I brush past them, drowning out my own steps. But the claps of fungus-clad feet are much louder, sounding like she's not too far behind me now.

I glance over my shoulder and immediately gasp. Because she's barely a yard behind me.

"AHHHH!" I scream, turning and pumping my legs faster.

"GWUH-UH-AHH-SCREEEEEE!" she shrieks like a fucking velociraptor.

I look back again and see her pouncing—she's midair with her biomass-coated arms reaching, her fingers curled like claws.

Then she slams into me from behind.

"GAH!" I cry as I hit the ground and skid.

I elbow her in the face.

"SCREEEAHHH!" she scream-roars as she tumbles off me. A split-second later, she's already scrambling after me on all fours.

I try to roll onto my back, but she tackles me halfway through the maneuver. "AHHH!" I yell, grabbing her squishy shoulders.

The barely human creature bares her bloody, plaque-caked teeth. "SKREEEAAAAARRH!" Savanna shrieks as she lowers her head toward my abdomen, her body shaking violently.

A beat later, her teeth sink into my flesh.

I wake up screaming, my body spasming as my eyes snap open to a blurry view of dirt bathed in faint orange light. I'm lying on my right side with my cheek pressed against my bent arm.

Groaning, I slowly turn my head left and find a wall of bushes barely a foot away. As I look up at the tree behind them, I realize how hard I'm shivering. Being in sweat-soaked clothes while it's this cool out is part of why I'm shaking so bad, but I think the main reason is this crazy high fever.

Why am I out… The thought trails off when I suddenly recall collapsing and passing out during a nighttime hike.

My teeth chatter as I turn my head farther left, squinting at the low sun peeking through the trees.

Is it morning or sunset?

It's gotta be morning, right? Because it was dark when I passed out… And the last time I woke up from a nightmare, it was still night.

Unless I somehow slept for a whole day…

That's about all my brain can manage. I'm too fucking delirious to drudge up anything else.

"Grrrm!" I groan as I start rolling onto my abdomen. My right side aches from being on the ground for however many hours, and the rest of me hurts from the fever aches.

Once I'm belly-down, my gaze drifts to my itchy right arm. It's wrapped in a T-shirt, so I start pulling it off to see if something's crawling on me. As soon as my forearm is exposed, I gasp.

Dear God, I think, staring in horror at the beige bumps rising out of the scabbed-over gashes.

Hazy memories flicker in my mind's eye. Suddenly, I remember which of my nightmares actually happened.

Infected…

I picture the biomass. The tentacles.

No… There's no way that wasn't a dream, right? I must've gotten infected some other way…

I shake my head.

Hospital. Get to a hospital. ASAP. Worry about the details later.

I try pushing up, but my arms shake violently. I only manage to get an inch off the ground before they give out.

"Koofugh!" I grunt as I slam against the earth.

I try again, only to fail immediately.

The third attempt is even more pathetic.

Fuck it… I'll try again in a bit, I think, rolling back onto my right side. *I wonder if I have reception now.*

My left arm trembles as I reach into my pocket and pull out my phone. The screen stays black when I double-tap it. Now I hold the power button. Nothing happens.

"Fuck…" I mutter, going limp.

My eyelids droop down ever so slowly. The moment they close, I feel myself drifting off.

No… Don't fall back asleep…

I force my right eye open just enough to peer through my lashes. But it slides shut again a second later.

Gotta stay awake… Just… get up… You gotta… get…

My thoughts, the sound of the birds chirping in the distance— it all goes quiet in an instant.

CHAPTER 14:
ON THE TABLE

DANNY HOLLAND
????

Something cold pouring onto my right forearm…

Faint stinging radiating from where the liquid hits…

Mild discomfort from laying backside-down on what feels like a wooden floor…

My morning wood being pinned against my lower abdomen by something heavy but soft…

Cold all over…

Damp fabric clung to my torso and thighs…

A sweet, floral scent filling my nostrils. A familiar scent.

As my consciousness slowly returns, I become aware of it all at once.

I try opening my eyes, but I can't. I'm too tired—more tired than I've ever been—and my eyelids feel too heavy to lift.

In the next instant, I'm hit with…

Bliss…

I feel amazing…

So fucking amazing…

Amazing all over…

Every inch of flesh is, like, humming around my bones…

My entire skeleton feels like one giant vibrating tuning fork, while also feeling kind of soft and noodly at the same time…

Feels like I'm floating…

Somehow, my body seems like it's both formless and solid…

Happy…

Fuck, I'm happier than I've ever been…

I'm also hornier than I've ever been…

So horny that I think I might literally die if I don't jerk it right now…

I try reaching down with my left hand, but something tugs at my wrist, stopping me before I can lift it even an inch.

The same thing happens when I try moving the other hand…

At the same time, skinny, soft fingers slide into my left hand and give it a gentle squeeze.

The touch feels electric.

Skin-to-skin contact has never felt this good. Being touched makes my skin buzz and sends dopamine surging through me.

I squeeze the hand back, rubbing my thumb against it.

Soft hand…

Girl's hand.

Thinking *girl* immediately makes me picture Morgan Gallagher holding my hand. Then I imagine kissing her. Fucking her. The fantasy makes my meat rod swell harder against whatever's pinning it down, and I squirm, blindly reaching down again with the free hand.

"Keep still, Danny," a young-sounding chick whispers from my left—a voice I don't recognize. "She's about to start cutting… If you feel any pain, just squeeze my hand, okay?"

Cutting? Cutting what?

Cutting me?

"Urrgh?" I groan, finally forcing my eyes into a squint, only to get blasted by bright-ass lights directly overhead. "Gurrr-mmm!" I squeeze my eyes shut and squirm against the hard surface.

Something cold—something metallic—touches the middle of my right forearm. It starts moving back and forth, subtly but fast, dragging down toward my wrist. A weird pressure builds as it pulls.

Then liquid heat spreads beneath the metal. Whatever it is starts dripping down my arm.

Bleeding… I think I'm bleeding…

My eyes snap open. Through the glare, I can barely make out two female shapes standing to my right. One's working on my arm—it's a blonde dressed in a black top. The redhead beside her has on something green and kinda loose.

After blinking the blur away, I see the petite blonde more clearly. She's an insanely gorgeous 20-something with the most captivating blue eyes I've ever seen. Thankfully, she's too focused on whatever she's doing to my arm to notice me gawking.

Hot, I think, twitching down below. *She's so fucking hot!*

It takes another second for my delirious brain to register that neither of them is wearing scrubs or masks—just gloves. The blonde has on a black T-shirt and matching leggings. The chick with reddish-brown hair is wearing a green sundress with white dots or flowers all over it….

When I finally force myself to follow the blonde's gaze, I see what she's holding to my arm—a slim, silver, pen-shaped tool with a blade at the end. A box cutter? Or maybe an X-Acto knife?

And then it clicks.

The hot blonde is slicing away a small chunk of my flesh.

"GAHHH!" I shout, yanking my arm back—only for whatever's strapped around my wrist to stop me.

The sudden movement makes her blade slip, and she carves out another inch of skin.

"Oh-shit!" the blonde screams as more crimson starts oozing from my arm. "Shit-fuck! I'm sorry! I'm sorry!"

"Jesus!" the girl in the sundress shouts at the same time.

The person to my left squeezes my hand twice in quick succession. "Look at me, Danny!" the girl says.

Seeing all that blood makes my eyes go wide. "AHHH!" I scream over them while thrashing. Whatever's wrapped around my ankles stops me from kicking. But when I buck my right hip up, the thing covering my lap slides off my crotch. My wood immediately springs up, straining against my boxers until it pitches a tent. And because my whole body feels insanely hypersensitive, having it drag against the fabric makes me shiver with pleasure. "Wha—what the fuck!"

"Lena, here!" the redhead shouts, holding out gauze. "Here!"

"Oh—thanks!" Lena pants, snatching it and pressing it hard against my wound.

Out of the corner of my left eye, I see a pillow drop onto my lap, concealing the embarrassing situation below.

"Hey, hey!" the girl on my left shouts, cupping my face with her left hand while squeezing my hand with the other. "Look at me. *Look at me*, Danny!"

As I'm turning away from the hottie, I realize that the light between her and the girl in the sundress isn't artificial. It's sunlight, pouring through a window. A window over a sink. My gaze drifts past the sundress girl to a stove and a fridge.

Kitchen… I'm in a kitchen, not an operating room…

"What the fuck is—" I start to say.

"Hey!" the girl on my left calls over me, gently forcing me to face her. "Look at *me*, Danny! Please, just look at me!"

I finally give in, slowly turning toward her. The girl holding my hand is this kinda cute, dirty blonde with grayish-blue eyes. Unlike the other two, she looks to be about my age.

"Wha?" I slur, looking from her to the clear plastic tube running from my arm up to an IV bag filled with a slightly white, cloudy solution. Then my eyes snap back to hers. "Who are— what's hap—"

"It's me!" she blurts out with a nervous smile. "Lizzy! From school! We met in the woods earlier, remember?!"

My face scrunches. "Lizzy? Wait…"

She looks… familiar…

I get a flash of her walking the halls of Yelm High. Then I recall seeing her sitting at lunch with the hottest girl in school, Piper Cummings, and with… a girl who always wore cat-eye glasses—Savanna Lockhart. The girl who disappeared.

After that, memories of creeping on her TikTok and Instagram while researching the disappearances come flooding back.

Friend of Savanna…

Jake Landau's neighbor…

The sister of the guy who went missing… Eli… Rutherford.

"Wait… Lizzy… *Rutherford?*" I mumble.

She nods, smiling wider. "Mm-hmm! Yeah!"

My face scrunches up even more. "We… met… *earlier?* In the… *woods?*"

Lizzy nods faster. "Yeah! We did!"

Another hazy memory surfaces—me lying on the forest floor, her and a bunch of insanely hot girls standing over me, the sun blazing behind them in a way that made them look almost angelic.

I sigh. "I thought that was a dream…"

The smiling girl shakes her head. "It wasn't! Listen, you're having trouble remembering things because you've got a really bad fever. Like, *really* bad. It's so bad that it's messing with your memory and making you hallucinate." She squeezes my hand again. "Just know that we're trying to save your life. But we can't do that if you don't stay completely still until Lena's finished—"

"Save my… *life?*" I glance down at this sheet, or whatever it is that's tied around my wrist.

"Yeah, you—"

My eyes snap back to her. "Why'm I tied to a kitchen table if you're trying to save—"

Lizzy opens her mouth.

"Wait!" I shout, cutting her off. "Is this… This is some witchcraft shit, isn't it?!"

Lizzy giggles nervously. "What?! No! We tied you down so you wouldn't hurt yourself! Because you keep blacking out, forgetting everything we tell you, and freaking out every time you wake up! And you keep forgetting that you asked us to bring you here—" She points at the girl with auburn hair. "—to my friend Allie's house!"

I shake my head. "That doesn't make sense… Why—why would I ask you to bring me *here* instead of to a hospital?"

"Because…" Allie pipes up. "When we told you we're probably the only people in the world who know about the *Flesh Forest*, and the only ones who might be able to stop the podification—I mean, stop the *infection*—from spreading all over your body, you *begged* us to bring you here instead."

"Whuh?" I whimper. "Wait… *Flesh Forest? Infection?* I've got an infec—"

Lizzy points to my right. "Your arm, Danny… Just look at it, and this'll all make sense," she says calmly.

Slowly, I turn my head. As I do, Lena lifts the gauze. At first, I only fixate on the blood.

So much blood.

"Look here," Lena says, rotating my arm and pointing to something slightly tan farther over.

It takes a second to pull my focus off the deep, bleeding wound and lock onto the beige, lumpy growths bulging out of the gashes. They're in an almost perfect ring around my forearm, each bordered by white, frosting-like spikes. Every fungus-looking glob is nearly an inch across.

Wait… I've seen that before… That looks like…

A hellish biomass swallowing acres of forest floor, with dozens of spiked stalks rising out of it…

The squawking corpse puppet—Savanna—at the center of it.

Trees and plants consumed by that same meaty, veiny tissue.

I see it all in my head, as clear as day.

Then a series of nightmarish memories flicker in my mind… Kyle, Gavin, Tucker—each of them going down one by one, getting ensnared by tentacles. Then this same growth spreading across every inch of flesh touching the biomass.

I remember how small these were last night. Before I blacked out.

"Oh fuck…" I finally mutter. "It got so much worse!"

"Yeah…" Allie says. "And it'd be way worse than that if you hadn't cut away the first bit of infected flesh. And because this stuff grows crazy fast, you need to let Lena remove the rest before it spreads more. Otherwise, you're gonna lose the whole arm." She pauses. "Or you might lose your life…"

My eyes go wide. "Oh God…" I look at Lizzy for some reason.

She nods. "Allie's tellin' the truth, Danny. This infection is what…" Her eyes flood with tears as her bottom lip begins to tremble. She looks so sad, all I wanna do is hug her. "You know about the people who went missing in the last few months? Like, you know about my brother—Eli—and Jake Landau?"

I nod. "Ye-yeah?"

"Well, *this* is what killed them."

My eyes damn near bulge out of the sockets. "Wait… ss-*seriously?*"

She nods, wiping a tear from her cheek. *"Seriously."*

"But I… I thought they disappeared. I thought no one knew what happened to them."

Lizzy shakes her head. "We're the only ones who know. And none of us made it public yet."

"But… why?"

She exhales sharply. "Listen, it's a long, fucked-up story. Too long to get into right now. Just know that if you wanna keep your arm—if you don't wanna die the most horrific way imaginable— you gotta lay still and let Lena cut out the infected tissue and pull out those roots. Okay?"

I nod rapidly. "Okay, okay!" Now I turn to Lena. "Do it! Please!"

"Alright…" Lena whispers, giving me a caring smile. "I promise this won't hurt much at all. If you haven't noticed, the, uhh… the *painkiller* we gave you is insanely strong."

I nod, glancing back down at my arm. "You're right… I didn't even realize until just now that I barely even felt you cutting into me earlier. And I barely feel my arm stinging right now…"

"Good," Lena whispers, bringing the box-cutter-like tool toward the next growth. But then she stops with the blade hovering an inch above it. "Alright. Here we go… Just close your eyes, and this'll all be over before you know it."

I nod and squeeze my eyes shut.

"If it hurts," Lizzy whispers, "just squeeze my hand, okay?"

"Mm-hmm," I hum.

The blade only briefly touches my skin before lifting away.

"Hey, Danny," Lena says.

I open my eyes into a squint. "Hmm?"

"Umm…" Lena twists her mouth to the side. "Since you're a little more lucid than you were earlier, I need to ask you this *one more time.* Are you *absolutely sure* you want *me* to do this instead of taking you to a hospital and letting a doctor do this?"

My eyes widen. "Wait… Are you not a doctor?"

She shakes her head. "No. But I am a PhD zoology and bio student. And I've operated on a lot of animals."

"Oh, what the fuck…"

"Before you answer her based off *that*," Allie blurts out. "I need to remind you of two things. The first is that there's a very strong possibility you'd get sent to some CDC quarantine lab once I show the doctors what this infection does to humans. And if that happens, there's a chance they might not let us treat you at all, or even make sure you're being treated properly—there's a chance you'll become a lab rat and that you'll never be seen again."

My jaw drops. "Oh shit…"

That's probably exactly what will happen…

"Yeah," Allie continues. "The second thing is, on the off chance you *don't* get quarantined by the government, the only *medication* that might be able save you is… something that the doctors likely will be hesitant to treat you with. Because it's… uhh… *experimental*—"

"Experimental?" I interrupt. "What—what is it?"

She and Lena exchange a look, then they both face me. "Uteroboscis slime," they answer in unison.

My face scrunches up. "Wait… Like, the milky goo from those giant uterine worms that turn girls into… sex zombies?"

Lena nods. "Mm-hmm." She points to the IV bag filled with a slightly cloudy solution. "A diluted version. That's what's got you feeling all euphoric and numb to pain. And… *turned on…*" She gestures at the pillow covering my crotch. "Hence why we put that over your lap."

Heat floods my cheeks, and the embarrassment makes me tense up. "Oh… But how do you even have that—"

"I'm the one who discovered the first Uteroboscis," the gorgeous blonde says, smiling with a bit of a wince.

My eyes go wide. "No fuckin' way…"

All three of them nod as I look to Lizzy for confirmation.

"She's not lying," Lizzy says. "Here, I can show you." With the hand not still holding mine, she reaches into her jean shorts' pocket.

"We talked about this before," Lena says, "so I know you know this. But the Uteroboscis slime—it has antimicrobial properties."

I nod. "Yeah. I saw TikToks and news reports about that. About how it kills pretty much every virus and bacteria."

"And every *fungus*," Lena adds as Lizzy holds her phone in front of my face.

On the screen is an article with a photo of Lena in a lab coat beside a tank holding a Uteroboscis. The headline reads: **The Florida Grad Student Who Discovered the Amazonian Uteroboscis.** It's a picture I've seen before. I can't remember if it was this Fox News article or another site, but I remember seeing it and thinking she was so unbelievably hot that I needed to follow her on TikTok or Instagram. But she didn't have any social media. At least, none that I could find.

"Oh shit…" I mutter. "It really is you…"

"Mm-hmm!" Lena hums, flashing me a faint smile.

"How is it that you're even *here*? *In Yelm, Washington*, of all places."

Lena huffs. "Long story…"

Allie nods. "One we'll tell you after your fever breaks."

"For now," Lena continues, "the only thing that matters is that I tested the Uteroboscis slime. *Thoroughly*. And because it's killed every single pathogen we've thrown at it, I think that there's a very strong possibility its antimicrobial compounds are the only things capable of stopping your infection. Emphasis on *possibly*."

My eyes widen again. "*Possibly*? As in… you don't know if this'll work?"

The two girls on my right shake their heads.

"Like I said," Allie mutters, "*it's experimental*… And we won't know if this will work until a few hours after we've removed the infected tissue and the roots. Because we need to wait and see if they grow back after the treatment."

"Danny…" Lena gives me a sad smile as soon as we lock eyes. "If it makes you feel any better, the one thing we *do* know for sure is that this treatment won't kill you. I've spent well over a year testing dosages on rats, pigs, and humans for both infection treatment and pain blocking purposes. And I've adjusted the dosage for your size and approximate weight, so you won't overdose on the opioid-like compounds or anything like that." She drags in a deep breath, then huffs it out. "With all that said, do you want us to call your parents and take you to a hospital, or do you want me to—"

"No," I blurt out. "I still want you to do it. Please. And hurry. Because we gotta get back to my friends so you can treat them too."

Allie and Lizzy give each other a weird look.

"Oh no… What?" I mutter.

"Urrgh," Allie groans. "My friend's in the *Flesh Forest* right now. Checking to see if she can help them. But we can talk about that later, okay? Right now, we all need to be quiet so Lena can focus. The last thing we want is her slipping or cutting a vein because she was distracted."

I nod, my stomach sinking. "Oh… Okay…"

Lena closes her eyes, takes a deep breath, then exhales slowly. "Alrighty. Here we go again."

I shut my eyes as the blade nears my arm.

"You got this, Danny," Lizzy says, sweeping her thumb back and forth against my hand.

Her touch makes me throb hard. Over and over.

I'm so glad they put that pillow over my crotch…

Just like before, all I feel is pressure and a strange pulling sensation as Lena cuts to the right of the last spot.

Don't think about it…

Don't think about her slicing chunks out of your arm.

Just focus on how good it feels having Lizzy hold your hand.

Now all I can think about is clapping Lizzy's cheeks.

By the time I realize that I'm subtly grinding against the pillow, I'm already on the verge of unloading.

Stop! Stop! Stop! It's already embarrassing enough that these girls saw you all bricked up. The last thing you need is them watching your quiver as you finish.

As that thought ends, I feel the blade scoop into my forearm, a sharp flash of pressure accompanied by some faint stinging.

"Sorry, Danny," Lena whispers. "This one grew deeper than the last one…"

"Huh?" I murmur, opening my eyes.

Before I can look, Lizzy cups my face and gently turns my head away. "Don't look. It's better if you don't see any of that."

I nod, give her a weak smile, and close my eyes again.

There's still no real pain. Just that dull pressure and a scooping sensation each time the blade cuts and lifts back toward the surface.

The longer I keep my eyes shut, the sleepier I get.

It doesn't take long for me to start drifting off again.

Their hushed voices gradually fade.

Then a flare of pain stops me from passing out.

"Argh," I groan, looking over at my arm.

My stomach churns when I see it—a ring of deep, bleeding gashes. Some are so deep I think I can see muscle. Zigzag grooves trail away from them. From one strip of missing flesh, Lena pulls out a black fiber. A root. A long one.

My stomach flips. I get crazy dizzy out of nowhere.

That's when Lizzy cups the side of my face and turns my head toward her. "Don't look, Danny!"

Too late.

"Blurrgh…" I dry-heave as my eyes roll up into the back of my skull. "Oh God…"

My eyelids flutter, then they slide shut.

My body goes limp.

Then everything goes black.

Cold, thick liquid pours over my right forearm, spreading slowly across my skin.

"Huh?" I groan, slowly forcing my eyes open.

"It's all over, Danny," a girl says from my left, giving my hand a gentle squeeze.

Instead of looking at her, I turn right. The insanely hot blonde in black is pouring a clear, milky syrup from a mason jar over my arm. It's so opaque I can barely see the gashes beneath it, just the blood blooming under the slime.

She smiles at me. "This is to prevent you from getting an infection and to help speed up the healing process."

Even though I'm confused as hell, I nod. "Oh, okay…"

"Ready for the gauze, Lena?" the reddish-brown-haired girl asks.

"Mm-hmm!" Lena says, setting the jar on the countertop.

Lena… The Uteroboscis Girl… And the other one… Allie? I turn to my left, and the dirty-blonde girl smiles at me. *Lizzy. Rutherford,* I think, smiling back.

"Hey, *you*," Lizzy says.

"Hey…" I whisper.

"Here," Allie says, gently gripping my wrist and lifting my arm. "I'll hold it up for ya."

"Thanks!" Lena says, unrolling the gauze.

As soon as she starts wrapping my forearm, my eyes shut. Not because it hurts, but because I'm drowsy, and because I can't handle seeing my arm all carved up like that, even with the slime obscuring the wounds.

I only feel her go around twice before I start drifting back off into a peaceful nothingness.

CHAPTER 15:
WHAT HAPPENED

DANNY HOLLAND
Date Uknown

As I stir awake, I'm hit with the worst grogginess ever. It's not, like, 'I slept like shit' kinda groggy. It's more like I'm so out of it that my brain feels like cotton and my body's all numb. Everything is weirdly numb. Except for my right arm.

Itchy…

My arm's so fucking itchy…

Bugs.

The thought makes my eyes snap open. My gaze drops straight to the white sheet covering me from the shoulders down. It takes a second to realize I'm lying in a narrow bed with gray guard rails on both sides, with another rail where a footboard should be.

"Whuh?" I groan, lifting my head and spotting a small flatscreen mounted near the ceiling on a white wall.

I look around at this unfamiliar room—a hospital room bathed in golden sunlight. The bed I'm in is the only one in here. The door to my left is shut, but the one perpendicular to it is open. Looks like a bathroom.

The fuck… What happened… The itchiness gets so unbearable that the thought evaporates.

I lift the bedsheet and suck in a sharp gasp as soon as I see my arm, my eyes widening in horror.

Everything from the edge of my gown's sleeve to my fingertips is covered in this yellowish-tan… *stuff.* Stuff that looks like melted flesh in some spots, with gross lumps scattered across it.

"What the fuck…" I whisper, hesitantly reaching out with a shaky hand.

The moment my fingers sink into what feels like squishy clay, my right forearm registers the touch. "GAH!" I shout, yanking my hand away. For some reason, the right side of my mouth doesn't open all the way.

Wait… This stuff isn't on my arm… It is my arm…

The realization makes my whole body tremble. My heart jackhammers in my chest.

Suddenly, the itchiness spreads to my abdomen.

"No…" I whisper, ripping the sheet the rest of the way off.

That's when I see my right leg—covered in the same corrupted flesh.

But my left leg… it's normal.

"Whathufuhh," I slur while scrambling out of bed.

As I stand, I lift the hospital gown and see it all at once—my entire right leg, the right half of my crotch, and the right half of my torso are covered in that same yellowish, swollen mass. The border between healthy skin and this shit that looks like Deadpool's face runs almost perfectly down the center of my body. *Almost.* The edge is raised and wavy, with little beige tendrils stretching across the healthy skin like roots.

Seeing that sours my stomach.

"Oh… God…" My voice comes out all breathless.

I start crying immediately, making that pathetic, whiny sound that precedes a full sob. And as my mouth opens ahead of this impending scream, the left side of my lips parts—but the right stays sealed shut, like it's glued together.

No, I think, reaching up with my left hand.

When my fingers touch my upper lip, it feels wrong. Spongey and lumpy. Like my right arm did.

No, no, no…

I trace downward, trying to slip a digit between my lips, but I hit something that feels like stretched gum blocking my mouth.

"No…" My finger sweeps right, and I find more of the same corrupted flesh all the way to my ear and the side of my head. That's when I bolt for the open door. "No, no, no!"

Everything spins as I bank right into the bathroom. It's too dark to see my reflection in the mirror, so I slap at the wall until I hit the light switch.

The fluorescent light snaps on. Then I turn and immediately gasp at what's staring back at me.

Two-Face from *Batman.* That's my immediate thought.

The right side of my face and neck looks just like the rest of my body on that side—gross, swollen flesh that looks like prosthetics layered over my skin. My lips on that side are fused together. My right eye is only partly open, and what little of it I can see is bloodshot and webbed with bulging veins.

"AHHH!" I scream, my normal hand shooting up to my face.

I claw at my nose, nails digging into the edge where it meets real skin. The tendrilled border peels up with a wet, sticky pull, like ripping off a Band-Aid made of lunch meat. It hurts, like a dull pulling-burning sensation, but I ignore the pain.

"What the fuck! What the fuck! Please come off!"

The tendrils tear free first, snapping off the healthy flesh like gum off a shoe. Then I yank harder, ripping the edge back farther. Unimaginable pain flares across my cheek as what's underneath stretches and tears away with the sound of wet, open-mouth smacks.

"RAAHHHHH!" I roar, pulling even harder.

When the thick flap of yellow meat finally folds away, I don't see healthy skin. I see beige muscle. Dark blood mixed with maple-syrup-looking mucus. And something ivory and hard-looking that's deep in the middle of the curved cavity.

Bone…

Cheekbone…

My skin's mutated down to the bone…

My hand slowly falls away.

Then I freeze for half a second.

"NYEEAAAAHH!" I screech louder than I ever have.

Screaming—I wake up already screaming before my eyelids even have a chance to lift.

By the time my eyes snap open a split second later, I've somehow gone from lying on my back to sitting upright, my head angled down toward my itchy-ass right arm. I'm so spacey from this overwhelming high, and so distracted by how unbearably horny I am, that I've already forgotten why I was looking at it in the first place. And before my vision can clear, a sudden wave of dizziness hits, forcing me to squeeze my eyes shut.

As I do, the itchiness gets so bad that it drowns out the arousal and the body-wide high. The sensation makes me picture my arm covered in a fleshy fungus.

No… My eyes snap open again, but things are still all blurry. So, I blink once really hard. Twice. One more time.

My vision finally clears, and I find that all the skin not covered by the bandages wrapped around my forearm looks normal. Pasty. Human. Without thinking, my left hand grabs the purple sheet and rips it off me. A dull pinch flares near the bend of my left arm.

Instead of looking down, my gaze snaps to the IV line taped inside my forearm. I follow the clear tubing up to the IV bag hanging from a coat rack. Nothing in my periphery suggests I'm in a hospital room. There are no monitors. No machines. Just the walls, furniture, and the kind of window one would find in a bedroom.

Not my room.

Not my parents' room.

Not one of my sisters' rooms.

Not one of my friends' rooms.

Just some random-ass, small bedroom with no pictures or anything on the walls or dresser, and a window with a bit of sunlight bleeding through the closed blinds.

"Whuh?" I groan, looking from the closed door ahead to my lower half.

Cargo shorts—dirt-smudge ones—are what I'm wearing instead of the athletic shorts that I usually sleep in. I sigh in relief when I see perfectly healthy skin from the shin down. Everything looks good when I grab the shredded hem of my sweat-drenched green shirt and pull it up. Finally, my hands shoot up to my face and I start frantically feeling around. Nothing feels weird.

"Phewww…" I breathe out, slumping over.

It was just another nightmare…

The panic melts away, and then this calming bliss immediately hums through every fiber of my being.

Or maybe this is just a dream too… I feel too floaty and detached for this to be real life… I feel too good…

My eyes drift back to my bandaged arm.

Wait… I dreamed about a bunch of hot girls surrounding me while one of them did surgery on my forearm… Maybe that part wasn't a dream?

Nah, it had to be. Because there's no way that actually happened. Right?

I scan the room again.

If it didn't happen, then whose house am I in?

The second I try to remember how I got here, my vision goes unfocused the way it does when I'm daydreaming. No matter how hard I try, all I can think about is how my dick hurts, like it's been swollen for a full day, and how sensitive it feels.

Fuck. Maybe I should just lock the door and take care of myself real quick.

One second, I'm thinking that.

The next, my right hand is in my boxers.

Wait, when did I…

The door suddenly bursts open, and in walks this kinda cute, dirty blonde girl.

"GYAH!" I yelp, yanking my hand out of my pants while awkwardly maintaining eye contact with her.

Her eyes widen. Her cheeks flush. Then she cracks a smile and spins around. "Sorry-sorry!" she almost squeals.

"I wasn't—" I grab the pillow beside me and slam it over my crotch, wincing as the stiffness bends. "—I was just… scratching myself!"

"Didn't see anything! Also, sorry for not knocking first!" she says, speaking a mile-a-minute.

"It's alri—"

"I only barged in like that because I thought I heard you scream and I was coming to help!" she continues, speaking just as quickly.

I sigh. "It's fine… You can make it up to me by telling me where the fuck I am and what the hell's going on."

"Umm," she hums, peeking over her shoulder at me. After eyeing the pillow, she turns back around and walks toward me with a spacey, high look in her eyes. She looks as out of it as I feel. "What's the last thing you remember, Danny?" Her glassy eyes narrow into a squint. "Uh-oh… The way you're lookin' at me makes me think you don't remember me. You don't, *do you?*"

"Uhh…" I stare at her for a second, my brain immediately drifting to a fantasy of me clapping her cheeks. When I force that thought out of my mind a moment later, a hazy memory comes back to me. "Wait… You're Lizzy… Rutherford. From Yelm High. Right?"

"I am! Guess that means the fever is done frying your brain." She presses the back of her hand to my forehead. "Hmm… You're still a little warm, but nowhere near as bad as you were earlier! That's a good sign!"

"Yeah… But umm… If you're really here, that means…" I gulp hard. "Me tied to a kitchen table while you held my hand and that other girl cut up my arm—that wasn't a dream?"

"Eww! We *literally* just met, and you're already having weird BDSM dreams where we're holding hands?!"

My eyes go wide. "What?! No! I—"

Lizzy snickers. "Relax! I'm kidding!" She starts cracking up.

I blow out a long breath. "Geezus…"

"Sorry. Figured I'd lighten the mood with a joke."

I huff. "As if walking in on me with my hand in my pants wasn't torture enough."

"It's not like your glizzy was out and in your hand or anything."

"That's something you'd only know for sure if you got a good look. Which means you *did* see something…" I almost growl.

She winces, then a naughty smirk creeps across her lips. Suddenly, she's looking at me the same way I've probably been looking at her, like she's currently thinking about hooking up. "If it makes you feel any less embarrassed, thanks to whatever the pinecone-tipped tentacle injected into you, your… uhh… *soldier* was *standing at attention* when we found you in the woods. So, it's not like that was my first time seeing your pants tipi…"

I glance down to the right, my cheeks heating up again. "Uh… I think that makes me *more* embarrassed…"

"Oh…" She lets out a nervous giggle as she sits beside me. "Then forget what I said! I saw nothing earlier! Or just now!"

I snicker. "I wish I could… Also…" I look back at her, frowning. "You said you *found me in the woods*? Thought that was a dream too."

"Nope, that happened. And unfortunately, what happened to you and your friends because of those tentacles—that wasn't a dream either."

My stomach sinks. "That's the only thing I knew really happened."

Lizzy places her hand on mine. "I'm so sorry, Danny…"

"So… My friends are—"

"Allie's gonna update you on that later, okay?"

I look down at the mattress, my eyes burning. "Oh… Okay…"

"Yeah…"

"So uhh… How'd you even end up finding me out there anyway? Last thing I remember was passing out in the middle of a trail that wasn't really a trail."

"Uhh… We were actually hiking to the Flesh Forest—I mean, to that place in the woods where the meaty biomass is growing— and we found you just laying there. Well, we didn't, like, stumble across you. We heard you yelling for help first. I guess you heard us coming. Then we hurried over, and there you were."

My face scrunches. "Wait, wait, wait… You were going *there*? *On purpose*? *Why*? And why does it seem like *Flesh Forest* is just a totally normal part of your vocabulary?"

She winces. "Uhhh… I'll leave that for Allie to explain too…"

I squint at her. "Why can't *you* tell me, Lizzy?"

She averts her gaze. "Because… Allie's the scientist who discovered the organism currently growing out of control in the woods, and I'm just a girl who graduated high school a few months ago. And because she only filled me in on everything, like five days ago… And because she made me promise to let her be the one to explain everything."

"I see… So… if she discovered it, does that mean Allie is responsible for the creation of the *Flesh Forest* then? You know, like how the girl who discovered the Uteroboscis is responsible for that outbreak."

Lizzy winces slightly, then shakes her head. "*No…* She's not."

I squint at her. "You sure? Because you didn't sound too sure."

"I'm sure. It's just… *complicated.* And she's the only one who can explain everything to you properly."

"Okay… Sooo, when can I talk to her then?"

"Uhh… She's busy doing science stuff right now, which is why I'm on patient duty," Lizzy says while reaching into her pocket. "But—" She pulls out her phone. "—I'll text her to come up as soon as she's done. She's been waiting for you to be more coherent before having *the talk*, and you're definitely all there now."

"Okay… Thanks."

"You're welcome!"

I glance over at the window. "Hey… Lizzy?"

"Hmm?" she hums, still looking down at her phone.

"Where even *are* we?"

She looks up and smiles. "At Allie's house!"

"Oh… okay. But, like… where is that *exactly?*"

"Oh! Ummm… You know where my family's ranch is? Rutherford Ranch?"

I shake my head. "Nope…"

She looks up and to the left. "We're uhh… like a mile or so straight north of Yelm Lake. Allie's house is right up against the woods."

"Oh… North… I was… going north before I passed out."

"I know. When we found you, we asked if you or your friends lived nearby, and you said no. Then you told us your friend said to go north because it'd be faster to get help if you went that way."

"I don't remember that at all."

"That's because the fever—and whatever that tentacle injected into you—had you super delirious."

"Delirious is an understatement."

"I bet…"

"How'd you even get me here if I was that out of it? Did y'all carry me? Actually, do you mind just filling me in on everything that happened from the time you found me until now?"

Lizzy nods eagerly. "Yeah, sure! I was actually about to do that anyway!" She giggles. "Okay, so… we were abouuut… three-quarters into our hike when we heard you calling out from around the bend? Yeah, around there. You were face-down on the ground with your infected arm stretched out, so me and Allie saw the pod-masses growing on your arm the second we ran up to you—"

"*Pod*-masses?" I interrupt.

"The biomass stuff—that's what we call it."

I slowly tip my head back. "Ah…"

"Don't worry, that'll get explained later too."

I bobble my head. "Figured as much."

She gives me a pitiful smile. "Yeah… Anyway… While we were helping you up, you started rambling about what happened to your friends. You were slurring something like, '*I know this is gonna sound crazy, but my friends are being absorbed by a giant fungal biomass with tentacles because we were drunk and trying to save some girl stuck in the middle of it all.*' Then you mentioned that you had pictures and videos as proof. That's when Allie told you she believed you and explained that we already knew all about the Flesh Forest and what those tentacles do to the people they grab. Right after that, we split up. Priya—Allie's roommate—led her group to the Flesh Forest to check on your friends and see if they could help. The rest of us helped you get back here."

I just sigh.

She shifts beside me, getting a little closer. "You were too weak and out of it to walk on your own, but not so bad that you needed to be carried. So we had you put your arms around Allie and Lena, and they basically helped you walk here. Actually, more like… half-dragged you. Most of the way, at least." She giggles nervously. "During the last quarter mile or so, you passed out, and that's when I grabbed your legs to help them carry you."

"Damn… I'm sorry y'all had to—"

Lizzy smiles brightly. "No need to apologize! Wasn't like we struggled or pulled a muscle or anything. There were three of us carrying you, so it wasn't that bad at all."

"Oh. Good. Well… thank you for that. I appreciate it."

"Of course!" She nods. "Oh, and before you blacked out, Allie explained that she knew what was wrong with you and that she and Lena might have a way to treat the infection. That's when she asked if you wanted us to bring you here or take you to the hospital. And after you picked the house, I asked if you wanted us to call your parents." She hesitates. "But you said your mom would probably freak out and drag you to the hospital. And you begged us not to call her because you thought if doctors got involved, they likely wouldn't let Lena help treat you."

I nod. "At least I was coherent enough to know that much."

She giggles. "Right?"

"So… Is that all?"

Lizzy bobbles her head side-to-side. "Basically? I mean, Allie did ask you how long it took you to get the tentacle off your arm, and you kinda mumbled about how you cut it away from the pod-mass before ripping it off. Then the last thing you said before passing out was that you used a knife attached to a stick to chop down tentacles on your way out of the Flesh Forest."

"I'm surprised I remembered all that, as delirious as I was."

"Same! Let's see… What else…" She thinks for a second. "Oh! You woke up for a little bit shortly after we got here. Because we woke you up to give you Advil and water for the fever. And you freaked out because you didn't remember us. After you calmed down, Allie explained everything again. Then Lena told you that Uteroboscis slime *might* save your life, and she warned you that, even though it was diluted, it'd make you crazy horny until the IV drip stopped. She also warned ya it might make you black out and, uh… mindlessly give yourself a *tugaroo*. You know, like how girls with Uteroboscises black out and have sex or diddle themselves."

"Oh…"

Explains why I didn't realize I was putting my hand in my pants earlier.

"Mm-hmm," she says with a naughty smile, staring at me like she wants to do to me what I want to do with her. "And then I assured you the worm slime was your best chance at surviving. After that, they asked you again if you were okay with all that. And since you said yes, like, a few dozen times, Lena hooked up your IV. We gave it a few minutes for the painkillers to kick in. Then, uhh… while we waited, you woke up freaking out a few more times. You almost ripped out your IV a couple of times too."

"Oh shit."

"Yeah… So we decided to tie you down. You blacked out shortly after we explained everything to you yet again. Then, right as Lena was sterilizing your arm, you started stirring."

"And then I woke up to Lena cutting into my arm."

"Yup, yup! And the rest you know."

I sigh while shaking my head. "It's so wild all that actually happened… Like… I can't believe that *Flesh Forest* is real. And that all the stuff that happened to me and my friends *actually happened.*"

"I know…" Lizzy says quietly. "Shit, I'm still in disbelief about everything too, and I've been basically dealing with this since Jake and my brother disappeared… When me and Allie first found the Flesh Forest four days ago—when I realized that Savanna was the girl in the center of the pod-mass—I just about had a mental breakdown."

"Wait… So… that really was Savanna?"

Lizzy's eyes get even more glassy, and her face scrunches up a bit like she's about to start bawling. "Yeah…"

"Oh shit… I'm so sorry…"

She sniffles, wiping away a tear as she turns away. "It's fine… I mean… *It's not fine.* But you don't have anything to apologize for. It's not your fault she died. It's…" She swallows hard. "It's basically my fault she's dead."

Then, she really is dead. Guess that means she was a corpse puppet…

"Wait… How's it your fault?" I whisper.

Lizzy sniffles again, then lets out a shaky breath. "Because… I kept something from her. Something I should've just been honest about. And now she's dead because I didn't tell her everything about the glizzy—I mean, about the organism Allie's going to tell you about in a bit."

"Umm… Did you just say *glizzy?* Like… as in… a dick?"

She winces. "Listen, I'm sorry to hit you with another cliffhanger like this, but I'm gonna need to wait until after Allie explains everything before I get into that. Okay?"

I sigh. "Alright. No worries, Lizzy." I give her a little smile.

She smiles back. "Thanks for being understanding."

"No problem. And thank you for carrying me and everything else."

"By everything else, you mean holding your hand and pep-talking you through a kitchen surgery?"

I snicker. "Yeah. That." A chuckle follows.

She laughs too. Then her phone buzzes on the bed. "Ooh! That's Allie!" She picks up her phone. "She'll be up in a bit!"

"Okay, cool."

"Alright." She grabs the digital thermometer from the nightstand. "I was supposed to check your temperature earlier, so let me do that quick before she gets up here."

"Copy that," I say, watching her turn it on.

Lizzy brings it toward my face. "Now open up and let me *stick it in your mouth,*" she says in a teasing purr.

I snicker. "Weirdo." I open wide, and she slips it under my tongue.

"And now we wait!" For some reason, she smiles shyly. Her spacey eyes flick to the pillow on my lap, and she starts nibbling at her bottom lip as she looks back up at me.

"Whut?" I mumble around the thermometer. "Nothin'…" Her faint smile widens into a grin as she squeezes her thighs together. "Just thought of another conversation we need to have later."

I arch a brow. "Abou'?" I mumble again.

"Don't worry about it. And stop talking. You're gonna fuck up the reading!"

I sigh and turn to the window, shaking my head as I do.

The reason I looked away wasn't because she's annoying me. It's because the longer I stare at her, the more I wanna make a move on her and live out this fantasy that's been running through my head since she walked in here.

But looking away didn't help. Not one bit. If anything, the urge is getting worse.

Damn this Uteroboscis IV drip!

And damn this girl for being so cute, and for looking at me with fuck-me eyes all this time.

CHAPTER 16:
THAT WHITE STUFF

DANNY HOLLAND
Saturday, August 27th

While I sit here against the headboard waiting for the thermometer to beep, I look around the room, stealing glances at Lizzy every so often. She's too focused on her phone to notice. Thankfully. And I'm so glad this pillow's on my lap, because I've been constantly twitching down there at the thought of me and her hooking up.

Damn this diluted Uteroboscis slime…

I know it's whatever's in this worm goo that's got me obsessively thinking about getting it on with her like this. Because I've seen her at school a few times, and I've creeped on her social media during my missing-person research, but I've never really thought about her like *that*. It's not that she isn't attractive. She is. It's just that there were always hotter girls to fantasize about. Like her best friend, Piper Cummings. Every straight dude at school talked about her obsessively.

But now? With this shit coursing through my veins, Lizzy suddenly looks just as hot as Piper, and it's driving me insane that we can't just hook up right here, right now.

Now that I know what girls with Uteroboscises are constantly dealing with, I feel bad for them.

The longer I sit here not getting to do what I so desperately need to do with her, the more anxious I get. And the guiltier I get too. It's not even guilt over what I did to Tucker. It's guilt over not feeling sad enough about what's happened to my friends. And the reason I don't feel more down is that the Uteroboscis-derived *medicine* flowing through my veins has me overwhelmingly happy—happier than I've ever been. Happy and thinking about hooking up with Lizzy instead of focusing on their well-being, or even thinking about them much at all...

Cognitive dissonance... I think that's what my psychology teacher would call this.

Light footsteps sound in the hallway just as the thermometer starts beeping. Before I can pull it out, Lizzy plucks it from my mouth for me.

"Okay!" she says, squinting at the display. "Hmm... You're still running a fever, but it's down a lot! Like, *a lot*, a lot!"

"What was it before?"

"A-hundred-six..."

"Holy fuck..."

"Yeah... But it's one-oh-three now. High, but not dangerously so."

Three soft knocks rap on the door as she finishes that sentence.

"Come on in," Lizzy says.

Allie—the auburn-haired girl in the green sundress—steps in with a laptop and a smile. "Hey, Danny! How ya feelin?"

I bobble my head as a sweet, floral smell fills my nostrils. A familiar one. One that somehow makes me even more turned on. "Okay, I guess."

That smells like...

Her face lights up. "Good, good!"

The closer she gets, the stronger the aroma becomes, and all I wanna do is pounce on her and do what animals do to keep the species going.

"That smell!" I blurt out when she's, like, a foot away. "You smell like that—"

"Hold that thought!" Allie interrupts, flipping open her laptop. She turns the screen toward me and sets it on the mattress. On it is a picture of a beige dildo with a skirt of starfish-arm-shaped leaves dangling around its stalk. "Have you ever seen one of these?"

"Yeah! We found one of those dong-shrooms near the Flesh Forest! And that's *exactly* what you smell like!"

She and Lizzy glance at each other, snickering.

"What?"

"Nothing!" Lizzy says. "That's just a really good name for it. I called it a *Flower Glizzy* when I first found one."

"But me and Priya—my friend who you haven't met yet—have dubbed it a Linga Flower," Allie adds.

Glizzy Flower…

"Wait…" I mutter, turning to Lizzy. "You started to say glizzy-something earlier before you stopped. Is this what you were gonna tell me about?"

Lizzy nods. "Yeah," she says flatly.

"Where'd you see one of these before, Danny?" Allie asks. "Like, which direction in relation to the Flesh Forest?"

"Ummm… We were coming from a neighborhood called Fox Hill, which is northwest of Yelm Lake."

Allie nods while glancing at Lizzy again. "Okay." She turns back to me. "Then we know which one you saw."

My eyes go wide, and my jaw drops. "I'm sorry… Did you say *which one*? As in, there's *more than one* of those things?"

Both girls nod.

I let out a short puff of a laugh. "Oh, what the fuck… Also, why do you smell like one of those dong-shroom—Glizzy-Linga-whatever things?"

Allie tilts her head. "Uhhh… I'll explain that in a bit. Just know I'm sorry for smelling like one, and that I can't wash the scent off."

"It's okay… Also, why are you sorry?"

"Because inhaling this fragrance while there's arousalin—the Uteroboscis compound that's making you insanely turned on—is probably making you *unbearably* aroused right now. And that's gotta be driving you crazy."

You have no fucking idea… You might need to tie me down before I zombie-out and do something I regret.

I subtly bobble my head. "No comment."

The girls smile.

"Don't be embarrassed," Lizzy says. "It makes us feel the exact same way you're feeling right now."

I think about what Tucker said—about bringing the dong-shroom to the lake and using the fragrance to get girls to fuck us. *Is Lizzy saying she's thinking about doing to me what I'm thinking about doing to her?*

"Oh…" is all I manage, failing to suppress a smirk. Then, mid-fantasy, guilt and sorrow twist in my stomach at the thought of what I did to Tucker. "Umm… Before you explain what this dong-shroom has to do with the Flesh Forest, can you please tell me what happened to my friends first?"

Allie's expression shifts from neutral to sad in an instant. "I can't. Not without giving you the background first. Otherwise, it won't make any sense."

I sigh. "Okay… But can you at least tell me if they're… dead? You can tell me if they are. After seeing Savanna encased in the biomass, I know what'll happen to them. And considering how fast that fungal tissue grew into my friends' flesh in the hour or two I was passed out in the Flesh Forest, I'm guessing they're already covered in the shit now that it's been nearly a day since I last saw them. So you can just tell me. I'm prepared for the worst."

Allie presses her lips together as her eyes get all glassy. "Your friends… They're not dead, Danny. Not yet, anyway."

"Oh…" I exhale. "Okay. Thanks for letting me know."

"Sure, no problem." She sighs. "Listen, I promise I'll make this quick so you don't have to wait too long to find out what happened to your friends—and so you don't have to suffer too long with this fragrance radiating off me. Before I begin, though, I know you have a lot of questions, and I know you're gonna have even more once I start, but I'm gonna ask you to save them for the end. Because I've got a presentation of sorts that should explain everything you could possibly ask. Okay?"

I give her two slow nods. "Yeah, I can do that."

"Awesome," Allie says with a warm smile. Then she takes a deep breath. "Okay… So… the Linga Flower actually comes in two forms. This one—" She points at the beige dildo organism on the screen. "—the main form. And then the Yoni Flower." She hits the spacebar.

What pops up makes my glizzy throb.

The video shows a flowerpot with a flower growing out of it—a *flower* that's slightly larger than my hand and made of the same meaty tissue as the dong-shroom. Same colors too. Its five red petals look like starfish arms, edged with this beige skin. Right in the middle is a vertical slit between two plump folds—vertically oriented *lips* that look like a pussy. Like, *exactly* like a pussy. There are even fleshy curtains between the folds bordering the slit, identical to a female's inner labia in both shape and position. There's also a little bump at the top that looks like a clit. Beneath it, a tiny pinhole that looks disturbingly like a urethra.

Anatomically correct is how my anatomy teacher would describe this flower's vagina-like appearance.

A Flower with a pussy. A flowussy, is the first thought that pops into my head. Because of TikTok, my generation throws -ussy onto the end of anything resembling the female reproductive organ.

The Allie in the video turns the flowerpot, showing the side profile. Connected to the backside of the meat flower, directly opposite the flowussy hole, is a thick tube that looks exactly like an upside-down dong-shroom. Its glans-shaped tip is attached to the same white fungal stalk the dong-shroom had.

It looks like someone inverted a dong-shroom, bent the tip downward, and jammed the stalk into its urethra-like hole.

When Allie spreads the flowussy's lips and brings the camera closer, light spills into a deep, ribbed, red cavity. The passage is wet-looking and lined with folds. It legit looks identical to every birth canal I've seen in porn, except the *flesh* is watermelon red. The passage seems just as deep and snug as a real one too.

It's basically a living fleshlight… That's what pops into my head the moment I see that tight, wet flesh tunnel.

Now all I can picture is me using it that way. And thanks to the Uteroboscis slime in my veins and that godly fragrance radiating off Allie, I almost splooge just thinking about it…

"Uhh," Allie groans, snapping me out of my trance. "You still with us, Danny?" She smirks.

I snap my mouth shut and nod. "Yeah… Sorry… Just tryna comprehend what I'm seeing."

Lizzy nudges my arm. "Keep your mind out of the gutter, buddy," she teases, giving me a wink after.

My cheeks instantly heat up. "I wasn't—never mind…"

She giggles menacingly. "Yeah, no point in lyin'. With this smell in the air and that womb-worm slime in your blood, we already know *exactly* what you're thinkin'. And it's okay that you're thinking that."

I sigh. "Can we continue, please?"

Another menacing giggle follows, and I don't know why I find it so cute. Wait. Never mind. I know *exactly* why. Worm slime.

"Okay, so," Allie continues, "the Linga and Yoni Flowers both emit the same intoxicating fragrance, with pheromones and *spores* mixed in. All of it works together to make mammals experience the same kind of maddening arousal the Uteroboscises cause in females. Now, as you might've guessed, the reason that the Linga Flower mimics the human male reproductive organ and emits that fragrance is because it *wants*—" She air quotes the word. "—females to get so unbearably horny that they eventually *ride it* the way they would ride a mate's erect phallus. And the Yoni Flower evolved to resemble female genitalia with a passage just as deep as a birth canal to—"

"Get guys so turned on that they *stick it in*," I finish.

Allie nods. "Exactly. Now…" She double-clicks the next mp4 file in line.

This video starts with the camera panning up from a wooden floor before settling on a dong-shroom growing out of a dirt patch in the middle of what looks to be a shed. Then a hand, presumably Allie's, reaches in and starts jerking it off…

And instantly, I picture her doing that to me.

"Umm," I groan, fighting the urge to reach into my pants again. Fighting that and the urge to pounce on Allie or Lizzy.

"Sorry," she says, "I know it's hella weird watching me give a fungoid-plant-thing a tugjob, but I promise this isn't some pervy shit. There's a scientific reason for me showing you this." She snickers. "And that reason is…" As her voice trails off, the dong-shroom twitches and starts oozing golden goo. "After enough stimulation, the Linga Flower secretes this sap. The same sweet lubricant coats the Yoni Flower's passage and drips out when it's stimulated too. If that sap is ingested or absorbed vaginally, that person gets even more intoxicated and becomes overwhelmed with an insatiable, consciousness-eroding arousal. And after the Linga Flower is stimulated enough…"

A beat later, the dong-shroom throbs hard in her hand. Then something like mayo explodes from its tip in a thick, rope-like stream, shooting a few feet into the air before splattering onto the floor.

"AYOO!" I shout. "What the actual fuck!"

"Before you ask," Allie says. "*Yes*, that Linga Flower essentially just ejaculated. And Yoni Flowers gush the same white slime simultaneously from their cavity and their urethra-like hole after enough penetrative stimulation." She pauses the video and points to the creamy goo on the floor. "That white stuff?" She gives me a serious look. "It's a viscous liquid filled with infectious, mutagenic material that alters the female reproductive tract once it's *released* into the birth canal. I'll tell you what it does later. For now, just know it *only* affects *female reproductive* tissue. If it gets on our skin, it wipes right off and nothing happens."

Lizzy nods, her expression suddenly serious now too.

"But," Allie continues, "if even a microscopic speck of that white slime touches *any part* of a guy's body, or a male animal's body, it doesn't come off. No matter how hard you scrub or what you try washing it off with. And then it does… something horrific. Something so incomprehensible you wouldn't believe it unless you saw it yourself. And even then, you probably still wouldn't believe it." She sighs. "Hell, I've witnessed it many times, and I'm still struggling to accept it as reality. And that's why we couldn't take you to the hospital and show doctors what I'm about to show you as evidence meant to get them to cut out your infected skin and let us treat you with Uteroboscis slime. They'd think it was some AI shit. Or worse, they'd believe it and quarantine you in some CDC lab for the rest of your days."

I gulp hard. "Uhh… Wha—what does the white slime stuff do to guys?"

"Watch this, and I'll explain while you do…" Allie says, reaching for her laptop. She stops with her finger hovering above the mousepad. "Wait… The tentacle that wrapped around your arm… Before you ripped it off, you said you cut it, right?"

I nod. "Yeah… Stabbed it with the jagged end of a broken branch until the stalk split… Why?"

She nods. "Perfect." Then she shakes her head and winces. "Sorry! I don't mean perfect like I'm glad that happened. I meant perfect as in this will make more sense to you, since you witnessed that!"

I force a smile. "It's okay. I know what you meant."

"Okay, good. But, umm… When you cut it, what gushed out of it?"

"Uhh, some pink goo… Some maple-syrup-looking shit. And… some white… slime…" My eyes go wide as I remember the white goo oozing from the black roots still stuck in my arm wounds. "Was that the same stuff as—"

"What shot out of the Linga Flower?" Allie finishes. "Yes. It was."

Lizzy nods.

"Oh shit…" I mutter. "So the stuff that was growing on my arm—"

"Is what the white slime turns your skin into," Allie says. "Which is basically the same tissue as the pod-mass—the biomass covering the ground, the trees, and Savanna's body."

"Wait," she says, turning to Lizzy. "Did you tell him about Savanna? Or did he figure it out from the license in her backpack?"

"Sort of both," Lizzy says. "His friend found her bag, so he already figured it was her. I only told him that she died because I didn't tell her what I knew, but I didn't tell him what that was yet."

"Oh, okay," Allie says, turning back to me.

"Hold on," I blurt out. "I know you said to save the questions for the end, but how is it that Savanna's skin and muscle turned into the biomass if she's a female? Was she not... *a female?*"

"She was," Lizzy answers. "It's just..." She glances at Allie.

Allie huffs. "Savanna didn't die because her body mutated into what you saw. She died first, *and then* her body changed into what you saw *because she died.*"

My eyes widen. "Oh. What the fuck..."

Allie winces. "Yeah... Don't worry, it'll make sense after this next part."

"Oh, okay. Go ahead. Sorry for jumpin' ahead."

Her expression softens into a faint smile. "No worries! I'd be doin' the same thing." She takes a deep breath, then exhales sharply. "Okay, so... once the white slime infects a guy's skin, it starts spreading all over his body. And if the infected flesh isn't cut away before it reaches the torso..." She double-clicks a video file titled **M. Barlow.mp4**. "Well, this'll show you what happens in one-hundred percent of all cases where the infection isn't stopped."

The naked, white, 20-something on screen... the shit covering his crotch and lower abdomen looks exactly like what was growing on me and my friends where the tentacle stalks touched us. The edges of the infected skin taper into skinny tendrils that look like spiky off-white frosting. But what's covering his boner looks different from the biomass. His entire dong is encased in something smooth that looks like beige candle wax...

It almost looks like...

Allie sighs. "This is a guy named Matty Barlow, four days after he got a spore egg—I mean, after he got *that white stuff* on his penis."

"Holy fucking shit… Wait… As in *Matthew Barlow*? Isn't that the guy who went missing from Seattle?"

She nods. "Actually, yeah," she says as the video cuts to another clip. "And… this is him three days later."

Now, most of his body looks like Savanna's, except it's more beige-tan and lumpier than the yellowish biomass in the Flesh Forest. But when I see his erect reproductive organ, my brain nearly breaks.

Allie skips ahead a few seconds. What appears next is something incomprehensible that's resting in a wheelbarrow, and there's something all too familiar growing out of it. Based on what she just showed me, I know what I'm looking at. But it's got me so fucked up that I can't make sense of what it is, or what it means for me and my friends.

"And this…" Allie almost sighs. "This is the end-stage of the infection."

"Wait—" I retch, then swallow hard to keep from puking. "No… So… my friends… If this treatment doesn't stop my infection… We're gonna turn into—into *that*?!"

Allie winces. "There's a strong possibility you won't. As for your friends… I'm sorry… But they will…"

Lizzy nods.

I shake my head fast. "No… Nah! How the fuck does someone go from what you just showed me to *this*—to whatever the fuck this is I'm looking at?! Like, where are his limbs? Where's his head?!"

"Let me show you," Allie begins, double-clicking on a video titled **Podling_Stage.mp4**.

What I'm watching this guy do in the middle of the woods doesn't feel real. But it still has me trembling and tearing up…

Then she plays a video called **Pod Dissection.mp4**. What I see inside the thing that the on-screen version of her cut open makes me sick. The shit she explains while it plays makes sense and doesn't.

By the end, I both understand how the infection progresses and can't comprehend how any of it is biologically possible.

Allie lets out a long sigh. "Three to five days…" she continues as the very first thing she showed me appears on the screen. "That's how long a guy infected with the white slime has before becoming a podling that does what you just saw." She places her hand on my shoulder. "And since the Flesh Forest's pod-mass is the same tissue the slime turns male flesh into, only growing inside out, once it starts merging with a guy's skin, the process accelerates, cutting the timeline from about three days to roughly one."

My jaw drops, and my eyes nearly bulge out of their sockets. "So… my friends only have, what… a few hours left?"

Allie nods.

I start crying immediately.

That's when Lizzy wraps her arms around me. "I'm so sorry, Danny," she whispers in my ear.

A pathetic whine slips from my throat. "Why?! Why didn't your friends save them right after you found me? Why didn't they cut them free from the meat-mat and buy them some time!"

"Danny," Allie whispers, rubbing my arm gently. "I can say with absolute certainty they were too far gone by the time you left them yesterday. And the reason I know that for sure is because on Wednesday, when we were measuring the Flesh Forest's growth rate and checking to see if we could save Savanna, there was no one fused to the pod-mass. But when we went back Thursday morning—wait… Do you know about the guy who went missing a few days ago? Ummm… Nicholas Crawford?"

I sniffle. "Actually, yeah. He's a teacher from my school who happened to live a few doors down from Kyle—my friend who was with me in the Flesh Forest… Speaking of… I forgot to mention earlier that we found Mr. Crawford's wallet in a pair of pants stuck to a tentacle stalk near the middle of the meat-mat."

"Okay. Figured you might've found that," Allie says quietly. "Well, like I was saying… On Thursday morning, we actually found Mr. Crawford unconscious and fused to the pod-mass, with a tentacle wrapped around his right wrist and one around each leg. And when I say *fused*, I mean his body was almost completely covered, except for his eyes and mouth."

"Oh fuck…" I mutter.

"I mean, his lips were covered too, but his mouth was still open, like Savanna's…" Allie sighs. "Anyways, based on the timeline you gave us for your friends, and given how much of Nicholas Crawford's body was covered in just one day, we estimated he was grabbed by those tentacles sometime in the mid-to-late afternoon… He still had a pulse when we found him. *A slow one.* And he was still warm to the touch. But no matter what we did, we couldn't wake him up. Then, when we went back Friday morning, his body was gone. Not absorbed into the pod-mass. Just *gone.*"

Lizzy nods, looking like she wants to cry.

Allie hits the spacebar, and what pops up is a scene I recognize immediately—a small clearing in the woods near where Kyle got that first little tentacle stuck to his leg. "And this is where we found him," she almost whispers. "Where you and your friends found him right before you stumbled across the Flesh Forest…"

"Holy fuckin shit," I mutter. "*That* was his—I mean, that was *him?!*"

Allie nods. "Without a doubt. Because there wasn't one there Thursday, and then that was there the next day… And uhh…. what we've learned from studying him is that once the pod-mass starts growing onto the head and the back of the neck, it's already too late. Just like with the standard white slime infection, once it reaches the brainstem, guys stop being themselves within a few hours and become what you saw in that video."

I picture my friends doing what that guy did in the video. My eyes burn. My body shakes. Guilt churns my stomach.

"Fuck… FUCK!" I scream, pounding my fist down on the mattress.

Allie sighs and rubs my arm again in that nurturing way my mom does. "I know this won't bring you much comfort, but it might help you to know your friends are not suffering. They likely haven't been conscious since you last saw them. Because whatever the tentacles and the pod-mass pump into people works like anesthesia. So for them, they're just in the deepest sleep of their lives, completely at peace."

I wipe the tears from my eyes. "I guess it does help knowing they're not suffering… Thanks for tellin' me that."

"You're welcome," she says softly.

I suck in a deep breath, then huff it out. "I wanna go back and see them. To see that shit for myself. Because I'll never be able to believe any of that was real until I see it in person. And I… I wanna say goodbye to them. I wanna apologize."

"Aww," Allie coos. "That's sweet, and I totally get that you want to. But that's not a good idea, Danny. Your fever's still *way too high* for you to be hiking that far."

"I can make it!"

She shakes her head. "Even if you were able to, IV bags need to be elevated for gravity to move the liquid into your veins. And we can't exactly hold it up for you the entire way there and back.

Also, stopping the Uteroboscis slime treatment, even briefly, could give the infection a chance to resume spreading."

I scoff, looking down at my arm. "Do we even know if this treatment's working? Like… have you checked to see if the pod-mass bumps grew back while I was asleep?"

Allie shakes her head again. "We wanted to let the bleeding stop before unwrapping your arm. And based on the normal growth rate of the standard pod-mass infection, it would take four to six hours for any microscopic infected tissue Lena may have missed to regrow to a detectable size. That's why we planned to wait. And it hasn't been that long yet."

"Oh, I see…" I drift into a trance as the things I saw in those videos replay in my head. "So… I still might be podifying or whatever right now?"

Allie winces and subtly bobs her head. "It's possible. And just to be completely honest, even though Lena cut away all the visibly infected tissue and removed the roots, the tentacle's spikes didn't just deposit the white slime *into the surface of your skin*. The slime was injected *into* your arm, possibly into your veins and capillaries. So we still don't know if any of that shit migrated elsewhere in your body, or if something's happening internally where we can't directly see it…"

I stare back at her with wide eyes, my body trembling. "Oh fuck…" I mutter as Lizzy hugs me again. "Wait, wait… I thought you said the slime changes skin and muscle first, before working on organs."

Allie half-nods, half-bobbles her head. "Yeah, but that's only based on cases where guys got the white slime on their penises or *directly on their skin*. The only case we know of where tentacles and the pod-mass fused to skin is Nicholas Crawford. Until two days ago, we didn't even know that could happen. And it's not like we cut him free, took him to the lab, and studied him. We wanted to. But he was gone by the time we got back with the wheelbarrow."

"Fuck…" My gaze drops to the pillow on my lap as my eyes start flooding with tears again. "I see…"

"Hey," Allie says, rubbing my back this time. "Before you start worrying yourself sick, there *is* something about your situation that makes me think the treatment is working."

I look up at her. "And what's that?"

Allie takes a deep breath. "When we were dissecting the flesh pod beneath that first Linga Flower that I found, Priya fell into it, and one of the tentacles inside of it wrapped around her leg and injected her with the same stuff that was injected into you. Even though the white slime didn't mutate her body the way it does to guys, whatever was pumped into her bloodstream gave her a severe fever. One as bad as yours was earlier. Her temperature got so high while she was at the hospital that she had a seizure and slipped into a coma for nearly a week."

My jaw drops. "Oh shit… So… the fact that my fever went down, and the fact that I'm conscious right now—that means the Uteroboscis slime is working?"

Allie shrugs and does another nod-bobble. "I think it's very likely. Especially considering males tend to have a worse reaction to the fluids produced by the tentacles and both flower variants. So either the Uteroboscis slime's antimicrobial compounds are doing their job, or you're not as sick as she was because you ripped the stalk off faster than we could get the tentacle out of—I mean… *off of* her. Or perhaps it's because you cut away the infected skin immediately, and then we excised even more afterward. Honestly, we won't know for sure until we unwrap the bandages and check to see if the pod-mass started growing back… We can do that now if you—"

"No!" I blurt out, yanking my arm back to my abdomen. "I'm not ready to find out yet. I just… I wanna keep believing it's working for a little while longer. Until after I see my friends one last time. We can check when I get back from the Flesh Forest."

Allie sighs, hanging her head. "Danny—"

"*I'm going*," I interrupt. "I have to. If we can't figure out a way to go with the IV bag, maybe you can, like, I dunno…" I glance at the thing taped to the inside of my left forearm. "Maybe we can just inject the Uteroboscis slime stuff into this port thing every few minutes or something?"

She twists her mouth to the side. "I mean… I suppose that *could* work. As long as we figure out how to match the IV drip rate so your blood concentration remains at these same levels. I'd have to run it by Lena."

"Awesome, thanks—"

"*But*," Allie cuts in sharply, "you're still too feverish to make that hike. If your fever spikes in the middle of the woods and you lose consciousness again, we'll have to carry you back. *In the dark.*"

"Umm," Lizzy hums. "We won't have to worry about that if I take him there on horseback!"

"*Horseback?*" I say as Allie starts bobbling her head side to side.

"Yeah!" Lizzy says. "Remember when I mentioned my family's ranch?"

"Mm-hmm."

"Well," she says, turning to Allie. "I can just grab a horse or two, and we can just ride down to the Flesh Forest. They'll be able to handle that trail no problem."

Thinking about her riding a horse makes me imagine it's me she's riding like a cowgirl. *Fuck…*

"Uhh," Allie groans. "Won't your parents question why you're taking their horses into the woods *this late?*"

Lizzy shakes her head. "No. Not if we say that you're paying to rent them or some shit. They've rented out horses for woodland rides before. And since they know I *work for you*—" She makes air quotes. "—they won't think anything of it. Plus, I'm pretty sure they're not even home right now."

Allie winces slightly. "I dunno…"

"Well," I say, "I'm goin' no matter what. So, can you please help me make this work, Allie?"

She lets out the same long, dramatic, exasperated sigh my mom does whenever one of us finally pushes her too far. "Fine."

"Awes—"

"Hold up!" she interrupts again. "There's something I need you to promise me first."

"Just name it."

"I don't want anything else to happen to you today, and you're my responsibility until I get you home to your parents. So I need you to promise me that, while we're out there, you will not, under any circumstances, step foot on the pod-mass, touch your friends, or do anything else I tell you not to do. Okay? That means no hero shit either. *Got it?*"

I nod rapidly. "Okay. I promise, Allie. Not that you even had to ask. Trust me, the last thing I want is to suffer any more than I already have."

Allie shakes her head then lets out another sigh. "Fine. Then we can take you back out there."

I force a smile. "Thanks so much, Allie."

"Mm-hmm," she hums. "You better not make me regret this. I won't be able to live with myself if anything happened to you out there."

"I'll be safe. Don't worry."

Lizzy slings an arm around me. "And I'll stick beside him the entire time to make sure he doesn't do anything stupid!"

I smile at her, genuinely this time. Mostly because her being against me like this has me all riled up.

"Good," Allie says, checking her phone. "Alright. We should hurry up and get to your place before it starts getting dark, Lizzy."

"Kay!" Lizzy says, springing up from the edge of the mattress.

"Umm," I groan. "Before you go… Where's your bathroom? I gotta pee."

Lizzy grins knowingly. "I'll take you there and help you with the IV!"

"While you're doing that," Allie says. "My friend Brandon left some clothes here. I'll grab his hoodie and jeans for ya so you can cover up a bit more. Just in case."

"Oh, thanks, Allie!" I say with a faint smile.

"You're welcome. Fair warning, he was a bit taller than you, so you're probably gonna have to roll up the jeans and cinch 'em up with a belt."

I nod. "That's fine."

She smiles, then heads for the door.

"Lemme just bring this closer," Lizzy says, dragging the coatrack-turned-IV-bag-holder toward me.

"Thanks," I whisper, scooting to the edge of the bed while keeping the pillow over my lap. "Uhh… You mind turning around for a sec?"

Her eyes flick from mine to my lap. "*Oh.* You need to adjust your… *situation*, don't'cha?" She smirks and then waggles her eyebrows.

"Uhhh… Yeah…"

Lizzy turns toward the door, pauses like she's listening for something, then twirls back around while I'm still tucking my *sausage* beneath the waistband.

"I didn't say I was done yet!"

She giggles, staring deep into my eyes.

"Do you mind?"

"Hold on a second," she says, placing a hand on my chest.

My eyes widen. "What's up?" I glance at the door. "Something wrong?"

She shakes her head. "I'm gonna ask you a super personal question, and I want you to answer me honestly. Okay?"

"Oh… kay… What is it?"

"Are you going to the bathroom to—" She mimes jerking off.

My eyes damn near bulge out of my head. "What?! *No-uh!*"

"*Danny…*" She tilts her head, arches her brows, and presses her lips together. "You've got Uteroboscis slime in your veins, so I know that smell coming off Allie definitely has you losing your mind right now. And the reason I know that is because I drank a little worm goo before I came in here, and I'm feeling *feral* as all hell right now."

"Are—are you serious?"

A shy smile plays across her lips, but her eyes are full of mischief. "Yeah."

I slowly tip my chin up. "Ahh… Now it makes sense why you seemed so spacey and smiley-smiley. And all touchy-feely."

Her eyes widen a bit. "Was it that obvious?"

"Most definitely." I snicker.

"Shit… I was hoping no one noticed. Also, please don't tell anyone. Because Allie and Lena don't want me consuming that stuff. Because it contains addictive opioids or whatever."

"Oh. Okay. I won't tell anyone. I promise."

She grins. "*Good boy.* And just so you know, I'm not a drug addict or anything. I've just been self-medicating with that stuff because I've been insanely depressed over my brother, Savanna, and Jake dying. And weed and alcohol haven't been cuttin' it."

"I get it," I say quietly. "I'd be doing the same. Or… I guess I should say *I will be* doing the same pretty soon."

She nods slowly, holding my hand and squeezing it. "We can self-medicate together until we're both done grieving."

I smile. "I like the sound of that."

Lizzy seems to get lost in my eyes for a moment. "Anyway… back to what I was sayin'… If I'm feeling this horny from just a gulp, there's no way you haven't been dying to go to the bathroom to *take care of your… situation* this whole time."

"Well, I'm not, so…"

She sighs and pouts. "Too bad… If you admitted you were gonna, I was gonna offer to help you out instead."

My eyes widen. "Wait… Are you fucking with me, or are you asking because that smell and worm slime have you talkin' crazy?"

"Ummm…" she groans, fighting off a smile. "Partially because of that. But also because you're having a really hard time right now, and I wanna do something to cheer you up—to cheer both of us up."

I stare at her for a few beats, blinking every other second. "Wait… Seriously."

She smiles harder, blushing this time. "*Seriously.*"

"Yes," I mutter, averting my gaze. "I was gonna… *you know.*"

She grins, spins away from me, and starts speed-walking toward the door.

"Uhh…" I groan.

Lizzy shuts it gently, then turns back, heading toward me with a slower strut. "You a virgin, Danny?" she whispers, reaching into her pocket.

My cheeks suddenly feel like they're on fire. "Uhh—"

"I am…" she says quickly, wincing slightly. "And yeah, it's super embarrassing being an eighteen-year-old virgin. So… it's okay if you are too. I won't judge."

I nod, swallowing hard. "Yeah… I am."

"Oh." She looks down and smiles shyly, her cheeks flushing. She then pulls out a condom. "Found this in your bag earlier. While I was checking to see if you had any medications you might need to take. So… you wanna…" She shrugs. "Wanna use it? Or you want me to just—" She mimes jerking off again. "I don't mind—" Now she mimes giving a BJ. "—if that's what you want. But fair warning, I've never done that before. So I might not be any good."

Seeing all that makes me throb so hard it hurts.

"Lizzy… Are—are you for real right now? Because if you're not…"

She looks away shyly, then nods as she sits beside me. "You just had the worst night and day of your life, and you literally just got the worst news imaginable. So I wanted to help make you feel better. And yeah, I'm feeling feral from the Uteroboscis slime and that smell, but I also really wanna just lose my virginity already. And I also want someone to help me feel better. And since I think you're cute and nice, I figured we could just help each other out."

Holy shit, she's definitely not lying, I think, staring deep into her eyes. *I knew I wasn't imagining that she was being weirdly flirty with me, a guy she doesn't even know.*

"Hold on… This isn't some *Make-A-Wish Foundation* thing, is it? Like, are you offering to hook up with me because y'all checked my arm while I was asleep and now you're trying to make sure I don't die a virgin without telling me what's wrong first?!"

She shakes her head quickly, giggling. "No! That's not what happened! What I just said? I meant it. Listen… if it makes you feel any better, I also kinda just want someone to help me forget for a little while too… Because I've been really depressed since my brother… disappeared—I mean, since he got infected and died…" She takes a breath. "So yeah… *Seriously.* We can do whatever you wanna do. *Dead-ass*. No cap. For real, for real." She giggles. "But if you don't want to do anything with me, we don't have to—"

"Of course I wanna do *that* with *you!*" I blurt out. "I mean, look at you! You're pretty as all hell! And it blows my mind that some guy hasn't already tried to hook up with you! The only reason I hesitated is because… we don't really know each other, and I didn't want you to feel like I was taking advantage of you while you were high on—"

She leans in suddenly and presses her lips to mine.

And damn, I don't know if kisses are supposed to feel this incredible or if it's the Uteroboscis goo in my blood making me hypersensitive, but this smooch somehow feels better than nutting.

Right as she starts fumbling with my belt, her free hand presses the condom into my palm. "Open that. *Quick*," she whispers against my lips. Then she kisses me again. Her tongue slips into my mouth a moment later, and it feels amazing.

Between making out with a girl for the first time and the anticipation of what's about to happen, my brain is swirling with so much dopamine that I suddenly can't remember anything that led up to this moment.

"Wow-*wuh!*" Lizzy says breathlessly during her dismount.

I wince, glancing from the ceiling fan to the smiling girl beside me. "Was that *wow* because it was that good, or because it was that bad and way too fast?" I say, sounding just as winded. A nervous chuckle follows.

"No!" She giggles. "Not that! As brief as that was, it was actually really good!"

"Yeah, right…"

"No, seriously! My body is all hypersensitive from the worm goo I drank. *Remember?!*"

"Oh," I mutter, nodding. "Right."

"Yeah! So it was impossible for me not to *really* enjoy every second of that. Hence the *wow*. Well, I said wow for that, and because I feel like a cougar." She turns to me with a troll grin.

"Ha. *Ha...*" I fake-laugh. "You're, what—barely half a year older than me?"

Lizzy snickers. "Probably about that." Then she starts cackling.

I shake my head and sigh. "Hey, was that really your first time?"

She gives me a shy smile, then looks up at the ceiling. "It really was. Why? Did I seem experienced?"

"You did. But that's not why I asked," I say quickly. "I just wanted to make sure you were telling the truth before I said thanks for..." I shrug. "I dunno. Thanks for picking *me*?" I can't help but snicker.

She giggles in that way I find so cute. "You're welcome?" Another quiet laugh follows. "Thanks for letting me pick you?"

I chuckle. "You're welcome?"

We both let out nervous laughs.

As her laughter fades, she abruptly looks down at my still-stiff *situation*. "Ooh!" Lizzy squeals, pointing at it.

I jump, and my eyes go wide as I look down at the rubber-sheathed appendage. "Ah! What?!"

She winces. "Sorry! Didn't mean to scare ya! It's just—it's a really good sign that your... *baby batter* is normal! It means that the infection hasn't spread *down there*!"

I look down at it, remembering what Allie explained about all the fucked-up shit that happens to a guy's nuts and wang once the infection spreads there. "Oh, yeah... I guess that is a good sign." A nervous snicker slips out.

"Mm-hmm! Also, since we're on the topic..." She smiles naughtily. "Lena wanted me to tell you that until the Uteroboscis slime is out of your system, you're gonna stay hard even after you've *reached completion*. So don't freak out and think it's a symptom of the infection."

"Oh, shit. Thanks for telling me. Because I was startin' to wonder why I was still so bricked up."

Three soft knocks tap the door.

"Clothes are on the floor by the door, Danny," Allie calls from the hallway.

"Okay!" I shout as Lizzy giggles beside me.

"Pssh," Allie blows out. "I can hear you giggling in there, Lizzy," she says, her voice lowering as she walks away.

Lizzy snickers. "*Shit*. She definitely knows," she whispers.

I grin, staring deep into her eyes. "Oh, for sure." A sudden surge of pressure in my bladder makes me wince. "Okay, I really do need to get to the bathroom now."

She springs up from bed. "Okay! Lemme put my pants back on and I'll help you!"

It isn't until I shut the bathroom door behind me that I stop thinking about that very brief, albeit gloriously amazing, life-changing experience I just had and start remembering what led up to us swapping V-cards.

Suddenly, I can't stop picturing my friends looking like the guys in those videos.

I catch my reflection in the mirror and immediately picture myself the way those other guys looked in the late stages of the infection. That's when my body starts trembling.

My gaze drifts down to my bandaged forearm.

You should look at it…

I reach for it, but then stop with my fingers just inches away.

No… Not yet… If it's bad, I won't be able to handle it.

I picture my arm looking all gross and fucked up.

The end-stage of the infection pops into my head.

The second I picture my friends inside something like that, my stomach churns.

And then I'm puking nothing but bile into the toilet.

From beyond the door, I hear rapid footfalls rushing toward the bathroom. "Danny?" Lizzy calls. "Did you just puke?! You okay?!"

Her voice snaps me out of it. Hearing her makes my mind jump back to the amazing 1-to-2 minutes we shared a bit ago.

"I'm good!" I croak.

"You sure? Are you feeling *sick*? Like, sick-*sick*? Should I get Allie?"

"Nah, I'm okay, Lizzy. I swear. I just thought about those videos and it made me nauseous. It's not the infection or anything."

"Oh, okay! Trust me, I get it. I hurled too right after she showed me that shit… But okie-doke! I'll go back into the room so you can have some privacy!"

"Okay… Thanks…"

Only once her footfalls fade do I drop my pants, aim my perma-wood at the toilet water, and start draining my bladder.

And just like that, I'm thinking about the Flesh Forest again.

You're going back out there. On purpose. All because you need to see them one last time. Even though you definitely shouldn't see them looking like… that.

But you have to…

You gotta go back and apologize, Danny. Just in case there's a chance they can hear you. They need to know how sorry you are…

I replay everything that led to me being the last one standing.

Especially Tucker…

CHAPTER 17:
IN 100% OF ALL CASES…

DANNY HOLLAND
Saturday Evening, August 27th

As if being back near the edge of this *Flesh Forest* wasn't surreal enough, the fact that it's almost sunset—just like it was when I escaped yesterday—makes everything that's happened since feel like a dream. Especially the part where I lost my virginity to a cute girl I barely even know, all because she happened to be high on Uteroboscis slime and that hypnotic smell radiating off Allie. That part feels more impossible than all the nightmarish shit I've lived through in the last day. But it happened. Thankfully. And me sitting here on the ground, holding her hand while staring at Kyle's mostly mutated body through a pair of binoculars?

Unfortunately, this is happening too…

And I really wish it wasn't.

Kyle's still lying on his back exactly where I left him a day ago, his perma-wood still pitching a tent in his shorts. Unlike Savanna's fully biomass-encased corpse, his body stands out against the lumpy tissue that's grown over every inch of him, except for his eyes and mouth. Every inch of flesh is covered, but that fungal, meat-like shit didn't grow over his clothes. Which is weird, considering the biomass grew onto my backpack and towel after I passed out. It's almost like it doesn't grow on non-living matter unless it's trying to reach living tissue…

But yeah, Kyle's clothes aren't why he stands out. He stands out because his mutated flesh isn't the same yellowish-tan color or texture as what's covering everything else. It's more of a beige-tan—identical to the shit that grew all over the guys in those pictures and videos Allie showed me. A mix between coagulated oatmeal and kombucha SCOBY is how she described the final form of infected skin, and she wasn't wrong.

If it weren't for the binoculars letting me see his chest slowly rising and falling, I'd think he was dead. Though, based on what Allie told me, he's basically a vegetable at this point anyway…

This can't be real… This can't be real, I think while lowering the binoculars.

Wake up, Danny. Just wake up. Wake up back in your bed on Friday morning. Let all of this be a nightmare. Please! I've been mentally reciting some version of that ever since we got here an hour ago.

But no matter how badly I want this to be a nightmare, I know it's real. Lizzy holding my hand is my proof. Her soft skin against mine. Her warmth. The sweat forming between our palms from holding on so long. The way her thumb gently sweeps back and forth against me every now and then. All that sensory input lets me know I'm awake.

That's why she's holding my hand—to ground me. To comfort me. And so I can comfort her too. It's not because she's fallen for me or anything like that. I know that for a fact. She basically told me as much right after she grabbed my hand.

Holding hands with her, plus how intense the wind feels against my skin—thanks to this Uteroboscis-slime-induced hypersensitivity—proves I'm actually awake and not trapped in another hyper-realistic fever dream. The sweet, intoxicating fragrance mixed with the meat-mat's mustiness is another clue.

"Urgh," I groan.

"You okay?" Lizzy asks, sweeping her thumb against my hand.

"Physically?" I say without lowering the binoculars. "Yeah. At least, I think so. Mentally? Far from it."

She leans against me. "Same, Danny… *Same.*"

That groan wasn't just because I'm getting sadder and more depressed the longer I stare at Kyle. It's because I'm getting increasingly more bitter. Not bitter at myself for failing to save him. Bitter at Savanna.

During the horse ride over here, one of the things Lizzy filled me in on was what Savanna did with the dong-shroom she found in the exact spot where she is now, and how that led to her death.

Which led to the pod-mass growing inside out and completely out of control…

Which also led to Savanna's brain forming a connection with the one buried 2- to-3-feet beneath her…

This is all your fault, Savanna, I think, looking from Kyle to her. *If you weren't such a fucking deviant—if you never did what you did—my friends wouldn't be suffering the worst fate imaginable. And I wouldn't be at risk of suffering it too.*

Out of nowhere, a squeal turns into a neigh behind us, and I jump. "Holy-fuckin-shit!" I shout, looking over my shoulder with a quick snap. "*Jesus*… Forgot your horse was back there."

Lizzy lets out that menacing giggle I'm starting to love. "Don't worry, I'm *totally* not judging you for getting scared by a very obvious horse noise. *But only because* it's kinda hard not to be jumpy when you're this out of it and standing in the middle of the woods."

I crack a smile, partly because what she said was kinda funny, and mostly because thinking about what happened between us is unavoidable whenever I look at her. "Thanks for being *sooo understanding*…" I say with heavy sarcasm.

She winks. "Don't mention it!"

As we get lost in each other's eyes, all I can think about is what happened between us. And judging by the faint smile on her lips and the flirty look in her eyes, I think she's thinking about it too. Either that, or the Uteroboscis compounds still coursing through her blood have her thinking about us doing it again.

"GAWUHH-UHH-UH!" the corpse-puppet squawks, loud as fuck—louder than ever.

We both jump this time.

Lizzy shivers beside me, squeezing my hand like she's trying to break it. "Ughhh… I hate hearing her make that sound," she croaks, sounding like she's on the verge of tears.

I stroke her hand with my thumb. "I can't imagine how hard this is for you," I whisper.

A click crackles from the walkie-talkie on her lap. "We've got movement!" Allie radios. She's on the west side of the Flesh Forest with Lena, opposite from where we are.

We spring up at the same time, hands still locked. As I bring the binoculars to my face, my heart races and my stomach drops like it's being sucked into a black hole.

Kyle's who I lock onto. I focus on him instead of the others because, aside from Savanna, he's the only one still fused to the meat-mat.

Because Tucker and Gavin are *gone*…

They were gone before we got here. But the tentacle Gavin fell on, and the two that wrapped around Tucker? Those are still there, just missing a bunch of their quills. The only real evidence they were ever here is the two body-shaped outlines of jagged meat-mass left behind when they… *departed*… along with their ripped shirts, shorts, and boxers scattered nearby…

The first thing I see through the lenses is Kyle thrashing, his arms sort of punching upward as he tries to sit up, the membrane fused to his head and triceps stretching with him.

It looks… stretchier than it did when he tried breaking free yesterday, I think as I pan the binoculars up toward his face.

I shudder when I see how wide and bulging his eyes are. His mouth hangs open in a way that reminds me of a baby waiting to be fed.

"*Wuhhhh-ughh!*" Kyle groans in the most ghastly, unsettling way possible.

"Oh, Danny…" Lizzy whispers beside me, squeezing my hand. "I'm so sorry…"

"UH-UHRR-GUHHH!" Savanna's corpse moans along with him, almost drowning Lizzy out.

"Fff-fuck," is all I can croak.

"Danny," Lizzy says, nudging me with her elbow. "You gotta record this."

I snap out of my trance. "Ra—right," I whisper, handing her the binoculars.

With the sweaty hand she just released, I dig into my pocket and scramble to pull out my phone. I'm not about to film this just because I want—no, *need*—evidence. I'm going to do so because Allie specifically asked me to as part of the favor I agreed to during the horse ride over here.

My hands are damp and shaking so badly that it's hard to even open the camera app. Switching to video and hitting record isn't any easier. But I manage. The moment I raise the phone, Lizzy grabs my free hand again and squeezes like her life depends on it.

By the time I get Kyle in frame, he's already gone from lying flat to partially sitting up, his violently shaking arms nearly fully extended in front of him. The membrane tethering his head, neck, and arms to the meat-mat is stretched so taut it looks like batwing skin.

"KYLE!" I cry out. "Kyle! Do you hear me?! What—what are you doing?!" I say all that because Allie told me to act like I don't know what's happening while filming.

In the blink of an eye, my zombified friend slams his torso back down, hitting the meat-mat with a wet thud. A split second later, his body shoots upright again in the most spastic way, his right arm punching out sloppily as he does. Then his left arm flails out while his torso twists to the right.

He does that again.

And again.

And again.

The entire time, he's groaning and wailing like something out of *The Walking Dead,* his eyes never blinking, his mouth never closing. Thick drool eventually starts pouring from the corners of his lips.

On his fourth explosive thrash, the membrane behind his neck and beneath his right arm rips with a horrendously wet *schlick*—the sound of juicy chicken meat tearing off the bone.

"Blerrgh," I retch in response.

Lizzy gags quietly beside me.

"GWAHH-UH-UHHH!" Savanna's corpse wails over us.

The next time Kyle's upper body lunges forward, the meat-mass membrane tears slowly from his neck to his wrist, strands popping one by one like rubber bands snapping.

The sight and sound of that makes me queasy as hell.

Maybe 30-thirty seconds later, the last bits of membrane snap free from his ankles.

Savanna wails at that exact moment.

"KYLE!" I scream as loud as I can.

My zombified friend doesn't react. He just staggers to his feet without using his hands, his torso swaying and his legs wobbling—moving like someone too drunk or too tranquilized to function.

Once upright, he looks down and starts pawing at his shirt. Pawing turns into clawing, and his groans shift into growling.

Then he pulls at it. Hard.

Eventually, his awkwardly bent fingers catch the neckline, and he rips the shirt straight down the middle.

Allie said podlings all strip at a certain point in the infection, I think, watching him shrug off the tattered fabric. *Shit… his body looks exactly like the ones in those pictures and videos she showed me…*

As the torn shirt slips down his arms, it snags on the severed tentacle wrapped around his left forearm—a tentacle which now looks darker than the rest and stiffer-looking, like it's turned into wood.

"GRUHHH!" he roars, tugging at it.

He pulls harder and harder until the sleeve rips free and falls away. Then he takes a step forward, stops, and looks down at his shorts. Now he starts clawing at those. His shorts and boxers eventually slip down past his knees. Then he spazzes out and falls face-first onto the meat-mat.

React, Danny. What would you be saying or doing if you didn't know what was happening?

"Kyle! Wha—what are you doing!" I shout out. My voice sounds believable. Because I really am trying to break through to him.

He doesn't even so much as look my way.

Instead of getting back up, Kyle thrashes, kicks, and squirms like a child—or a chimp—that doesn't understand how to undress. He keeps doing that until his shorts and underwear come off, along with his shoes. Without missing a beat, he rolls onto his stomach and pushes himself up into a kneeling position. Then he stands again the same way as before, without using his hands.

Earlier, Allie told me podlings always migrate away from light once they reach the last stage of the infection. That's why she had us position ourselves near the eastern edge of the Flesh Forest—so Kyle would come toward us instead of us having to chase him across the meat-mat. In case she was wrong, she stationed others to the north and south to make sure we didn't lose him.

Since the sun was already dipping below the tree line when we got here, I thought he might not move east at all.

But as soon as Kyle gets up, he raises his arms to shield his face from the slivers of sunlight breaking through the canopy. Then he turns and starts waddle-stepping toward us. Well, not directly toward us, but in our general direction.

That's when I see the only part of his lower half not covered in lumpy tissue resembling coagulated oatmeal—the stiff appendage *down there* that's encased in smooth, beige, waxy *skin,* with 5 massive bumps forming a perfect ring around its base.

It looks just like Matthew Barlow's, I think, my gaze snapping from it back to Kyle's vacant eyes and hanging mouth.

Zombie-Kyle doesn't walk in a straight line. He swerves toward a gap between the tentacles ahead of him.

"GAH-UHH-UHHH!" Savanna cries as one tentacle slaps against his left thigh and another whips across his right arm.

Both recoil instantly.

They didn't wrap around him or stick to him, I think, turning to Lizzy, who looks just as stunned as I feel. *It's like the tentacles sensed he's made of the same shit as the biomass…*

Every tentacle he passes strikes him, then immediately pulls away. He grunts and swats at them, but never stops swerving toward the eastern edge of the Flesh Forest. Not once does he blink. Not once does he close his mouth to stop the thick, cloudy drool from pouring out.

Gone… He's already gone… That's not Kyle anymore, Danny…

When he's about halfway to us, it looks like he's about to come straight at us. Then, a few yards later, he veers sharply to the left.

By the time he reaches the point where the meat-mat transitions to regular ground, he's maybe 10 to 20 yards away, in an area thick with bushes and clustered trees. That's when I start following him from the trail. Lizzy moves with me without missing a beat, still holding my hand, staying just out of the camera's view.

We're walking parallel to him because I don't want to push through all that foliage and risk getting grabbed by a hidden baby tentacle the way Kyle did near the dong-shroom yesterday.

With each step he takes, he looks around aimlessly with those unblinking eyes, like he's searching for something specific while drunk and hallucinating. Along the way, he bumps into trees and scrapes past bushes, growling at them each time he does.

Another 10 or so yards later, I spot a narrow path free of foliage and biomass that cuts through the trees toward where Kyle's wandering. So I bank left, pulling Lizzy along with me.

Even though I'm freaking out and high as fuck from the Uteroboscis compounds in my blood, I check the ground carefully before every step. I don't jog like I want to. I don't run. I creep towards him. Because Allie doesn't know what guys this far gone will do to another male. Like, we don't know if he might bite me or scratch me like a real zombie and re-infect me. So I move cautiously, trying not to let him see me coming.

It's only once I'm a few yards away that I see them—the quills jutting out of his arm and left calf. Not only are they much longer than the ones on the tentacle stalks, but branches are sprouting from them now. And they're woodier. Like roots instead of rubbery, chopstick-looking spikes.

If the quills that grow into flesh turn into that…

I can't help but picture these same roots bursting out of Tucker's eye and Gavin's back…

Dear God, I think, gagging quietly.

Kyle comes to a dead stop out of nowhere, like a dog whose leash has gone taut. Then he slowly turns, waddling side to side. Once he's facing roughly the direction he came from, he starts heading back, scanning up and down and left to right with every dragging step.

The fuck's he doing?

Kyle doubles back another 5 or so yards before freezing again, like his brain just fucking shut off. A second later, he starts sniffing rapidly, his gaze drifting to a large tree on his right. He stares up at the leafy branches, then takes two unsteady steps toward it—only to stop abruptly, like he just ran into something invisible.

Suddenly, his head drops in a spastic motion, hanging forward as though the muscles in his neck just gave out. He stands there like that for a few seconds. Then he drops to his knees while reaching for the ground. The moment his fingers sink into the soil, he starts clawing at it—feverishly digging like he's trying to save someone buried right there.

As Lizzy squeezes my hand, my gaze wanders left, to where the edge of the meat-mat lies 5 to 10 yards away. Then my eyes snap back to where Kyle is digging near the base of the tree.

It's just like Allie said. I glance at Lizzy and find her staring back at me with tears in her eyes. *She told us he'd pick a spot opposite the sun, near a tree, and less than fifteen yards from the meat-mat… And he did exactly that.*

"Say something," Lizzy whispers so low I can barely hear her.

When I look back over at Kyle, I catch Allie and Lena in my peripheral vision, watching from behind a tree to my left. They're not hiding from him—they're hiding to stay off camera.

"Ky—Kyle…" I stutter as tears fill my eyes. I reach toward him, then yank my hand back a beat after it appears on my phone screen. "What the fuck are you doing, bro? Stop! Please stop!" I'm not acting anymore. This is a genuine plea.

He turns toward me, staring with those vacant, unblinking eyes for a moment. Then he slowly turns back to the shallow hole in front of him and resumes digging.

"Hey, bro…" I croak. A sniffle follows. "I—I don't know if you can hear me, but… I'm sorry, Kyle. I'm so sorry I couldn't save you from those tentacles and that meat-mat, brother…"

He doesn't react this time. He just keeps digging feverishly.

That's when I start crying silently, struggling to keep my phone steady and the camera trained on him now that my vision is all blurry. Beside me, Lizzy snivels and whimpers under her breath.

It takes a few minutes to get myself under control. By the time I blink the tears away, Kyle has somehow already dug a pit that's almost a foot deep and nearly as long and wide as his body.

Moments later, he lifts a handful of dirt to his mouth and takes a bite out of it. Then he starts moaning and smacking like a feral animal, gulping noisily every so often.

"What the fuck…" I mutter.

He's doing exactly what that guy did in the video Allie showed me…

Every so often, he stops digging just to shovel more dirt into his mouth.

It takes about 15 minutes for him to deepen the pit another foot, widening it as he goes.

A few scoops later, he stops digging and starts crawling around the man-sized grave on all fours, like a dog trying to find the right place to lie down. Not long after, he suddenly goes still.

Then he drops flat onto his stomach and slowly rolls over in a disturbingly squirmy way, groaning as he does.

Once he's on his back, he goes still. He freezes with his eyes wide open, his dirt-caked mouth hanging slack, and his fingers curled like claws. The only movement now is the muddy drool spilling down the sides of his face.

Is he… dead?

The thought barely finishes forming before Kyle abruptly sits up with his arms stretched toward the pile of dirt at the edge of the pit near his feet. His arms quickly snake around the mound, and then he just rakes it all in toward himself.

He does it again.

And again.

First, his legs disappear beneath the soil.

Then his waist.

Then his abdomen.

When the dirt reaches his neck, he claws chunks from the pit's wall until it collapses inward, burying his chest… and then his face.

"Kyle!" I scream as his face disappears beneath the dirt.

A second or two after that, he starts pulling his arms down into the dirt. His limbs twitch and bend awkwardly as they sink into the earth, the soil above him bulging from side to side as though he's shimmying his body beneath it.

I just watch in horror as his fingers finally disappear—until the soil caves in behind the tips of his digits and covers the last traces of him.

And just like that, he's gone…

I just watched Kyle bury himself alive, I think, ending the recording with a tap of my thumb.

Lizzy's hand leaves mine at the same time, then she quickly wraps her arms around me. "I'm so sorry, Danny," she sobs, pressing her cheek against my chest.

I'm so in shock that it takes nearly 10 seconds before I manage to hug her back.

And as I'm squeezing her against me, I start sobbing harder than I ever have in my entire life.

In a hundred percent of all cases, all males infected by that white slime turn into podling zombies, wander into the woods, and then bury themselves near the base of a tree so its black roots can feed on them and the surrounding plants… And then… Now I picture the beige, waxy-skinned appendage that will sprout from Kyle's grave within the next day.

I think back to what Allie explained during the horse ride over about what happens once podlings bury themselves near the meat-mat. She said that when the biomass grows over buried flesh pods, their black roots extend toward each other and connect. Then, neuron-rich tissue spreads from both the pod and the meat-mat until they fuse together, forming a continuous nervous system. And once that happens, the intact brains inside those underground flesh pods connect to Savanna's—and to everyone else who's become one with the pod-mass—forming a circuit of comatose minds that control the tentacles, dong-shrooms, and any Yoni Flowers above.

What she said at the end of that was, *"Essentially, the pod-mass is a giant superorganism with a nervous system and multiple functioning brains… Human brains… So if one Linga Flower connected to the pod-mass is jerked off or ridden by someone, theoretically, all the brains will experience the pleasure simultaneously. Just like how Savanna and your friends all experienced pain when you cut those tentacles."*

I imagine Kyle, Gavin, and Tucker linking up in some shared dreamscape—a biologically generated simulation where they all think they're living normal lives. Or worse, where they're trapped together in the same nightmare.

What happened to Kyle happens to a hundred percent of those infected, I think, looking down at my bandaged arm. *And I'm infected.*

I picture my body being overtaken by the pod-mass.

I imagine mindlessly wandering back here and doing what Kyle just did.

Now I imagine what it'll be like when my zombified mind links up with everyone else who's become part of the meat-mat hivemind. The scenario I play out next is me searching for my friends in that shared dreamscape, only to never find them.

I imagine people walking across the meat-mat, and me feeling it like footsteps moving across my own body.

Is that what's gonna happen to me?

The thought makes me cry even harder.

Please. Please. Please don't let that happen to me, God! Please!

A hand gently grabs my shoulder.

"Hey," Allie says. "I'm sorry you had to witness that, Danny. No one should ever have to experience watching a friend go through *that*…"

I sniffle while slowly pulling away from Lizzy. "You don't have to be sorry," I croak. When I finally blink the tears away, I see Allie's all teary-eyed too. "I *chose* to come here. I *chose* to come say goodbye and apologize…"

With her lips curled into her mouth, Allie nods. "I know… But I'm still sorry." She nods toward the trail. "Come on. Let's head back to Lizzy's horses and the others so we can get you back to the house and check on that arm."

"No! We still have to find out where Tucker and Gavin buried themselves!"

Allie shakes her head. "Not tonight… It's about to be pitch black out here, which means it'll be hard to find them. And more importantly, your parents haven't heard from you in over a day, and I need to get you home before they worry themselves sick. So here's what we'll do. The girls and I will look for their *burial sites* tomorrow—before the pod-mass grows over them. Once we find them, we'll come get you and bring you back to say goodbye. Okay?"

I suck in a deep breath, then let it out in a sharp, defeated huff. "Okay. *Fine…*"

Lizzy takes my hand again, interlocking her fingers with mine. And when I look at her, she gives me the saddest smile I've ever seen, her bottom lip trembling like she's barely holding it together. "You're gonna be okay, Danny. We're gonna get through this fucked-up trauma together, okay? I'll help you get through it, and you help me. Alright?"

I force a faint smile. "Okay. We'll help each other get through this," I whisper back.

"*Promise?*" she says in a childlike tone.

I nod. "I promise."

"Good!" she says with a nod. Then she turns and starts walking.

I fall into step beside her, my gaze drifting between the two girls ahead and the ground beneath my feet.

After what I just witnessed, I can't stop wondering if we're walking over the places where Tucker and Gavin buried themselves.

I can't stop imagining burying myself alive.

I can't stop picturing these girls one day finding my burial site.

If one hundred percent of infected guys end up like that, what are the odds some fucking worm slime makes me the exception?

Slim to none, I think as my arm starts itching like crazy.

Odds are, you end up in the ground in three to five days…

Odds are you'll become part of the meat-mat superorganism—you'll become one with your friends and Savanna…

In an instant, the flashlight-lit path ahead blurs behind tears, and I start sobbing uncontrollably.

FIND OUT WHAT HAPPENS TO DANNY IN:
BLIGHT OF THE YONI FLOWER

"A few minutes of pleasure can lead to a lifetime of pain and a nightmarish threat to humanity…"

Thanks to the deviant acts of perversion that Allie Hannigan and Lizzy Rutherford engaged in a few months ago, the Yoni Flowers and the Linga Flowers have spread, taking lives and mutating bodies each time a new one pops up.

Because of what they did, one girl's unspeakable act with a Linga Flower ends with her untimely demise. And that death triggers a mutation that causes the horrific biomass beneath the soil to grow uncontrollably and spread across the forest.

As Allie, Lizzy, and Priya Singh work with the Uteroboscis experts—Lena Anderson and Angela Henry—to try and solve each other's problems, the nightmarish Linga-pod-overgrowth that they've dubbed the *Flesh Forest* consumes everything in its path like a sentient blight.

And just when things seem like they can't get any worse, another unexpected mutation results in the most horrific monstrosity that humanity has ever witnessed…

A year before Allie Hannigan stumbles across the Yoni Flower, Lena Anderson has a horrific encounter in the Amazon Rainforest…

"Some organisms should remain undiscovered…"

Since she was young, Lena Anderson's dream was to get a degree in biology and explore the Amazon Rainforest. Unexpectedly, on the day of college graduation, her travel blogger best friend, Derek, made the second part of that lifelong dream come true by surprising her with an all-expense-paid trip to the one place she's always wanted to visit.

The only thing that'll make Lena's life complete now is if she can somehow discover a new species during the two-week expedition through the uncharted and restricted Vale do Javari region of the Amazonas. On the last day of their adventure, just as she's losing hope that she'll make a new discovery, Lena breaks away from the group for a potty break only to take a tumble down a muddy hill and splash down into a stream without her friends realizing what's happened. It's there in that body of water where she discovers a giant, phallic worm the likes of which the world has never seen…

Then that worm races up between her legs and discovers a passage to the perfect habitat…

Little does Lena know, she may not be leaving that jungle empty-handed after all, because her dream adventure might end with her going home with the creature of her nightmares living within her womb…

Author's Note:

Thanks for reading *Flesh Forest!* And thanks to all of you readers out there who have been emailing me and commenting on my posts, praising my stories, and asking me when the next book or books are coming out! Your comments, emails, reviews, and Reddit posts have kept me going and inspired me to keep writing these deliciously messed-up tales! I hope you enjoyed the read! And I hope the death of Danny's friends didn't hit you too hard. Honestly, writing Tucker's accidental demise at the hands of Danny was one of the hardest character deaths I've ever written…

For those of you who've been reading my books since the beginning, I'm sure the biggest twist of all with this story is that I—B.L. Overman—wrote a body-horror set in this universe without writing any smut this time haha. I thought it'd be nice to take a step back from all the naughtiness for once and just focus on the psychological turmoil and the horrific shit that happens to the [male] body after a guy stumbles across the Yoni/Linga Flower and its innards **without** doing anything naughty with any part of it. Figured that a sort of coming-of-age story-turned-impromptu-rescue-mission where a bunch of high school seniors are trying to save a girl from a Lovecraftian horror would be a nice way to showcase that even those who resist the pheromones and practice extreme restraint can still fall victim to the horrors of the Linga flower and its variants. I also figured that toning down the spicy stuff would make for a good way to share this universe with new readers who aren't into spice.

For the record, this book with Danny and friends was planned since the very first chapter of Lizzy's Flower Glizzy, where she mentions Yelm Lake and the 'secret parties' kids from school throw there. And this *Flesh Forest* story was planned ever since I was writing the part of *The Yoni Flower* where Priya fell into the Linga Flower's flesh sarcophagus, then got grabbed by and *invaded by* that very first pinecone-tipped tentacle. I've been aching to write this story and finally show you all how the pod-mass *behaves* once it grows out of control. I hope the *Flesh Forest* didn't disturb you too much because you'll be returning there a few more times in *Blight of The Yoni Flower*. **Hint, hint**: The Flesh Forest is a blight caused by the Yoni Flower, but it won't be the only one. If you think the Flesh Forest is the worst thing to spawn from Allie's *flower*, you ain't seen nothin' yet!

And speaking of *Blight of The Yoni Flower*, you won't have to wait too long to find out what happens to Danny or to see the meeting between Allie and Lena! I'm aiming to get done by end of spring/early summer at the latest. Also, if you thought the first 5 books were full of bonkers-ass, WTF moments, wait 'til you see what the girls will have to deal with next…

A special thanks to everyone who's purchased *Flesh Forest* and my other twisted novels. Seriously, knowing you all love these stories enough to buy them with your hard-earned money during these hard times warms my heart! I love and appreciate you all so much that there are no words to describe it! And if you'd like to reach out to me on Twitter @BLOverman99 or email (BLOverman99@gmail.com) to chat, feel free to message me!

If you've enjoyed *Flesh Forest* and/or any of the **Primeval Ones Universe/Deviant Ones Universe** novels, if you could be so kind as to leave a review wherever you purchased them, that'd mean the world to me! Also, if you'd like to keep up with the rest of the series, please head on over to my publisher's website [https://www.scirotic.com/bl-overman] and sign up for the email list. I promise there won't be any spam, only routine updates on my books, messages from me, and **FREE** bonus tie-ins that'll be sent out whenever available.

With love and appreciation,
B.L. Overman